Academy Mystery Novellas

Volume 1
WOMEN
SLEUTHS

Academy Mystery Novellas

Volume 1

WOMEN
SLEUTHS

Edited by
Martin H. Greenberg & Bill Pronzini

Academy
Chicago
Publishers

Published by The Reader's Digest Association, Inc.,
1991, through special arrangement with Academy
Chicago Publishers.

Library of Congress Cataloging-in-Publication Data
Main entry under title:
Women sleuths.
    Contents: The toys of death/G.D.H. & Margaret Cole—The calico dog/
Mignon Eberhart—The book that squealed/Cornell Woolrich—The broken
men/Marcia Muller.
    1. Detective and mystery stories, American. 2. Women detectives—Fiction.
I. Pronzini, Bill. II. Greenberg, Martin Harry.
PS648.D4W6   1985   813'.0872'08352042   85-18558
ISBN 0-89733-157-5 (pbk.)

Academy Mystery Novellas are collections of long stories chosen on the basis of two criteria—(1) their excellence as mystery/suspense fiction and (2) their relative obscurity. This second criterion is due solely to the special limitations of the short novel/novella length—too short to be published alone as a novel, but too long to be easily anthologized or collected since they tend to take up too much space in a typical volume.

The series features long fiction by some of the best-known names in the crime fiction field, including such masters as Cornell Woolrich, Ed McBain, Georges Simenon, Donald E. Westlake, and many others. Each volume is organized around a type of crime story (locked room, police procedural) or theme (type of detective, humor).

We are proud to bring these excellent works of fiction to your attention, and hope that you will enjoy reading them as much as we enjoyed the process of selecting them for you.

Martin H. Greenberg
Bill Pronzini

Contents

THE TOYS OF DEATH

by G.D.H. and Margaret Cole

I

You will not know where Quartermouth is, and I shall not tell you. It is as well, for the comfort of those of us who do not like large crowds, that not too many people should know where to find, on the South Coast of England, a place that is more like a Continental casino than a seaside resort—a place where there is a real little town of some antiquity with a real harbour and a quay where fishing-boats land, a Fore Street of old grey cottages and smelly fishing-nets, and a High and other streets of clean modern shops where visitors can purchase all necessary and unnecessary objects. A place, moreover—and this is the point—where the Mrs. Grundy of the seaside has not found a home, where the bathing restrictions are *nil,* where the licensing hours are long and loosely enforced, and where the public-houses, one and all, possess as well as their stuffy little bars for the fishermen, small or large courtyards or gardens, hung with fairy lights, where one can sit for hours, German or French fashion, sipping at a long drink in the evening, in the soft southwestern air.

It would, you will agree, be a pity if too many people—since there are forty million people in England, at least a quarter of whom, it would seem, have money to spare for a charabanc trip—if too many people knew how to find a place like this, so I will not tell you. Besides, anyhow, it is very likely already spoilt for the connoisseur. Since the "Crampton-Pleydell Drama"—ah, that begins to remind you, doesn't it?—it will have become crammed, if I know my country, with hot and shrill pilgrims anxious to carry off a loose bit of his house, or a leaf from his garden, or even just to stand and gape up at the wall behind which the drama was played; and there will be no room or peace to enjoy oneself in a civilised manner. I should not myself go there again—for some years, at any rate. But a year ago it was as I have described—unique among English watering-places.

Quartermouth has two hotels, not large but old and comfortable. It also has several superior guest-houses, and many cottages and bungalows available for renting by artists, successful and unsuccessful, and by those who like to meet artists during the summer. And all, or nearly all, of the inhabitants of these buildings used to drift, at various times of the day, but particularly before and after dinner, to one or other of the public-houses which I have mentioned, their choice, for the most part, being dictated by Crampton Pleydell's fancy of the moment.

For Crampton Pleydell was Quartermouth's Great Figure. He was not, perhaps, at the very zenith of his fame; there were some unkind people who said that his leaving London had not been dictated wholly by the sordid and vicious quality of London life, but by its inadequate appreciation of Crampton Pleydell's genius. But these were only a few malignant whisperers, who did not, thank goodness, often come to Quartermouth. At any rate, his novels, with their gift of tearing the heart out of anything he chose to describe, whether it was the Middle Ages, Russia before the Revolution, a stud-farm, or a typing agency in East London, still sold well, and brought him in royalties enough to enable him to inhabit Chalgrove Field, the fine old house and garden which he owned a quarter of a mile from Quartermouth town, up on the low cliff above Quarter Creek, to act as Lord Bountiful to the young shoots of literary and artistic appreciation in Quartermouth, and to stand rounds of free drinks whenever the spirit moved him to come down and foregather with visitors and summer residents in the pub gardens.

As it often did. For Crampton Pleydell, except when he was actually working or was visited by one of the fits of divine gloom which are the penalty of genius, was a gregarious creature. He liked to drink, and to talk, preferably to as large a circle as his fine resonant voice would reach; he liked to tell the young about the glories of the past, about his own experiences in many capital cities, and to warn them of the abysses into which literature was rapidly sinking. And there were always, among the visitors, a certain number of young would-be writers who had come to Quartermouth on purpose to find Crampton Pleydell, to get a glimpse of his leonine head, with its beaked nose and full mouth, and of his strong white hands moving in eloquent gesture over the iniquities of mankind.

On a hot August night of last year those of the guests and residents who had been fortunate enough to choose the Spaniard's Inn for their rendezvous had had a field-day. For Crampton Pleydell, after having remained in his house for some days—he had been entertaining a party, among them his brother John, a coarser, more bucolic-looking edition of himself, and an old friend, Nigel Herdman, a lean, dark silent fellow with a curiously twisted smile—had suddenly emerged, full of radiance and bonhomie, shepherding the remains of the party for a final drink at the Spaniard's. Once there, he had drawn into his orbit, with a splendid sweep of the arm, the half-dozen or so people who were already seated there, including Lady Wishart, the widow of the iron-monger peer, who had known Pleydell these many summers, and could always be relied on to lead up to his best stories; including a poet called Oliver Something-or-other, who was an intense and avid follower of Pleydell's theory of the arts; including Vivienne Murray, his scarlet-lipped and scarlet-fingered admirer, Vivienne Murray's lack-adaisical blue-blooded mother, running now to fat, and a cousin or swain of Vivienne Murray's, who had to endure with a smile his nose being put out of joint by the hero; and including, incongruously enough, the distinguished private detective, James Warrender, and his small, elderly mother, whom he always took round with him to whatever place he had selected for his holidays.

There, at any rate, they all were, sitting round in the slowly cooling evening, with the tiny red and blue and green lights doing no more than just break the dark, ringed round, encompassed, and enfolded in Crampton Pleydell's voice. Pleydell himself seemed excellently pleased with the way the evening was going; he had just ordered another round of drinks, and with unusual expansiveness had gone the length of inviting the whole company to come to an alfresco supper in his garden in two days' time—"to cheer me when these dear people leave," he explained with a wave of his hand to the remnants of his own gathering. Oliver Something-or-other gasped and breathed heavily, as though the prospect of so much ecstasy were altogether too much for him; whereupon Pleydell underlined his hospitality by demanding a personal acceptance from everyone present, being particularly pressing to the Honourable Mrs. Murray (at which her daughter hunched herself and looked sulky) and to little Mrs. Warrender, who gave a very small start. She was so accustomed to being overlooked. However, she had the presence of mind to accept with a smile, and, sipping with a feeling of slightly guilty pleasure at a tall glass of very cool lager, gave herself up to contemplation of the night. She was not really listening to the conversation. Literary and artistic principles were rather above her head; and besides, Crampton Pleydell's voice, with its rotund sonorities, belonged to a type to which she had, unfortunately, never been able to listen for more than ten minutes. Not since she was a child in church, and had been told not to wriggle during the sermon. She rather wished he would not go on drowning the sound of the sea, which was just audible from the pub garden if you kept quiet; and she anticipated with some fear having to listen to that voice, probably for two or three hours on end, in its own home. However, she consoled herself, perhaps she could look at the garden. Crampton Pleydell's garden was said to be exquisite, and Mrs. Warrender loved gardens.

At this point her thoughts received an interruption. Pleydell had left the subject of literary theory and was turning to politics. She heard the words "Spain" and "Catalonia"; and pricked up her ears to listen. For one of the events in Mrs. Warrender's uneventful life was when she had spent three weeks with a friend in Northern Spain; and anything connected with or suggesting Spain always roused her romantic feelings.

Pleydell was talking with contempt of something which he called the Catalan Separatist movement. "*Dear lady,*" he addressed some distant figure in the darkness, "do not deceive yourself. There is nothing genuine in it—nothing whatever—nothing but a conspiracy of criminals and crooks who for their own ends persuade that poor old noble people that they are being led towards independence. The old war cries, the old colours, the old flags—they bring them out, I grant you—and use them to deck out bankers and Bolsheviks! Once, ah once," he sighed, "there was a *real* independence movement among the Catalans. I remember it so well, twenty years and more ago, when I was a young fellow tramping it in Catalonia, not knowing and not caring where I should get a bed the next day. I remember in a little *estaminet* in Santander—"

"But surely," Mrs. Warrender's voice squeaked a little in her excitement, "Santander *isn't* in Catalonia." There was a sudden silence. "I mean," she was forced to continue, "it isn't in Catalonia at all. It's in Castile, miles the other side."

The silence continued and grew more grim. Then the great man recovered himself. "Dear lady, of course," he said. "How right you are! How strange it is— memory. Here is a thing etched on one's mind— irrevocably etched, with all the emotion and the realisation plain as though it were yesterday. And then . . . just a little thing like a name, and one has forgotten. Of course—of course it was not Santander . . . it was . . ."

"Oh, never mind what it was! Try Barcelona," Vivienne Murray snapped. Slowly the stream of words reformed and flowed again. Mrs. Warrender heard an infinitesimal chuckle at her left shoulder.

"Oh, dear," she whispered, turning to the chuckler in distress, "Oh, *dear!* What a dreadful thing to have said!" Nigel Herdman chuckled again. "Yes, you've rather done it now. Put him right out of his stride. Never mind, I shouldn't worry about it. Does them good to be deflated every now and then."

"But it's so *rude* of me!" Mrs. Warrender said in an agonised sort of hiss. "I don't know how I came to—it seemed to slip out. And just after I had been invited to dinner!"

"I shouldn't mind. Look here," said Herdman, taking pity on her, "let's walk down the road to the sea, shall we? Nobody'll notice if we clip out the back way for five minutes."

"I can't possibly go to dinner there," Mrs. Warrender said, as they stood on the cobbled pavement. "Not after having interrupted him like that."

"Indeed you can. What's more, you'll have to," Herdman said. "You'll have to go, as a penance, and look sorry for having remembered an unimportant fact right. If you don't he'll begin to think perhaps it *was* important, and that'll worry him no end. He may even feel he'll have to go to Catalonia and find out where the place really is."

"Oh! *Hasn't* he been, then?"

"I shouldn't think so," Nigel said. "Of course, you never can tell. But I think I know my Pleydell."

"Yes, of course. You're very old friends, aren't you? You would know him."

"Don't you? You look to me as though you'd know about people."

"Oh, dear no. I've only met him and read one or two of his books. Besides, I only know about ordinary people—girls, and servants, you know, the kind I have to meet."

"I see. Well, tell me about Vivienne Murray," said Nigel abruptly. "Or isn't she ordinary enough?"

"Oh, she is. Very ordinary. I mean—that sounds so rude! I mean, she is quite a—a usual sort of girl, only she doesn't get on with her mother, and she hasn't any money or any work to do, and that makes her cross. She's quite a nice girl, you know, really kind and friendly, in herself, and she would be quite happy if she had something to do, only she has no money and no training, so it would have to be something that depended entirely on personality. And I don't think her personality's really strong enough yet, poor child."

"Um. Yes."

"Of course," Mrs. Warrender pursued, "just now, she's simply in love with Mr. Pleydell, and nothing else."

"Oh. You think that?"

"Oh, yes. She can think and talk of nobody else,

which is rather hard on Mr. Archibald, who is a nice young man, even if he *is* a bit dull. I dare say you haven't noticed, because of course since Mr. Pleydell's party came we haven't seen so much of him—how lovely the harbour looks, doesn't it? But before that they were together a very great deal."

"Yes. Come for a run?" said Nigel, putting his hand on the gunwale of a motor-boat that was moored to the quay, rocking faintly on the high tide.

"Oh, is that your boat? How nice!" Mrs. Warrender said. "I should love to, but not tonight, after I've been so rude already. I must go back."

"It's your only chance," the boat's owner said. "She'll be gone tomorrow."

"Oh, are you leaving? What a pity! But I really couldn't. I ought to have gone back already."

"They'll be another half-hour yet. Trust me," Nigel said. "We'll just go for the shortest possible nip round the harbour, to blow the anecdotage out of our brains. Believe me, I'll get you back in time for all the proprieties.

"What about Pleydell?" he asked when they were seated. "Is he as smitten too, do you think?"

"Oh, well, you wouldn't expect a man like him to be very much interested in a girl of twenty, would you? As a matter of fact, I thought he liked her a good deal; but, now you mention it, he did seem a little standoffish tonight. I do hope," Mrs. Warrender mused, "that if he has got—tired of her he'll be kind. You see, she's *very* young, and—and he doesn't look as though he'd always be considerate."

"He doesn't," Nigel agreed rather absently, and began suddenly to talk of other things. He proved a very entertaining companion, and Mrs. Warrender, when they landed, thanked him very gratefully for her trip.

"How sad that you must leave so soon," she said. "Where did you say you were going?"

"I didn't say anywhere," Nigel said. "I shall cruise round a bit, probably, and then put her in at a port where I can pick a liner for South America."

"*South America?*"

"Buenos Aires. I've got a small show there—sort of agency—run it as De Rosas, at 34 Strada Olivada. By the way, nobody knows that here—I don't know why I should bother you with it—"

"I see," said Mrs. Warrender, not seeing at all.

"—Here we are, anyway. Come up and see how Pleydell will press you to come to his party—just to show you your little mistake doesn't matter."

II

Good manners notwithstanding, Mrs. Warrender had much ado not to giggle at the exactitude with which Herdman's prophecy was fulfilled. The party broke up soon after their return, and when Mrs. Warrender, feeling like a school-child who has been naughty, came to bid her host farewell, Crampton Pleydell fixed her with his large blue eyes, bowed low over her hand and kissed it, saying in a rich, carrying murmur, "*Good*-night, dear lady. So charming to have seen you again—and this is not to be the last. You will not fail me on Thursday night, will you?" Indeed, Mrs. Warrender felt, she was being handsomely forgiven for knowing something of the geography of Spain; and she hoped very much that nobody else had wanted to laugh.

But they did not. They took it seriously. Lady Wishart spoke to her with respect, and her son informed her, on the way back, that Vivienne Murray, on hearing the farewell, had flounced off home in a temper.

"Oh, dear! But she can't imagine—oh, the *silly* little thing, why should she take any notice of what Mr. Pleydell says to an old woman?" cried Mrs. Warrender in some distress.

"That's just it. Because you are an old woman, and she's a silly little thing. Anyhow, her hero didn't even chuck her a bone this evening," James said, "and you've seen yourself she's gaga about him. Little fool she is, too. Of course, Pleydell's a bit flyblown nowadays—you notice how he's had to come down to bragging to parties of summer visitors, so as to keep up the illusion that he's a great genius; but he can still fly at higher game than little Vivienne."

"Then he oughtn't to have taken her up and made such a fuss of her, if he was going to drop her as soon as he got bored. It isn't fair to a child as young as that!" said Mrs. Warrender indignantly.

"All right, all right, I never said it was. It's just his way and they say it always has been, to pick up women—men, too, for that matter—and let 'em go when he's had enough. Great big egotists these writers are," said James. "Who was that?" as Mrs. Warrender gave a soft "Good-night" to a girl who had just passed them.

"Miss Gray. The girl at the library."

"*What* library? How you do collect acquaintances!"

"The circulating library, dear, in Ferry Street. She's such a nice, clever girl, and so good at helping me to choose books that you'll like. I'm sure she must be very bored here—she's much too good for the sort of work she's had to do, and she's been a proper librarian once, in Plymouth, or somewhere like that. I asked her if she wouldn't like to go to London and get some more interesting work—I'm sure she's good enough for the *Times* Book Club; but she said she wouldn't, I can't think why."

"Very wise of her, too," James said with a yawn. "Damn silly, all these girls and young fellows who come dashing up to London thinking the place is made of gold—and then can't get work and have to go crawling home with their tails between their legs. Well, my dear, I hope you're getting on happily—what with provincial bookshop girls and Great Literary Lights, your acquaintance ought to be varied enough. Come along in; it's getting late.

"This *is* a nuisance," he remarked a few minutes later, having opened and read his letters. "I say, mother! I'm awfully sorry, but I'm afraid I shall have to cut things here a bit short. You know I left a particular case in hand when I went away—well, the long and the short of it is that it's turned into two cases; at least, it's divided into two trails, and one's in England and one in France. So Edwards can't handle it all himself—anyway the French people don't know him well enough and he hasn't had enough experience that end to deal with it. So I'm afraid there's no help for it, I must go off to Paris. You'll be all right for a week or so by yourself, won't you?"

"Couldn't I go home?" Mrs. Warrender who, though perfectly competent in her own home, was liable to attacks of panic outside it, suggested. But she was rebuked.

"No, you couldn't. The servants have got to have their time off—anyway, I shall be much too busy to be able to get them back before I go. And I certainly shouldn't dream of letting you stay there by yourself. Surely, mother," said James, with pardonable impatience, "it isn't such a dreadful thing, to stay on here in the hotel for ten days? You know the people now, and you've got your bookshop girl and Pleydell to talk to."

"Oh! And there's Mr. Pleydell's party, too!" cried Mrs. Warrender, in great alarm. "Really, James, dear, I *couldn't* go by myself to that! Not after making such an exhibition of myself, and the embarrassing way he behaved about it. I should feel so *foolish*, by myself."

"Well, you won't have to be," James said dryly. "I'll stay over Thursday night; there's no such appalling hurry, and Edwards can get the papers ready for me, and not fuss so much. There's no real need for me to come tearing home, if he'd only keep his head. Besides," James added, "I'd like to see Pleydell's place, now I am here; I'm not likely to get another opportunity, and they say he's got some really extraordinary stuff there he's picked up. Plants and shrubs, too, mother—you'll like that. So don't you worry; I'll come to the party, and if the gentleman's too gallant for you I'll put him over my knee and spank him."

"I wish that nice Mr. Herdman was going to be there," Mrs. Warrender remarked, as she turned to go upstairs.

"Oh, isn't he? I didn't know he was going," James said. "Do you like him? Bit cynical for my taste. Of course, I suppose it may come of being a failure."

"*Is* he a failure? He didn't sound like one."

"Well, anyway, he's never done anything, and he was supposed to be a brilliant chap when he was younger. Dr. Tetley was telling me about him the other night—he was a contemporary of Tetley's and Pleydell's up at the 'varsity, and started out to be a first-class scientist of some sort or other. But then it all seemed to come to nothing, anyway, nothing anybody ever heard of. I expect he had some cash of his own, and was just too lazy to work—it's the devil and all, these young men with independent incomes. Tetley says he hasn't any idea what he manages to live on—not that he knows him well."

"Bu—" Mrs. Warrender opened her mouth to speak, and shut it again. She had just remembered that Nigel Herdman had told her that nobody in Quartermouth knew of his South American activities; and she doubted very much whether he would wish Dr. Tetley, whom she knew well to be a most flagrant gossip, to hear anything about them. It gave her a small thrill of pleasure to keep Nigel Herdman's secret for him.

"Well," she said, with unusual firmness, as she walked up to bed, "even if he isn't as successful a man as he ought to be, I'm sorry he's going away. Good-night, James dear. I'm getting nicely sleepy."

She did not, however, go to sleep very soon. She was an old lady who did not like to hurt even the most unimportant of human beings and she was distressed to find that, however absurd it was, she should have been the source of pain to Vivienne Murray. It was a shame that the girl should be made unnecessarily miserable, and in the morning, she resolved, she would at least put that right.

She had to wait until the afternoon, for Vivienne did not come to breakfast, nor had she put in an appearance by the time Mrs. Warrender set out to change her library book, and to pass the time of day with the assistant. She had really taken quite a liking, she admitted to herself, for the slim fair girl with the quiet manner, who was so patient with old ladies who could not remember exactly what book it was they wanted, but knew it wasn't a detective novel and that the author's name began with a B or an M—and yet had a good deal of knowledge of more serious works on tap. But the girl looked tired this morning, and her answers, though pleasant, were listless. Perhaps she was feeling the heat.

So Mrs. Warrender, not wishing to be a nuisance, left the library, and went into the photographer's just opposite to choose some photographs of a play which had been performed the previous week by the West Country Players in the garden of the hotel. She thought the photographs disappointing, and said so, in which opinion she was unexpectedly supported by the assistant, who served her, a tall, dark, rather good-looking young man with a very melancholy face, but extremely obliging manners. For, finding out that she particularly wanted some pretty photographic memorial of Quartermouth to send to her sister in Australia, he ransacked the shop's whole store of photographs until he had produced a view of the bay which was exactly what she wanted, and much more attractive than the dramatic groups. "Really, how *nice* people are to one!" she reflected as she walked back to the hotel in a pleasant glow, all ready for tackling Vivienne Murray.

Vivienne was having lunch. She looked ill and tired, as if she had hardly slept at all, and she seemed determined to be rude to Mrs. Warrender. But Mrs. Warrender knew enough about sulky young people not to be lightly rebuffed, and after lunch she easily got Vivienne into the garden, and even, over coffee and a liqueur, induced her to smile at the foolish way in which old ladies liked to air their bits of knowledge at the most inconvenient moments and at the exaggerated, *almost* offensive courtesy with which Mr. Crampton Pleydell had covered it up.

So far, so good. But it was not to stop there. Having lost her frown, Vivienne Murray went on to stumble over a half-apology for her rudeness at lunch, and, when she was assured that it did not matter in the least, to observe, in the tone of one about to burst into confidence, that she knew she was awful, she was just rotten to everybody, but she couldn't help it, she was going crazy, and she'd just be clean nuts if that job didn't come along soon!

"Job, my dear? What kind of job? I hadn't heard of it." Mrs. Warrender was relieved; if there were really a job on the horizon, how much better than Crampton Pleydell! But the next words dispelled the relief.

"Why, the job Crampton Pleydell's finding me, of course!"

"Oh! I didn't know he was."

"Well, he's got to. There's nothing else for it," Vivienne said roughly, staring very hard at a large bush of escallonia. "He's got to go back to town sometime; he doesn't like being here in the autumn. And I can't possibly live in town, not near, unless I've got paid work. You know mother and I haven't got a sou; we couldn't stay here at a place like this if Lady Wishart wasn't paying because she likes mother and she's so sorry for her. We don't live in town, we live in a dismal hole of a flat in Wembley. That's no good; but, you see, if I got a job mother'd have all the money, and she could go and live in a private hotel in Kensington, which is what she'd like, and I could find some place near him."

"But . . . my dear . . ." Mrs. Warrender hesitated, perplexed and alarmed. "Do you think—you are certain—that he—"

"I know he can't get on without me!" Vivienne cried. "I—I—I'm *necessary* to his work. If you don't believe me, he said so! He *said* nobody'd ever helped him so much as I have. Didn't you know I'd been helping him all this time—he calls it being a model—telling him what it's *really* like to be a blinking little aristocrat trying to keep it up on two pounds a week in a cheap boarding house: he can't know that for himself. And he *never* guesses at things; he always finds out—that's why his books are always right, he says, he just goes to the people themselves. And we haven't half done—the book's not nearly finished, and it can't be finished without me. And anyhow"—she cupped her chin in her hands and looked at Mrs. Warrender with an expression of conscious determination—"I'm damned well not going to live without him. Now I've tried it." She stared defiantly.

"Oh, my dear—"

"It's no use your sitting there looking like mother," said Vivienne. "I thought you'd see that I know what I mean to have and it's no use being Victorian about it. Of course I shouldn't say anything like this to mother; she'd have a fit. But I thought you—don't you understand I *must?*"

"It isn't quite that," said Mrs. Warrender. "But are you really sure—"

"Of course I'm sure! But I know what you're thinking!" Vivienne burst out. "You're thinking I'm making it up—just because we haven't had time to see one another so much lately—just because I was a fool last night! What mother keeps saying to me—'he doesn't really *mean* it, dear.' Oh, it's all such nonsense! As if people had to live in each other's pockets just to show they're getting on all right! *You* can understand that, can't you? Oh, well," getting no reassurance from Mrs. Warrender's face, "if you don't believe me it's all right by me. It's *so,* that's all; and I'm not g-going to sit here and let him go away without me, and nobody need think it!"

She stared at Mrs. Warrender, as though she would convince her by the power of the human eye; and then, suddenly, her eyes faltered, her lips quivered, and she broke into a passion of angry weeping, in which at first no words were distinguishable. Mrs. Warrender, distressed if not surprised, moved nearer to her and stroked her shoulder and her bent dark head.

"Oh, God!" the girl sobbed. "I do love him so frightfully, and I can't bear it! I want to touch him, and to be with him, all over and all the time—it sends me crazy just to look at him. I—I didn't know loving anybody could *hurt* one so much. And he won't . . . I don't know what it is—I haven't done anything, it isn't me! *Why* should he change—why does he look as though he didn't care? Oh, Mrs. Warrender, I can't bear it! I'll just go clean off my head if I can't have him! . . . But I will—I will! I won't let him go—I'll kill him or kill myself—I can't *bear* it! What *am* I to do?"

What indeed? Mrs. Warrender did not feel that there was really anything that she could do. She did not for a moment believe that Crampton Pleydell had any intention of taking Vivienne Murray to London, and she felt that the utmost to be hoped was that he would have the decency to let her down gently. But even that, she was sure, he would not do if he were screamed and shouted at; he was the type whom hysteria quickly turns into a brute. So she devoted all her energies to calming the immediate storm, and eventually succeeded to a certain extent, though she was very doubtful about the success of tomorrow's supper party. She did not think the girl would be able to get through a whole evening of Pleydell in his present mood without breaking down.

"It would really be the best thing for her, poor child," she reflected, as she went back into the hotel after her ministrations and stood for a minute looking out into the street, "if Pleydell could die quite soon, so that she could go on believing that he really cared for her, and start again. But that's not very likely—though I can't say I think he'd be very much loss. . . . Hullo, dear! Had a good bathe?"

"Not too bad," James said. "Beach a bit over-crowded, though. I forgot it was early closing. That's rather a nice-looking wench over there." His eye was roving after a slim girl in white tennis clothes and a primrose blazer, who was walking past the hotel in deep conversation with a dark-haired youth. "What are you grinning at, old lady?" as she gave a small chuckle.

"Only that's the girl you asked me about last night—my nice Miss Gray from the library. I'm so glad you think she's attractive," said Mrs. Warrender demurely. "And she's got a young man too—isn't that nice? Why," in a ladylike squeal, "it's the young man from the photographer's—"

"Wah!" said James, an indescribable noise compounded of amusement and exasperation.

"—the one who was so kind to me this morning! So *that's* why she doesn't want to go to London."

"Jumping to conclusions a bit, aren't you?" James said.

"Oh, no, dear, I don't think so." Mrs. Warrender nodded her head firmly. She had seen the expression on the girl's face as she looked up at her taller companion; and she knew. Whether he (the companion) did was, of course, quite another matter.

"Well, how about tea?" James said.

III

Mrs. Warrender had been full of apprehensions about the evening party; but when the time drew near it seemed that the worst of them might not be fulfilled. Vivienne Murray came downstairs looking subdued, and evidently intending to behave well. She had made up with less violence and more care than usual, and she showed considerable patience with her mother, who was being particularly trying. The Honorable Mrs. Murray, as befitted an impoverished aristocrat, was liable to fits of helplessness, and on that evening she was totally unable to make up her mind whether it was going to rain or not, and whether, in consequence, she should wear an evening cloak which would be irretrievably ruined in a downpour, or a more serviceable object which was less becoming. She changed her mind half a dozen times, calling for support in each decision as she made it, and complaining all the time of the weather—and indeed it was a sultry night—and of the terrible headache which was besetting her. Mrs. Warrender was sure, from the look in Vivienne's eyes, that her head was aching no less badly than her mother's; but she said nothing of it, but meekly arranged and rearranged the two wraps from every possible angle, once even throwing Mrs. Warrender a glance which seemed intended to be reassuring.

At last Mrs. Murray professed herself satisfied, and they packed into Lady Wishart's large car, which held all but the young man called Oliver and Vivienne's discarded admirer, who were walking up the hill expecting to be overtaken. But owing to the delay of the hotel contingent they had arrived first; and when the others reached Chalgrove Field and were conducted through the house to a broad lawn surrounded by sombre evergreens alternating with bushes of bright blue hydrangea, they found the two young men standing alone and rather awkwardly by a table laden with cold food of various kinds.

"Hullo! Where's Crampton?" Lady Wishart asked.

"We don't know. He isn't here," one of the young men said.

"The naughty fellow! And it's late already. However," said Lady Wishart, sinking into a chair, "I suppose we can have a drink while we're waiting for him. Bar-

ney!" she called to the butler who had shown them out.
"We needn't wait for our drinks till Mr. Pleydell comes,
need we?"

"Certainly not, my lady." Barney handed them
round. There was a few minutes' silence, during which
Mrs. Warrender, who did not take cocktails, walked
round the lawn looking for another kind of flower. She
was not particularly interested in hydrangeas. But there
was no other flower on the lawn. With the tail of her eye
she noticed Vivienne take the cocktail that had been
meant for her.

"Phew!" said Lady Wishart at last. "I don't *like* this
lawn. All those black trees give me the creeps, and what
a horrid colour the flowers are!"

"It's the light," said James Warrender. "There's a
storm coming up."

"Oh!" squeaked Mrs. Murray, and put her hand to
her head.

"I believe you're right; it's so hot. That's why my
cocktail's coming straight out through my skin," said
Lady Wishart. "Let's have another, Barney. I suppose,"
she added, as she helped herself again, "your master's not
forgotten all about us? He *is* somewhere about?"

"He is in the study, my lady, to the best of my belief," said Barney, taking the tray round again.

"To the best of your belief! Don't you know?" asked
James in surprise; and Lady Wishart said, "Haven't you
told him we're here? The study's right down at the bottom of the garden," she explained to the company. "He
wouldn't hear us come."

"No, my lady. We've orders never to disturb Mr.
Pleydell when he's working in the study. But he knows
your ladyship is expected. He ordered supper to be put
out on the lawn for eight."

"Looks almost as though he might have to take it in
again," another of the party observed as a flash, followed

by a long growl, lit up the southern sky.

"Well, isn't that just the limit of Crampton?" Lady Wishart observed without much surprise. "How long has he been there, Barney?"

"Since breakfast, my lady. I laid out his lunch for him there before he went down, and I have not seen him since."

"Well!" said Lady Wishart, and sat down again. The rest stood staring at one another. James Warrender looked at his watch. Vivienne Murray drank Mrs. Warrender's second cocktail. There was another and much brighter flash, and a clap, instead of a roll, of thunder.

"*Oh!*" cried Mrs. Murray. "Oh, my *head!* I can't *endure* storms!"

"Nor can I," said Lady Wishart, rising suddenly to her feet. "At least, not in the garden. Look here," gathering her courage together, "let's all go down to the study and rout Crampton out. It's quite clear he's either forgotten all about us or he's playing one of his dreadful tricks. No, Barney," to the butler, who was hovering uneasily about, "we won't go and wait in the house; we've waited long enough. You can take the food in if you like—in fact, I should think you'd better; but we've done enough waiting. Come along, all of you. I won't go alone." It showed the force of Pleydell's personality, Mrs. Warrender reflected, as they hurried across the lawn, that even his old friend did not venture to challenge his privacy without support.

Beyond the lawn a long path led through herbaceous borders to a rose garden, through which they passed to twisted alleyways of flowering shrubs, which Mrs. Warrender would have been glad to linger and examine, had not Lady Wishart been in such a hurry and the storm evidently coming up so fast. The study must have been two or three hundred yards from the house; at least, they seemed to have walked immense distances in the sullen light before they came to it, a big, curious building of wood, with painted and twisted pillars at each corner, roofed with green glass slates like the bottoms of bottles, with overhanging eaves and a giant skylight like a studio's. It stood in a sort of open space covered with long grass, with a low wall behind it and beyond that the mutter of the sea. The door was facing them, and on the right of the building a path led away into holly bushes black with the coming storm.

Lady Wishart trotted up to the door, knocked on it, and called, "Crampton! Crampton! We're tired of waiting!" There was no answer. She waited a moment, and then knocked again, and tried the handle.

"It's locked! Bother him, what can he be doing? Crampton! *Crampton!* Oh, dear," as a large raindrop fell with a plop on the threshold. "This really is too bad! He can't have gone out. *Crampton! Crampton!!*" She battered on the door and shook at the handle. "*Crampton!!!*"

Suddenly they all jumped, and turned their heads as a high piercing shriek tore the air.

"Vivienne! What's the matter?" quavered Mrs. Murray. Vivienne Murray, who had gone to the side of the building and peered in through an open casement, was looking back at them with a chalk-white face and eyes staring out of her head. She screamed again and again; but no words came.

"*Stop that noise!*" James Warrender shouted, and she checked it. "Now what's the matter?"

"He—he hasn't gone out! He's in there! But he can't hear you! He can't hear you *at all!* Oh!!" She began another scream which was cut short as she put her hand to her throat and stumbled retching and choking into the grass. "Keep her quiet, mother." While his mother moved to the girl's assistance, James Warrender took a couple of strides to the open window and bent his head to peer into the dimness within.

"He's in there, all right," he said, after what seemed an interminable time; "and I'm afraid it looks as though he's been taken ill. We shall have to get in somehow, even if it means breaking the door down." He stood back a second or two, measuring the window with his eye. "It's too small for me, but I believe you could wriggle through, Oliver. Have a try. The rest of you had better get back to the house; it'll be pouring in a minute." The young poet, shivering like an aspen, approached the window and peered in, while from round a curve in the path by which they had come appeared a ludicrous trotting figure, black and white with flapping tails. It was the butler, who must have heard the screams from the house.

"Oh, Barney, there you are. I'm afraid your master's seriously ill—a fit or something. I can't help what his orders were; we shall have to break in. You'd better come, if you can—if there's anybody up at the house to look after these ladies. It's been a bit of a shock for them, and they've had nothing to eat. Is there anybody up there?"

"Yes, sir. The maids are there," said Barney in an apprehensive voice.

"Good. Archibald, see to that, will you, and as quick as you know. Get Miss Murray away, mother, if you can; she can't stay here. Now, then, Oliver, what are you waiting for?"

"I c-can't!" Oliver, after his glance into the room, was shaking and looking nearly as sick as the girl whom Mrs. Warrender was now leading away with an arm round her shoulders.

"Rubbish. Pull yourself together. We've got to get in, and I don't want to break the door down if it can be helped. Here, I'll give you a shove. That's right. Drop down as lightly as you can, and don't touch him. Can you see the door?"

"Uh."

"Is the key in it?"

"Yes."

"Good. Go straight across, will you, and open it. Come, Barney."

In a second or two the door was open, and a white-faced Oliver appeared on the threshold. "All right," said James, with a hint of contempt, "you can cut along now." He stepped in and looked about him.

Even in that fading light it was a strange room, a collector's room. It was forty by thirty feet at least, and as tall as a small chapel. The roof rose high to a ridge of sea-green glass, and sloped down low on either side to the casement windows, some of which were fitted with coloured glass like old-fashioned conservatories. There were Bokhara rugs and skins on the floor, carved and in-laid tables and chairs about, two divans, and an enor-mous oak settle covered with papers; there were book-cases full of books, and glass-doored cabinets full of strange objects of various kinds. But neither man spared the room more than a quick glance, for their eyes turned almost instantly to its owner. Crampton Pleydell lay on the floor, about three feet from the open window.

"He—he looks to be *dead,* sir," Barney stammered, having stared at the prone form in horror. Pleydell's body was twisted and awry, as though, having fallen, he had made desperate efforts to shift to a more comfortable position. His wide-open, staring eyes were turned towards the window, and there was froth upon his mouth. "Sir!"

"Oh, yes, I think he's dead. We'll make sure in a minute," Warrender said without much concern. "But first I want you to look round the room and tell me if you see anything odd about it—anything gone or out of place, I mean."

Barney blinked and stared. "No, sir," he said at last, "I can't say that I do, though I'm not very conversant with the way things usually are. I mean to say, I'm not

supposed to come in here very often, so I don't often get
a chance to see them. As far as I can tell, it seems to me
much as usual, except for that chair that's fallen over."
He stepped forward to pick it up.

"Don't touch it, you fool! Don't touch *anything*.
Don't you realise, we may have to have the police in
here?"

"The police! Oh, sir . . . but the master—"

"All right, we'll have a look at your master now."
He stepped across and laid two fingers on Pleydell's bare
forearm. "He's been dead for hours; he's quite cold," he
said. "Barney—pull yourself together, man. I know it's a
shock, but you can't help him by snivelling—when your
master came—when your master came down here this
morning, was he dressed like that?"

"Yes, sir," Barney sniffed. "He liked working in that
sort of shirt and his old army slacks."

"Didn't you say you'd put him out some lunch?
Where is it?"

"If he's not eaten it, sir, it'll be in the alcove, behind
that curtain," said Barney, switching on the light. "Mr.
Pleydell didn't like food lying about." Warrender strode
to the curtain and pulled it back. Behind was a table,
holding a cold meal which had not been touched.

"Um. Looks as though he had died some time during the morning. Hullo!" When the light was turned on
it rendered visible a small object lying on the floor
by Crampton's hand, which he had not noticed before.
He crossed back and stood regarding it with a serious
face.

"Barney," he said, "do you know if your master was
worried—troubled—upset—at all?"

"No, sir, not that I'd noticed, not anything special.
Of course, he had his ups and downs, like all of us. But
what—you don't mean to say, sir—"

"Do you know what this is? No, don't touch it. It's

a hypodermic syringe, the kind of thing you use to inject stuff—drugs—into yourself. And it looks uncommonly to me as if Mr. Pleydell died of poison. . . . Well, we've anyhow got to get the police along. Will you go and ring them up? Don't let everybody know what you're doing."

"Th-there's a telephone here, sir, if you'd like to do it private," Barney, who evidently did not want to do it himself, suggested. "In the alcove where the lunch is."

"Good." Wrapping his hand in a handkerchief, Warrender went to the telephone and manipulated it. "That's all right," he said, turning back after a minute or two; "they'll be along directly. You'd better go up to the house and be there to let them in. I'll stay on guard here; but you'd better not let any of the other visitors go till the police say you may. You might bring or send me down a coat sometime; there's no sense in getting soaked."

IV

Barney shuffled off. Left alone, James Warrender stood for some time in the middle of the room, as though making an inventory of his surroundings. Then he crossed back to the corpse and looked at it for some time, a puzzled frown slowly gathering on his face, until he knelt down and peered more closely at it, particularly at the bare arms and the neck and chest showing through the open shirt. He did not, however, touch any part of it, and after a while he rose to his feet, walked over to the alcove, and cut himself a substantial helping from Crampton Pleydell's lunch. James Warrender was not sentimental, and it would certainly not help his late host in the least for him to be starving when the police arrived.

After a commendably short delay, they came—an astonishing number of them, James thought, not realising at first that Superintendent Martin, though of course properly shocked and horrified to learn of the death of one of the county's most spectacular figures—whatever views he might privately entertain about the said figure—was yet quite aware that the death, whatever should turn out to be its cause, would make a noise, a very big noise, in the papers, and that it was a grand opportunity for what he flattered himself was really one of the most up-to-date and efficient forces in the country to show how neatly it could handle any unexpected situation. For this reason, he had delayed a few minutes— having ascertained that his superior, the chief constable, for whom he had little or no respect, was dining out forty miles away across country—until he had collected quite an imposing paraphernalia of instruments and assistants; and for this reason also he was grateful to James Warrender, of whose profession he was already aware, for having promptly taken charge and preserved everything intact until his arrival.

"The butler tells me you think he killed himself," he remarked, having first taken Warrender's statement about the finding of the body, and set a photographer to take a photograph of it before he let the doctor have a turn.

"Um. It does look a bit like it," said James thoughtfully. "You see that syringe by his side; it may have his fingerprints on it—" The superintendent, full of pride, beckoned to a man who had been standing in the background with an attaché case, and motioned him to the corpse. "You can see the puncture on his forearm where the needle went in. And, by the look of him, I should think he died of poison of some sort."

"Is that your opinion, too, doctor?" the superintendent asked of little Dr. Tetley, who was now on his knees beside the body. James had been much amused to find that the police surgeon should turn out to be one and the same person as Crampton Pleydell's garrulous medical attendant and fervent hanger-on. The sudden change of role appeared to embarrass him; indeed, it had almost reduced him to stuttering.

"Oh, yes, yes. Probably. Yes. I—I must move him, of course. But I should say—cursory glance—I should say cyanide. All the s-signs of it. Syringe, too, smells . . . But—but of course I couldn't say, without a post-mortem."

"Quick-acting stuff," James said.

"Oh, yes. Depends on the amount taken, of course."

"How long would you say he had been dead, sir?" the superintendent asked.

"I—I—I couldn't be sure." The doctor gibbered a little. "Eight—nine—possibly ten hours. I don't think more."

"That fits," said the superintendent. "Ten o'clock, the butler said he went down here, and nobody's seen him since. And his lunch—hullo, what's this? I understood he hadn't eaten his lunch?" James nonchalantly confessed the liberty he had taken.

'I see. Um. It seems to point to suicide. But—have you any idea why he should commit suicide, either of you? Barney hasn't—I've asked him." The doctor shook his head, and the superintendent was turning to James, when an inarticulate murmur from one of his own men caused him to swing round in indignation.

"Jones," he said, "how often have I told you I won't have any of your dirty gossip? If you know anything I ought to hear, say it; if you don't, keep quiet!"

"I'm s-sorry, sir," said the man addressed, with an unmistakable Welsh hissing of his consonants; and Martin turned back to James. "You were saying, sir?"

"I wasn't saying anything. In fact, I didn't know him well enough to offer any opinion on that point. But, as you've asked me, I did think something looked rather queer." He crossed over to the body again. "Look here, Tetley—look at that puncture a minute. Isn't it rather a queer place to choose to give yourself an injection?"

"On the arm? I don't see . . . Oh," said the doctor, "you mean he couldn't get at the place with his other hand."

"So as to pinch up a fold of the flesh when the needle was going in. That's what you do generally, isn't it, when you give injections?"

"Yes. But," said the doctor, "you do that so that you shan't feel the prick of the needle, not for any other reason. And if you were going to kill yourself you wouldn't mind much about the prick of a needle."

"I'm not so sure—I should have thought instinct would still have made you avoid it," James said. "However, that's not much to the point, because, as it happens, he *did* pinch up the skin. Look at the arm."

"By George," said the doctor, "you're right. The mark on the arm's quite clear. Curious that it should have retained the pressure so long . . . But—in that case, he must have done it that way—I don't see what——"

"Then what did he pinch his arm with?"

"I—I don't know," said the doctor.

"You mean to suggest, sir," interrupted the superintendent, whose wits seemed more at command than Dr. Tetley's, "that he *didn't* give himself the injection."

"That's what I'm suggesting. And if Dr. Tetley will look on his chest and shoulders, I think he will find a mark or two that seem like bruises and something that looks to me like a splash or two of acid," James said. "I saw them just now; but I didn't examine them closely."

"You mean that somebody else gave him the injection?"

"Doesn't it look rather like it? And," said James, "I feel I should like to know where that somebody is now."

There was a silence that seemed very long. Then the superintendent pounced. "You again, Jones! What is that now?"

"I wass only saying, sir," said the unrepentant Welshman, "that it wass not so hard to find a reason for murder, at all."

"Murder!" The superintendent boggled over the word, and then went over and looked at the body. "Uh!" he said. "But, look here, sir. There's another mark, here, on his chest, which looks to me quite fresh. Mayn't that have been where he really pushed it in?"

"*Is* that a needle-puncture, Tetley?"

"N-no; certainly not," the doctor said. "That's a scratch—made by a pin or a thorn, or something of that sort."

"Well, mightn't he—"

"Hardly," said James. "Even if he did kill himself with a poisoned thorn—which sounds rather like a detective novel, doesn't it?—there's still the puncture on his arm. And a syringe of cyanide to be accounted for."

"That's so," the superintendent sighed. There was silence for a minute or two, until he spoke again.

"Well, whatever turns out to be the fact, it looks like being a very serious business," he said. "I'll have to seal this place up, as soon as we've got the body out of it, so that Dr. Tetley can make his examination—you'll do it as soon as possible, sir? And find out where everyone was this morning—you weren't either of you here, I suppose?" he asked James and the doctor, who shook their heads. "And see whose syringe that is, and whose prints on it. And where the cyanide might have come from—" He was ticking off the points, methodically, in a notebook, when the irrepressible Jones was heard to remark, "Surely to goodness photographers wass using the stuff every day, in their businesses?"

For a second it looked as though Jones was about to be annihilated; then Martin, with a worried face, said, "Never mind about that now," and wrote something more in his book. At that moment the fingerprint man, who had been standing by the window after performing on the syringe, remarked, "There's some funny bits of glass down on the floor here, sir. Shall I pick 'em up?"

"Get them on a sheet of paper," said the superintendent, handing him one. "They're very thin," he commented, poring over the broken slivers. "What would they be? Bits of a watch-glass, now?"

"They're much too fine for that," Warrender said. "In fact, I've no idea what they are. I don't think I've seen glass as fine as that outside a museum or a laboratory. Probably they're bits of one of Pleydell's curios—perhaps his visitor squashed it," he conjectured cheerfully. "Well, superintendent, if you don't want me any longer I think I'll be getting back. Good hunting."

"Is it true, James, that the poor man killed himself?" his mother asked him when he came to say good-night. She knew better than to ply him with questions downstairs.

"They've not decided yet whether it was suicide or murder," James replied.

"And what do *you* think? Or mayn't I ask?"

"Oh, it was murder all right," said James with a yawn.

"Oh, how dreadful! And does that mean you won't be able to go to France?"

"Of course it doesn't. I'm going to France on business, and that can't wait. I've no time to do local policemen's jobs for them. Besides," he said, "I think, from the look on the man's face, that he's got a pretty good idea already who's responsible, so he'll be able to pin him or her quick, if he can prove it."

"Oh!" said Mrs. Warrender, with a little shiver. She had never really learned to like the process of the law. "Oh, James, dear," she said suddenly, "I nearly forgot to ask you what I ought to do with this. I picked it up in Mr. Pleydell's garden—my foot knocked against it and I slipped it into my bag, and when I came home I found I'd still got it with me. What do you think it can be?"

"I don't know. What a curious thing!" James looked at it with some interest. It was a round glass ball, nearly two inches in diameter, and made of glass of very great translucence and with a faint tinge of blue. It was almost perfectly smooth, save that on one side there was a narrow elliptical ridge, in shape like a small slot, which was sharp to the touch, with a few tiny splinters of thin glass sticking up. "I've no idea what it can be. It's very good-quality glass—and it must be solid, it's so heavy. It can't be a paperweight, because it would roll; and I can't think what that roughness is—it looks as though something had broken off, but it must have been something very thin."

"Is it an old stopper, do you think, with the part that went in the bottle broken off?"

"No bottle ever had a neck as narrow as that," James said. "It must be a curiosity of some sort. I wonder"—he looked at it again—"there were some slivers of glass on the floor in Pleydell's studio. I wonder if this and they are part of an ornament that got broken."

"Oh! Do you think I ought to show it to the police?"

"Oh, sometime, perhaps. They'll have their work cut out for the present, and I don't suppose they'll want to be bothered. It wasn't in the studio, was it? Where did you say you found it?"

"In the long grass, between the studio and the hollies," Mrs. Warrender replied. "It was when I was—looking after Vivienne Murray," she added delicately.

"Yes, in the end. But she was dreadfully hysterical, and really made herself quite ill. We've put her to bed now, and I hope she'll be better in the morning."

"I hope she'll be quieter, for her sake as well as everyone else's," James said. "Well, good-night. I've told the police that I'll stay until lunchtime tomorrow, and after that I really must be off."

"Good-night, dear." But in her bed, and just as she was turning over to go to sleep, his last words recurred to her with a meaning which caused her to sit bolt upright in the dark. "*Oh!*" she whispered to herself. "He couldn't have meant that—poor child . . . oh, no, it's quite impossible!" But she could not feel quite certain that it was.

V

James Warrender called round at the police station in the morning, and found Superintendent Martin looking very well pleased with himself. "Not too badly, not too badly, not too badly," he said in response to an enquiry. "We're not getting on too badly; and I must say it's largely thanks to you, sir, that we've been able to be so quick off the mark. Dr. Tetley's done the p.m., and it's as we supposed. He was killed by a good strong dose of cyanide, which was injected into him, and he died between half-past ten and eleven, as nearly as the doctor can make out. That's all plain sailing. But then there are those splashes of cyanide on his chest, sir, as you pointed out, and the marks on his arms and shoulders, which look like a struggle of some sort—they're pretty definitely the marks of hands, not of furniture or a rope or anything like that."

"It doesn't sound like much of a struggle, as far as I remember them," James said doubtfully. "He was a big strong fellow; wouldn't he have put up more of a fight?"

"Not if the poison was working in him *already*, sir," the superintendent said earnestly. "What it seems to me is, that his assailant jabbed the needle into him when he wasn't expecting it, and so got his dose in, and that the struggle was Mr. Pleydell trying to hold him, or get to the telephone and summon help, or something. But the symptoms come on very quickly, sir; he wouldn't be able to struggle long. And it wouldn't have taken a man of great strength to do it either," he added, with emphasis.

"Oho! So you have somebody for the part, have you? I thought I saw it in your eye. Anything to do with photography, by any chance?"

"I properly took the hide off that young Jones," said the superintendent. "Blurting things like that out in front of everybody! But, yes, as a matter of fact, we have got more than an idea; and, if you'll promise to keep it to yourself, sir, I don't mind telling you what there is to it—knowing that I can trust you. It's a fact that there *is* a young fellow resident in the town who's been heard more than once to utter threats against Mr. Pleydell. Very serious threats indeed," said the superintendent.

"Such as?"

"Such as that Mr. Pleydell was no better than a

murderer himself, and if the law wouldn't act, decent people ought to take it into their own hands."

"Oho! And what was all that about?"

"Well, sir"—the superintendent looked down at his desk and seemed rather embarrassed—"it's not really a very pretty story, but . . . I don't know whether you're aware of it, but the late Mr. Pleydell—well, he was a bit of a free and a friendly gentleman, particularly with the ladies, and, not to put too fine a point on it, he sometimes went further than was called for."

"You don't surprise me," James said, and the superintendent lifted his head again.

"Matter of fact, sir, he was a terrible one for taking up people—young lads, too, as well as girls, and just dropping them like hot cakes when he'd had enough. You know, I'm not saying there was necessarily anything *wrong*—what we'd call wrong—about it, only it turned their heads and made them all upset and that's a fact. And I don't call it right, myself, not if you were fifty times a famous artist—but, there, people are made like that and you can't stop it.

"But I'm wandering. The long and the short of it is, there was a girl in the town called Irene Gray—and a pretty, taking little thing she was too. She worked in the beauty parlour in Market Street, and my girls said she was clever as paint at her job, and sharp too. Bit saucy with the boys, maybe, but nothing to matter much. And she was earning good money and keeping company or whatever they call it now with a young chap called Edward Fenton, a steady clever fellow, if he is a bit on the quiet side.

"Now, about a year ago—when he was here last summer, to be precise—Mr. Crampton Pleydell took Irene up, and I'll say he did take her up. She was forever being called for by him and going around to his place, and she got above herself—a lot too much above herself for some of our tastes. I don't say she actually gave young Ted the chuck, but she came pretty near it, and to the best of my belief she told him that if he wanted her he could wait until she'd had her fill of Mr. Pleydell or some rubbish of that sort.

"This went on for some time, Ted swallowing it, more or less, because he couldn't do anything else, and she getting more and more up in the air, and hinting she was going to set up for herself in London or somewhere, this place not being good enough. So nobody was very much surprised when one fine morning she never turned up to work at all. Everybody assumed she'd gone to London; and though the beauty-parlour was a bit fed-up with her not giving any notice, they just shrugged their shoulders and said she'd been getting so slack about her work they were going to fire her anyway.

"Only she hadn't gone to London. She hadn't gone anywhere. After a few days, of course," said the superintendent, "there began to be enquiries made, and we put Scotland Yard on to it, and they broadcast for her; but she never turned up—not until, weeks after, her dead body was found under some bushes in the woods some way out of the town. She'd never gone to London at all; she must have died, I suppose, the day she disappeared."

"Oh! And what did she die of?"

"The coroner returned an open verdict," said the superintendent. "Privately, he and the doctor were pretty sure she must have taken some poison whose traces disappear quickly—one of the vegetable poisons, probably. The alternative was that she died a natural death, but there was nothing wrong with her and you don't die of exposure at the beginning of September. But after so long there was nothing to tell by, so we let it be. No sense in shaming the girl after she was dead."

"But Mr. Fenton, he didn't let it be? He said Mr. Pleydell had murdered her?"

"Murdered in the sight of God," the superintendent corrected. "I should have said that Mr. Pleydell had left for town two or three days before she disappeared, and it came out afterwards in talk that in those two or three days she'd been pretty down in the mouth—probably he'd given her the chuck already. No, all Ted meant was that if she'd killed herself it was Mr. Pleydell's fault— and, you know, there was some truth in that, one must admit."

"I see. And you think this is his revenge. Waited a good long time for it, hasn't he?"

"Well, he hasn't had so very much opportunity," the superintendent pointed out. "Mr. Pleydell's been away all winter—only came down again and opened up his place about a month ago. And you could hardly expect Ted to get busy the moment he turned up again. But I know he started talking this silly talk again as soon as he did come back—and he's still talking it just as hard as he did last winter."

"And I can't say I'm surprised he should," James commented. "So you think you've got it all sewn up for him?"

"Oh, no, I wouldn't say that, sir. It's a long way from being proved yet, though there *are* one or two other things. For instance, the cyanide. Young Ted is assistant to Hollins, the photographer, and he's a keen youngster who experiments himself in his spare time; and you can't deny it's a coincidence it should have been cyanide, being the one quick poison Ted could get hold of without any trouble. Then again—yesterday morning he asked if he could go out, because he wasn't feeling well, and old

Hollins, thinking he looked pretty dicky, let him go. And he was away from ten to twelve without anyone knowing where."

"Where does he say he was?"

"Don't know. One of my men's going to ask him," said the superintendent. "Of course, if he turns out to have an alibi, that'll bust it; but I *think* we'll find that he was taking a walk all by himself and met nobody, and I *guess* that this walk was in fact round the old cliff path to the creek that leads to Chalgrove Field grounds."

"From which he could get up to Mr. Pleydell's study?"

"As easy as falling out of a tree. The path goes straight up; it don't go anywhere else, and, moreover, there's no other way out of the creek, and the place is lonely and overgrown; the path's none too safe, nowadays, and there's a warning notice on it. So it would be pretty easy to come up secretly. It's a pity that last night's storm will have washed away any traces of anybody coming that way."

"Um. I see. And the syringe—was that his?"

"We don't know anything about the syringe, yet. It doesn't seem to have been Mr. Pleydell's, at least, his man never heard of his using one; and it's a pretty common pattern. I've wired to Mr. John Pleydell to come back, and he may know something about it. But," said the superintendent, "I'll tell you one thing. That syringe had Mr. Pleydell's fingermarks on it and nobody else's—*but* the marks weren't placed so that they could have been made by anybody using the syringe for business purposes! Now what do you make of that, sir? If you hadn't tumbled to the way things were so quick, we might never have thought of looking. And I'm sure I'm very grateful to you for all the help you've given."

"Ye-es. I'm not so sure that I'm so grateful to my-self," James murmured, as a few minutes later he took his leave. "I'm not sure that my feelings, as regards the late Crampton Pleydell, aren't much the same as the photographer's."

VI

Not very dissimilar were the feelings of Mrs. Warrender, as she sat on the hotel lawn after tea on the following evening, talking, or rather being discoursed to, by Lady Wishart. She had sought the lady out, in the first place, because she was anxious to enquire after Vivienne Murray, whom she had not seen for nearly forty-eight hours, since she had helped to put her to bed, in a collapsed condition, on the evening of Crampton Pleydell's party. Lady Wishart replied with some asperity that she had despatched both Vivienne and her mother on a charabanc tour round the beauty spots of the west country, and added (which made Mrs. Warrender's gorge rise) that anything was better than to have that silly girl languishing around and trying to get herself into the middle of the picture.

"Pretending she had an affair with Crampton!" Lady Wishart said.

"I didn't think there was much pretence about it," said Mrs. Warrender.

"My dear Mrs. Warrender, it was all pretence from the beginning to the end! You don't suppose *Crampton* would ever have taken a child like that seriously? Why, he could have his pick of women in any continent he chose! And to imagine, because he talked a little to her about his work, where his work touched upon her experience, that she had any *claim* on him, any right to suppose he was smitten with her—quite frankly, it makes me sick. If she had any sense of Literature," said Lady Wishart, with a capital L, "she would have been glad and proud to think she was being of service—quite apart from anything he did for her, and you can't honestly say you think that was nothing!" Nor could she, in fact. "The most sickening thing about Literature," said Lady Wishart, "is the way leeches fasten upon you all through your life and think that if they've helped you once, they are entitled to prey upon you forevermore. Poor Crampton was preyed upon more than any writer I ever knew, while he was alive—and I thought I would at least make sure that that girl didn't make capital out of him when he was dead. . . . Goodness me! Whatever was that striking?"

"Six o'clock," said Mrs. Warrender.

"You're sure? Oh, really, that's too annoying! Now the library will be closed, and I want to change my book. That stupid girl there gave me the wrong one this morning, and I'm sure I said the name perfectly clearly!"

"She looked very tired this morning, I thought," said Mrs. Warrender.

"She's no business to be so tired she can't listen—or, if she is, she ought to get someone else to do her work," Lady Wishart retorted. "She gave me a detective novel, and she ought to know by now that I can't abide them—and it's Sunday tomorrow!" She finished in a wail, reviving, however, to continue in the same strain until she saw a servant from the hotel coming out in search of her. "Well, what is it?"

"If you please m'lady, the young lady from the library would be glad to speak to you for a moment."

"Well, I never!" said Lady Wishart inelegantly. "Do

you suppose she's *remembered*?"

In a very few minutes she was back, wreathed in the smiles of her own natural good-nature, and followed by the pale, slim figure of the girl from the library. "This good young woman," she said, "recollected the mistake she made this morning, and has come all the way up to put it right—isn't that kind of her? And she's asked me if she could have just a few minutes' talk with Mrs. Warrender—you won't mind, will you?"

"Of course not" — "Don't get up, please," said the girl. "Well, then, *you* sit down," said Mrs. Warrender, smiling and pointing to the chair which Lady Wishart had just vacated. The girl sat, poising herself on the very edge, and twisting her cheap handbag between her fingers. As the light fell on her face, she looked very tired indeed.

"You wanted to see me?" said Mrs. Warrender after a long pause.

"Yes. . . if you will forgive me troubling you . . . I'm afraid it is very . . .but is your son Mr. Warrender the detective?" The last words came out in a sudden rush.

"Yes, he is."

"Could—do you think he would possibly see me for a minute?"

"I'm so sorry," said Mrs. Warrender, "he's not here."

"Oh! Is he—could you tell me when he'll be back?"

"I'm afraid he won't be back. He's gone."

"Oh!" A stone might have sunk into the water. "I wonder," said the girl, obviously plucking up all her courage, "if you—would it be too much to ask if you could let me have his address?"

"I am so very sorry," Mrs. Warrender said; "I don't

know where he is. I could let you have his London address, but I'm afraid that wouldn't be much use, because I don't know when he'll be back. You see, he's gone to France—I'm so sorry."

"It doesn't matter. I'm so sorry to have troubled you. G-good afternoon," the girl said, rising. But there was an unmistakable quiver in the last words, and as she turned to go she stumbled, and put out a groping hand.

"My dear!" Mrs. Warrender rose from her seat and made a step towards her. "I'm afraid you're in trouble. Won't you—isn't there anything I can do to help?"

The girl choked a little, and blew her nose miserably. "Was it something you wanted to ask my son about?" She nodded. "I'm so *very* sorry he's away."

"It d-doesn't matter—I don't suppose anybody could help us."

"What is it? Won't you tell me, at least?"

"Oh, you are *kind*," said the girl, turning back and wiping her eyes. "I knew you were, the way you spoke to me in the library, and it's a shame to bother you. It's only. . .only that a friend of mine's probably going to be arrested for murder, and I hoped—"

"*Arrested for murder?*"

"Yes. You know about Mr. Crampton Pleydell—that people are all saying he was murdered?" Mrs. Warrender nodded; even in two days the opinion represented by Police Constable Jones had seeped as far as the hotel population. "Well, they've been asking my friend lots of questions, and he thinks—"

"Your friend from the photographer's?" Mrs. Warrender interrupted; and then blushed at her inquisitiveness.

"How ever did you know? Never mind, it doesn't matter. Only—they think he did it, you see. And I thought—perhaps Mr. Warrender could tell us what to do. Only he's gone." There was another catch in her voice.

"But, my dear child, I don't understand." Mrs. Warrender was completely at a loss. *Why* should the kind young man from the photographer's have murdered anybody?

"I'm so sorry; of course you don't," said the girl. "You see, he wanted to—I mean, he hoped he would die, at least—ever since my sister died last year."

"Your sister?"

"Yes, my sister. Irene Gray. I'm Daphne Gray." And then it all came out, substantially the same story as that which James Warrender had heard from the superintendent on the previous day, only told from another point of view. "And so, you see," she finished, "if—if Mr. Pleydell *was* murdered, there's only one person who's likely to have done it, and that's him."

"But do you mean the police really suspect your fiancé?"

"He's not my fiancé; he was my sister's," said Daphne Gray quickly. "He's only my f-friend—" "I beg your pardon," said Mrs. Warrender. "—I don't know for certain, but a policeman came round and asked him a great deal of questions, about where he was on Thursday morning—because he wasn't at the shop."

"And where was he?"

"He was with me," said Daphne Gray, and looked her straight in the face.

"Did he tell the policeman that?"

"Yes."

"Oh, my dear!" said Mrs. Warrender. "*Please*—whatever he has done or whatever you think, *don't* let him tell lies to the police! Really . . . it is not nonsense.

My son always says it makes things very much worse for anybody that they—that they aren't quite sure of. *Don't* let him do it."

Daphne tried to look at her again and gave it up. "It doesn't look as if I was being much use to him," she said. "Only—if he can't say where he was, what will they do to him?"

"But surely he must know where he was, Miss Gray," said Mrs. Warrender. "Forgive my asking you, but do you yourself—are you *sure* he couldn't have—I do beg your pardon."

"You needn't. Anybody would want to know. I'm quite certain," said Daphne Gray steadily. "He couldn't do anything like that—I've known him a long time, and he couldn't. He's not that kind of man. All he meant was that Mr. Pleydell ought to have been punished—and so he ought! But that doesn't mean that he won't be— arrested. Lots of people get punished for things they haven't done! Don't they?"

"But where *was* he, really?" Mrs. Warrender was trying to think what James would have done under the circumstances, and not feeling at all competent.

"He—well, as a matter of fact, he's waiting outside now," Daphne said. "I—I asked him to come too, just in case Mr. Warrender could see us. I wonder . . . would you very much mind if he came in?"

Mrs. Warrender did mind; she was nervous. But she could not well refuse, and in a minute or two the dark-haired young man appeared, more pale and distracted than when she had last seen him, and looking as though he were helplessly following the lead of his friend.

He was not much help. He was unhappy and hope-less. He agreed that it was foolish to tell lies to the police; but he said he didn't think it would have been much better if he had told them that he had spent the morning walking distractedly up and down, thinking of possible ways in which Crampton Pleydell could be punished. And this (with a slight touch of defiance) was just what he had done. Ever since Pleydell had returned to Quartermouth, looking just as if nothing had happened and going on the same way as before, he had been growing more and more desperate. He couldn't fight the novelist; he wasn't big enough. And yet he felt he *had* to do something. On that morning he'd been awake all night, thinking and wondering; and he'd asked leave from the shop because he didn't feel he could speak decently to a customer. And he'd just walked up and down, nowhere in particular; he didn't know where he'd been. All this in slow jerks, and partly in response to questions. "They won't believe me, of course," he finished. "Don't know why they should."

"*Don't*," said Daphne, and pressed his arm.

"Don't you bother about me," he said. " 'Tisn't worth it." Daphne looked at Mrs. Warrender in mute appeal.

Mrs. Warrender was distractedly trying to think what James would have done. She did not think that the boy looked like a murderer, though he did look like a neurotic. Perhaps it would be truer to say that she did not think much about him at all, because her sympathies were engaged, not with him, but with the nice girl who was so obviously in love with him and who had been very kind to her. But how could anybody do anything unless they knew what all the evidence was against him? James would know—but James was far away. And the police would know.

At this point, having spoken some of her thoughts aloud, she discovered to her alarm that Daphne was eagerly begging her to ask the police what the evidence was. She was apprehensive; she mistrusted her own powers, and she was not very certain what the evidence would turn out to be. But Daphne's pleading overcame her, and almost before she knew what she was doing she found that she had promised to go to the police—not on the next day, a Sunday during which law-abiding policemen in country places would presumably be at church and not in their stations, but as soon as possible—and ask them what it was. And she would meet Daphne Gray during the Monday lunch-hour when the library was closed, at Ye Kosie Korner Koffee-House, and tell her what there was to tell. The extravagant gratitude with which this suggestion was received caused her to feel more incompetent than ever.

"I don't care," Fenton, who had been silent for some time, suddenly burst out, "I don't care if they do hang me! I'm glad—he ought to have been killed. But I didn't do it."

"Never mind, Ted," said Daphne, taking his arm. "Come and have your tea. You know you're frightfully tired."

VII

Mrs. Warrender was quivering a little as she entered the presence of the superintendent, though she was less a-fraid of the police than of most people, having come into contact with them a good deal by reason of her son's occupation, and having always found them amiable and considerate. Still, to provide coffee for a sort of colleague of James's was one thing, and to seek information from an entirely strange policeman quite another; so with some vague idea of enlisting his interest, she took with her the strange glass object which she had found in the grounds of Chalgrove Field, and laid it in front of Superintendent Martin's nose, much as though he were a cat, and she were offering him a sardine.

The superintendent was very amiable. He was grateful to James Warrender, and disposed to be kind to his mother, if, indeed, he had not himself possessed a weakness for old ladies. He examined her exhibit with gratifying attention, though he did not seem to think very much of it. "It doesn't seem very likely the gentleman was hit on the head with a marble," he observed genially. "And you say you found it outside the study. Well, thank you very much for coming to mention it, madam." He pushed it to one side. "I'm sure we're very much obliged to you for taking the trouble."

But when she came to the real purpose of her visit, she found him much less genial. Not that he was unkind, not even that he refused to give her any information, as he might well have done. But he had obviously made up his mind; he did not like Ted Fenton—or else the young man had got across him in some way—and his chief concern was to warn her, speaking as one who would not like to see James Warrender's mother, any more than his own mother, making a fool of herself, not to be deceived by young men with plausible manners. Young men, he indicated, could always bamboozle old ladies, particularly when they were young men in danger of their lives, and as to not looking like a murderer, why, all the murderers he'd ever known (he talked as though he had known dozens) looked as though butter wouldn't melt in their mouths. He would advise her *most strongly*, if she didn't want to get into serious trouble—and, he hinted, seriously compromise her son's reputation—to go home and have a nice cup of tea and not bother her head about young Fenton.

Mrs. Warrender, as nearly annoyed as she could be

at being treated as if she were on the verge of the grave or of a home for the feeble-minded, argued the point with an obstinacy of which she had not known herself capable; and so irritated the superintendent (who did not feel free to lose his temper with her) that he ended by telling her more than he had intended to of the case against Fenton, notably the fact, up till that point unknown to her, that cyanide of potassium had been the cause of Crampton Pleydell's death. Mrs. Warrender let slip a small sigh as this information sank in.

"Besides," said the superintendent triumphantly, "who d'you suppose was likely to do it, if he didn't? Let alone the threats he's uttered time and again against Mr. Pleydell. There's nobody else bore him any sort of a grudge. No, my advice to you, madam, is to——"

But before he could repeat his advice for the fifth time there was a loud and angry noise outside, and almost immediately there burst in a loud and angry man. Mrs. Warrender recognised him, though she had only seen him once or twice, and on those occasions he had not been nearly so red in the face. It was Mr. John Pleydell, and he was very cross indeed, so cross that he did not even notice that anybody else was there, as he came storming up to the superintendent's table.

The superintendent rose to his feet. He was willing to be very conciliatory; but for a time he and his visitor were at cross-purposes. For he assumed that Mr. John Pleydell was angry at his brother's murder and with the police for not having prevented it, whereas it gradually became clear that what was really annoying Mr. John Pleydell was the disappearance of certain objects from his brother's study.

"Never even noticed—never even *saw* there was anything gone! Fools!" he shouted. "Asked Barney! *Barney*! What does he know? Fool! Most valuable things in the place—gone—may be anywhere by now! Fools!"

"I beg your pardon, sir," the superintendent said, "but what exactly are the things you say are missing?"

"Best pieces of glass-work—modern glass-work—in England! Collectors' pieces—absolutely irreplaceable," John Pleydell growled. "Look here, Mr. What's-your-name, do you mean to tell me you don't know that my brother was once one of the best makers of fine glass in England? Gave it up, of course, years ago—that's why these are irreplaceable. Used to sell it, of course—specimens all over the place, in collections and so forth. But he kept the finest bits himself—wouldn't sell 'em, wouldn't let anybody touch 'em—kept 'em locked up in the little case in his study. Now they're gone—clean gone—and nobody's taken any notice of it! Preposterous! . . . What's that? *There?* Of course they were there! Saw them with my own eyes, before I went away. Now they're gone. Pinched. And what are you doing about it? Nothing whatever!"

The superintendent was heard to murmur something about murder being more important than robbery.

"Murder my foot," John Pleydell retorted. "What I want to know is why the dickens aren't you paying any attention to the robbery? Here you go, messing around with some footling village idiot who you think may have killed my brother, and all the while there's a thumping motive for murder staring you in the face. Hang it, man, don't you realise the things were *valuable?* You could have got almost any price for them, and Crampton would never have let anybody have them except over his dead body. You get the man who pinched Crampton's glass and you've got Crampton's murderer—no need to go fussing round any further."

"Perhaps," said the superintendent, taking up his pen, "if you'd kindly describe them—"

"*I* can't describe them," said John Pleydell. "Glass things they were—beads and toys and things like that. If you want 'em described you'll have to ask that Herdman feller—oh, I *do* beg your pardon, madam!" In his excited gesticulating at the superintendent he had dealt a swinging blow to Mrs. Warrender, of whose presence he thus became conscious for the first time. From the look which the superintendent turned on her, it seemed to Mrs. Warrender that he also had been oblivious of it for the last few minutes, and she made all haste to remove herself, taking with her, after a few seconds' hesitation, the round glass ball. She was slightly uneasy about doing this; but soothed her conscience with the reflection that the superintendent had not seemed at all interested in it, and perhaps Mr. John Pleydell might be. For might it not be part of one of the missing glass trinkets, dropped in the grass by the thief as he made his escape?

At any rate here was a new and possible explanation of the murder—a very attractive one, since the police could hardly suspect Edward Fenton of wanting to steal valuable glass—it would not fit with a motive of revenge. Mrs. Warrender, trotting along to seek her rendezvous with Daphne Gray, anticipated with pleasure how she would cheer her up with her new suggestion, and how she would write to James's office in the hope of getting his opinion.

But, as she proceeded, her satisfaction gradually grew less and less. It was a good idea to assume a burglary—and if Mr. John Pleydell was right, the glass was certainly worth stealing. And burglars, if interrupted, did sometimes kill the owners of the property. But did burglars, even murderous burglars, generally poison the owners with cyanide of potassium? Perhaps she had better not tell Daphne Gray about this new idea just yet—though she could find out if she knew anything about the glass.

This was easily done, because Daphne Gray knew nothing whatever, had no idea, in fact, that Mr. Pleydell owned any glass, though she knew, as everybody did, that he had a lot of valuable things.

"You see," she said, "being away when it all happened I wouldn't have known about what he had, unless Irene'd thought to tell me, and she didn't generally put things like that in her letters."

"Oh, were you away? I hadn't realised that."

"Yes," said Daphne, "it was when I was working in Plymouth. I didn't—I didn't know anything about it, even, until three days after she—didn't come in. And then they sent over a policeman to see me in Plymouth, and the same night I got a letter from Ted, begging me to tell him where she'd gone, because he was going nearly off his head, and he thought I knew where she was—but, of course, I didn't."

"How dreadful for you! I suppose you hadn't any idea?"

"Oh, I thought she'd gone to London after Mr. Pleydell. But the police went and asked him soon after—as soon as they thought they could go bothering anybody as important as that—only of course *he* didn't know where she was. And then they broadcast for her—it was queer, hearing Irene described on the wireless—and nothing happened. And then I heard this job was going again—I'd left it to go to Plymouth, you see—and so I applied for it. I couldn't somehow stop in Plymouth, and besides I thought Ted would really go off his head if he hadn't somebody to talk to—it was awful for him, you see. And all the time she was dead," said Daphne, biting her lip.

In a minute or two she had recovered, and was putting on the table a large fat envelope which she had brought with her. "I don't know if they'd be any use to you at all," she said, "but I've brought Irene's letters, the ones she wrote to me when I was in Plymouth. I—they—I haven't shown them to anybody, I mean—I don't know if they'll be any good."

"Not even to the police?" Mrs. Warrender asked.

"No! I mean, afterwards . . . when they found her, they didn't ask any questions, much, or ask to see anything. And I didn't want to show them, and perhaps have them read out. It would only have made it harder for Ted, you see—at least, you'll see if you read them. But don't if you don't want to."

"Would you rather I didn't?"

"I don't . . . it's silly to mind, now. And if it could be any good to him—that's her photograph, taken in the summer. I put it on the top," Daphne said.

Mrs. Warrender took it and studied it: the head of a laughing girl with hair waved scrupulously in last year's fashion, wide-open eyes below a broad forehead like her sister's, white teeth, and a general air of vivacity. Perhaps there was a hint of hardness about the mouth, if it had been closed. Difficult to tell. But she must have been very pretty.

"Younger than you?" she asked.

"Four years. She had a very nice colour—a lot more than me. It doesn't show in the photograph," Daphne said in a level voice.

"I suppose—I ought to have looked after her better. Only—it's difficult to look after people when they're getting more money than you are."

Mrs. Warrender gave one last look at the photograph, and put it aside. Underneath was the broadcast description, from a newspaper cutting—as unilluminating as descriptions of wanted persons usually are. Underneath that was the first of the letters, of which there were seven or eight, all dated from Quartermouth during the summer of the previous year.

As she read them, Mrs. Warrender ceased to wonder why Daphne had not wished to show them to the police, or to produce them at the inquest. Not that there was anything out-of-the-way about them, either in content or in style. Irene Gray was not a *littérateuse*; the phrases were commonplace and half the story untold. But such as it was it was plain enough, and would not have been pleasant reading for Edward Fenton.

It began with a "pick-up" by Crampton Pleydell, who had come into the beauty parlour to have a manicure, and got into conversation with the lively assistant on the subject of her work. Then, the letters showed, she had been invited up to the Chalgrove Field study—"a funny old room like a cross between a studio and a chapel, with a lot of old junk in it"—asked to supply more details of a manicurist's life, "drawn out," if that were the proper phrase, until her head had been completely turned. As the letters went on, she became more and more excited, and more and more convinced that she was on to a good thing, and that Crampton Pleydell would do something handsome for her, in return for the services she was rendering—she hinted that what she hoped for was a beauty parlour of her own in London. Mrs. Warrender looked for the references to Fenton, which Daphne had not wanted him to see; but found only one, and that obviously in response to an enquiry. "Of course Ted's making a fuss," Irene wrote; "you know what he's like. But I've told him where he's going to get off if he bothers." Only one—but quite enough. Reading the letters, Mrs. Warrender wondered whether Daphne realised exactly how much of a gold-digger her little sister appeared in them. She glanced quickly up, and from her expression felt quite certain that she did, and that only Ted Fenton's danger would ever have induced her to show the letters to anyone.

With the last two the tone changed. Crampton Pleydell, having finished his book or the preparations for his book, was clearly beginning to cool off. In the first letter Irene was annoyed at some breaking of an engagement or lack of attention, and was indicating to her sister that she proposed to teach her patron manners; the second, written about ten days later, was a mixture of rage and despair. He was trying to chuck her, he was going to London that day, and he wouldn't see her. He was a devil—she'd as good as lost her job for him, and he was going to make hundreds out of her. He was a devil; but he shouldn't get away. She'd *kill* him—many times underlined—before he did. And there, in a scrawl, the letters ended. Two days after the posting of the last one, Daphne said, Irene disappeared.

Mrs. Warrender sat for a minute staring sadly at the letters, which seemed to tell her nothing at all, except a commonplace story of no credit to anyone. For a moment, the tone of the last one had reminded her painfully of a conversation held, less than a week ago, with Vivienne Murray. *Mutatis mutandis,* the story was the same, and she hoped very much that Vivienne would not . . . However, that was no help to anyone; in fact, the letters, beyond proving definitely to her mind that Crampton Pleydell was better dead—which was not very useful—told her nothing fresh.

At the bottom of the envelope lay a sheaf of newspaper cuttings containing the report of the inquest on the girl's body. Largely because she had nothing to say, she began to read through it, but found little. The body had been found in a deep ditch, covered with brambles—identified by the clothes—very much decomposed—

nothing to show cause of death—no signs of a struggle, except that there was some broken glass which appeared to be the remains of a string of red and white beads—

"Glass beads," said Mrs. Warrender, unaware that she had spoken aloud.

"That was a bit queer," Daphne said. "Because Irene never wore beads in her life. She was funny about it, couldn't bear anything round her neck. I suppose it must have been something Mr. Pleydell gave her; but she never said anything to me about it."

"Glass—glass." Mrs. Warrender's mind stumbled over the word, feeling as though it ought to tell her something, if she could only find out what it was. Glass—glass—why should that bother her? Glass beads round the girl's neck, and Mr. John Pleydell making all that fuss about glass. Perhaps Irene Gray had had one of his missing museum pieces—no, hardly, he'd said that Crampton would only have let them go over his dead body. But—wait a moment—hadn't James said that there *was* glass—slivers of broken glass, by Crampton's dead body? Mrs. Warrender stared into a whirlpool of confusing thoughts.

"My dear," she said, suddenly breaking the silence that had fallen, "did you ever think—did it ever occur to you that your sister might have been killed?"

Then she got a shock. Daphne Gray went as white as death, and gave a little cry. "Oh, no—*no!*" she said. "He—he *couldn't* have!"

VIII

Mrs. Warrender could have whipped herself for her carelessness. Of course, it was the obvious conclusion to draw—but she had not been thinking of Ted Fenton at all. She had been thinking, if it could be called thinking, in some vague way of a mad collector who had tried to get hold of these museum pieces, who had killed Irene Gray in a struggle for one, and Pleydell to get hold of the remainder. Put into words, as she had put it, in order to repair her blunder, it sounded abysmally idiotic; but Daphne, who was desperately catching at any straw which was going, jumped at the idea of a burglar, and before she left the teashop Mrs. Warrender found that she had promised to talk to that explosive person, John Pleydell, and find out some more about the glass objects that had disappeared. This, she felt, being unable to offer Daphne any other consolation, she was bound to do; but she refused to let any suggestion be passed on to Ted Fenton, saying, with as good an imitation of James's manner as she could manage, that it would be very unwise, if there was anything in it, that it should be mentioned.

"All right. I'm afraid Ted'll go right off his head, though," said Daphne. "There's the inquest tomorrow, and he's frightened to death of it."

"All the more reason for not upsetting him, don't you think?" Mrs. Warrender said.

On the way back, she herself found that she was very apprehensive about what she could possibly say to Mr. Pleydell, or what excuse she could give. She hadn't a theory; as far as she had anything, it was a confusion between two mutually inconsistent and equally silly ideas. There was glass—she tried to put her thoughts into some sort of order—valuable glass, that had disappeared, and could only have been taken over Crampton's dead body—only that was probably a picturesque phrase. Anyway it had gone, and Crampton was dead. She supposed there were thieves who stole valuable glass. Barney—could he have taken it and murdered his master? But he didn't look like it.

And then there were two people, the man and the girl, found dead, and each with bits of glass by them. Irene Gray's glass *might* have come from the Pleydell collection, and Pleydell's almost certainly did—perhaps even from the thing that was now in her bag. At any rate she could show that to Mr. John Pleydell, and see if he was more interested in it than the policeman. And Pleydell had been murdered, and the girl—well, she might have been murdered too. But *why?* Who on earth—ruling out Ted Fenton—could have wanted to murder them both? Not a glass thief, certainly, that was too ridiculous. *Who?* Especially the girl; with Pleydell it would be easy enough to think of lots of reasons. (Since reading the letters, Mrs. Warrender had become fully convinced that Crampton Pleydell was a social danger, a man who ought certainly to be put out of the way as soon as possible. She had been indignant with him for playing fast and loose with Vivienne Murray; whatever people might say, she thought that there was no excuse for that sort of thing in a grown man. But to find out that he had done it before—and probably, she said fiercely to herself, at least a dozen times before—changed the action from a piece of heartless selfishness into a crime. If Crampton Pleydell had not been dead, Mrs. Warrender, at that moment, would almost have been prepared to poison him herself.)

But that did not get one any further forward. One could not suppose both an insane burglar and a man who for some reason—no, *not* jealousy, for that would point to young Fenton—for some other reason desired to murder both Crampton Pleydell and Irene Gray. One must choose; and unfortunately either choice seemed equally ridiculous. Mrs. Warrender did wish that she had more adequate brains. Her head was going round and round; and what on earth was she to say to Mr. John Pleydell when she found him? Particularly if he roared at her.

However, Mr. John Pleydell did not roar. She could not get hold of him until the afternoon of the next day, because he had spent the morning attending the inquest, which had proved a great disappointment to the more avid among the visitors and the inhabitants. The coroner, who sat by himself, did not ask anybody any awkward questions. He took evidence of identity, and Barney's and the superintendent's statements about the finding of the body. Then he turned to the doctors, ascertained the cause of death and that they were satisfied that the deceased had not killed himself. And then, without further parley, he delivered a verdict of Wilful Murder by some person or persons unknown, which most people thought a shocking anticlimax. He did not call Ted Fenton or anyone else; he asked nobody about motive, or the state of the deceased's mind, or anything of the sort; he did not even adjourn the inquest for further evidence; he shut it all down without more parley. And the only explanation he offered of this inconsiderate conduct was a few words addressed to the press, in which he indicated that he was not a police-court, and did not propose to usurp a police-court's function. His duty was to ascertain the cause of death and he had ascertained it; and with that he brought the ceremony to an end.

Lady Wishart, who had gone to the court anticipating to be called on, as she had already been called on by the police, and prepared to act as Crampton Pleydell's heartiest defender, was extremely indignant at the whole procedure, and told Mrs. Warrender so again and again. Mr. John Pleydell, she added, looked as though he wanted to burst—a report which did not make Mrs. Warrender feel any more happy. But, as already indicated, Mr. John Pleydell, if he wanted to burst, did not want to burst at Mrs. Warrender. Indeed, he went out of his way to be particularly nice to her, first because he had been brought up in a proper public-school tradition of respect for old ladies, and secondly because he was genuinely distressed at having hit her in the superintendent's office and wanted to efface the memory. So he was both anxious to help her and pleased that she should enquire about the glass, and all the more sorry that he was not able to provide any very exact information.

"I'm very sorry," he said, "but the fact is I don't really know what there was there. I'm not much of a connoisseur in glass myself, and I never looked at it particularly. I only know my brother set great store by it, and I happen to know that Laverstoke glass—that's what they called it—fetches very good prices. But what exactly it was, more than it was fine stuff and mostly small things, I'm afraid I couldn't tell you. Nigel Herdman's the chap who'd know—it's an awful nuisance his having disappeared into nowhere like this."

"Why would he know?"

"Why, because he was my brother's partner in the Laverstoke firm when they made it all. Didn't you know? Oh, well, it was a long time ago, and I dare say people have forgotten about it. It was when they were quite young. Herdman and my brother got very keen on glass blowing, and they got some other fellers to put up some capital, and they bought a glass-blowing place and did pretty well with it. All arty stuff, you know, very fine and expensive—sort of thing I'd never dream of buying, get it smashed in two twos—but there are people who'd buy anything. They stopped doing it years ago, fifteen or twenty at least—I believe there was some sort of row about it, or else Crampton got bored or thought of something better to do—I never bothered to find out; but that's why the stuff's so valuable now, because none of it's been made for ages. But, as I say, Herdman would know exactly what it was that's gone—it isn't everything, only the contents of one small case which I know Crampton set particular store by."

"You don't know at all what was in it?" Mrs. Warrender asked.

"Oh, in a general way. Small things, you know, mostly—wine-glasses, amulets, charms, or whatever you call the things. I remember a green glass seahorse—quite a pretty thing, but goodness knows what it was meant for. And some crystal globes."

"Would that be likely to be a piece of one of them?" Mrs. Warrender asked, showing her glass trophy and explaining its history. John Pleydell examined it, scratched himself slightly, for he was a clumsy man, on the projecting scraps of glass.

"Confound the thing! I beg your pardon . . . It might be—but I really can't say. It's got something of the same colour—kind of bluish tint—that some of his stuff used to have. But I couldn't swear to having seen anything like it. Where'd you find it, did you say? *Outside*, in the grass? My God, isn't that just like the police? Of course, the thief dropped it making his getaway—and they pay no attention to it at all! Fools! Dunderheaded idiots! However," he chuckled, "I think I stopped them trying to get a murder charge against that young fellow right away—can't do it till they've cleared up what I told them about the robbery. But I'm sorry I can't tell you more about the other things—know 'em if I saw 'em, I dare say; but that's about all about it. Nuisance that Herdman feller being away. Tell you what, though—they were imitations, most of 'em."

"How do you mean?"

"Not the real thing, you know. Copies. Copies of old Venetian stuff and suchlike. Crampton had a lot of books and plates about it once and they used to reproduce Italian Renaissance stuff. Pretty well they did it, too; that was what fetched the prices. Particularly—y'see, it's beginning to come back to me—particularly one feller old Crampton was especially keen on—obscure sort of feller—Vic—Vitt—something—wait a moment, I'll get it if you wait a moment . . .Vetturi! That's what the name was. Niccolo Vetturi; I knew I could remember it if I tried. Now, then—dash it all, why did I want to remember it? . . . Oh, of course. Well, I'm afraid that's not much help to you, but if you *did* want to know what the stuff was like and could get hold of old Vetturi's book—must be somewhere—that might tell you. Though what help you think it's going to be, I must say I don't quite see." Nor did Mrs. Warrender, really.

"You don't happen to remember," she said, drawing a last desperate bow, "whether there was a necklace among the things—of red and white glass beads?"

"Well—dash it, now you say it, I believe there was. Stop a moment, let me think . . . Well—Bless my buttons, that's a queer thing. You don't mean you've found a red and white necklace?"

"No," said Mrs. Warrender, becoming excited. "But, if there was one——"

"Well, there was, and there wasn't—that's the point, and it's very queer you should ask about it. Because, you see, I would have sworn there was one there—rather showy sort of thing, with a great big bead in the centre—sort of thing you'd remember. Only last time I saw the case—this time, I mean—it wasn't there! Gone!"

"Are you certain, Mr. Pleydell?"

"Certain as no matter. I remember noticing and thinking, Why, that necklace thing's gone, and asking Crampton about it. And he—I can't remember what he said, but it was something about cleaning and repairing—anyhow I never thought of it again till you mentioned it now. Queer you should hit on the very thing."

"It is," said Mrs. Warrender; and with a word of thanks she scurried off to the library, so as to catch Daphne Gray before closing time. She had never heard of anybody called Niccolo Vetturi; but if he existed, possibly a librarian who had worked in a public library might know something about him. At any rate, if it was a clue, it must be followed.

She found Daphne Gray involved with two customers whose wishes seemed more than usually indeterminate, and had to wait until they had finished rejecting all her suggestions in favour of the book that had been mentioned first. When they had gone, the girl looked up at her with a face so white and exhausted that she put her question as briefly as she could. Clearly, the strain of the inquest had been almost too much.

"Niccolo Vetturi? I've never heard of anybody called that," said Daphne, her eyes turning quite plainly to the door on the opposite side of the street from which at any moment a tall young photographer might be expected to emerge. "But I could try and find out, if you think it's important. I beg your pardon—of course it must be, if you're asking. I'll try as quick as I can." She squeezed out a smile, and Mrs. Warrender departed, feeling very much like apologising. It made her very nervous to be treated as an oracle.

It made her even more nervous when she got back to the hotel and had time to think things over. For what, when she came to consider, could she expect to gain from getting information about Niccolo Vetturi? What on earth could an Italian glassblower of the Renaissance have to do with the death of Crampton Pleydell? The only reason that she was even interested in glass was just that those glass beads had been (or might have been; there

was no real proof that they had) round Irene Gray's neck
when she died; that they might have been given to her
by Crampton Pleydell and that they might (if they were
the same beads) have been made in imitation of something made four hundred years ago by Niccolo Vetturi.
Absurd. And anyway, if she *had* been killed, what could
the beads have had to do with that? Nor—to take the
other line of thought—was information about Vetturi
likely to put one very much further upon the track of a
glass robber—if robber there had been. And at this point
a thought struck Mrs. Warrender so suddenly and with
such a shock that she dropped three stitches and let out
an agitated squeak which disturbed the wireless
programme—but she was so agitated that she almost
omitted to apologise. For she had remembered, as she
cogitated, Mr. John Pleydell saying distinctly that the
missing glass objects had been made by a firm in which
Crampton Pleydell and Nigel Herdman were partners.
So probably Nigel Herdman was part-owner of them.
And Nigel Herdman had been staying at Chalgrove
Field—and immediately after his departure they were
found to be gone. Wasn't that the most obvious
conclusion—indeed, the only possible conclusion—that
Nigel Herdman had taken them with him? And, if so,
what happened to ideas about murderous burglars?
Truly, she was a foolish old woman, and she had set
poor Daphne Gray to work on answering a fool's question. Mrs. Warrender felt very depressed indeed as she
went up to bed.

The next morning saw a sudden change in the
weather. The temperature dropped fifteen degrees; it
rained, and the wind blew very cold; and Mrs. Warrender, who had a slight cold and was very much afraid of
what would happen to her if she dared to get bronchitis
in James's absence, decided to stay indoors, not having

any idea, indeed, what she would do if she went out. So for that day and the next she remained incarcerated, avoiding, as far as she could, the many inhabitants of the hotel who wished to discuss with her the details of Crampton Pleydell's death and what on earth the police were going to do about it now; and it was not until the Friday evening, a week after James's departure, when she was told that a young man was asking for her in the lobby, that she was again brought into contact with her most unsatisfactory case.

It was Edward Fenton, as she had half-expected, sitting in the lobby. He rose to his feet as she entered, and she saw to her satisfaction that his face seemed more animated than when she had seen it last. He looked, however, anxious and troubled; and his first words took her completely by surprise.

"Where's Miss Gray?" he asked, almost fiercely.

"*Miss Gray*! But—I don't know at all. Why, isn't she at home?"

"She left the library at lunch-time on Wednesday," said the young man; "and she never came back. She hasn't been back since, and they don't know where she is!"

"But where she lives—don't they know?"

"No, they don't!" The young man raised his voice suddenly, and fearing an awkward scene in the lobby, Mrs. Warrender took him up to her sitting-room.

"Now, Mr. Fenton," she said, "please tell me just what's happened."

"I don't *know* what's happened! That's it," Ted Fenton replied. "It's just what I told you. She went out at midday on Wednesday, and she hasn't come back, and nobody knows where she is. Her lodgings don't; they say she must have taken her things—I mean her night-things—sometime, but they never saw her, and she never said she was going."

"Well, but if she's taken her things," said Mrs. Warrender, "she must have been going somewhere."

"But *where?* And why didn't she tell anybody? I thought *you'd* know," said the young man.

"I? Why should I know?"

"Because," he said, "the last time I saw her, on Tuesday evening, she said there was something you'd asked her to do. So I thought you'd probably sent her—wherever she's gone."

"I didn't, indeed. I only asked her about a book."

"Then *where's she gone?*"

"Truly, I don't know. But, Mr. Fenton, aren't you getting anxious rather quickly? It's only two days, and—"

"I don't know! But I feel awful," said the young man, getting to his feet and beginning to pace up and down the room. "It's—it's so like what happened before—and they never found her. Besides, Mrs. Warrender, it isn't *like* Daphne to go off without saying a word to anybody; she's not—she wouldn't do things like that, I mean, and let people worry about her. It isn't *like* her. And"—he turned suddenly to face her—"I can't help feeling it's my fault. You see, whatever she's been doing she's been doing for me—if I hadn't talked like a fool and got myself into a mess she wouldn't have had to bother. I feel I've been a frightful nuisance to her all this time, bothering her and letting her do everything for me—"

"And I'm glad you're beginning to find that out at last, young man," said Mrs. Warrender to herself.

"—And I feel—if anything's happened to her through doing it, I should never forgive myself!" He sat down abruptly, and buried his face in his hands. Mrs.

Warrender looked at him sympathetically, though she could not help feeling that his anxiety was a trifle excessive. However, she would prefer him to be over-anxious rather than completely unconcerned.

"You know," he said, raising his head after about a couple of minutes' silence, "I don't know if you've noticed it, but Daphne—Miss Gray, I mean—is very kind to people."

"She is indeed."

"I used to think she was just clever, and oh, good at doing things," the young man pursued. "I didn't think she cared about people, at all. She's always—well, she *seems* rather stand–offish, if you know what I mean. I dare say you've noticed it yourself; but, do you know, she isn't really at all. I'm sure she was really quite upset when Irene died, though she didn't show it like some people would. She was very good to me after it, though I didn't seem to notice it until just now." Mrs. Warrender suppressed an inclination to laugh; he was so evidently in earnest, even if he *was* silly. "So I—I—I don't know what to do, if anything should have happened to her through doing something for me. And I don't know what can have happened—it's not like her not to say anything—"

He was obviously just going to begin all over again, and Mrs. Warrender was relieved when there came a knock at the door. She went to it, and found a maid outside, who gave her a brief message.

"Certainly; bring her up at once," Mrs. Warrender said, and then, turning back into the room, "That is Miss Gray, below. So you may set your fears at rest."

"Thank God," said the young man.

A minute or two later Daphne Gray stepped into the sitting-room. She was in outdoor clothes, rather muddy and untidy, and her coat was glistening with rain. Her face was very white; her eyes looked dazed and she swayed a little as she stood. In her hand was a large wet envelope, which she held out to Mrs. Warrender.

"I got—what you wanted," she said. "It's here. I'm sorry—to have been so long. I was as quick as I could."

"Daphne! Where on earth have you been?" cried Ted Fenton.

"I? Oh—only to Lond—don," said Daphne; and suddenly slipped down to the floor.

IX

"It's all right; she's only fainted," said Mrs. Warrender to the agitated youth. "Leave her a moment; she's very tired, and I expect she's had nothing to eat. There's some brandy in that flask over there, and some biscuits in the cupboard. You get them out, there's a good boy, and I'll make her some tea on the spirit-stove. There, you see, she's coming round already. Take her coat off and put her on the sofa. It's all right, my dear; take a sip of this and don't try to talk for a bit."

In a very few minutes Daphne was nearly recovered, and trying hard to apologise for her lapse and to explain it. But Mrs. Warrender brushed her remarks aside. "Not a word until you've eaten something and had a cup of tea; it won't be a minute. Just a little more brandy for her, Mr. Fenton, and then you can feed her with a biscuit. There, that's better. Do you take milk and sugar, dear?"

"I'm so sorry," Daphne repeated between mouthfuls of biscuit. "It was silly of me to come rushing to you like that, only I thought you ought to have it at once."

"It was very good of you, dear. But you really ought

to have had something to eat."

"I hadn't any money," Daphne confessed. "You see, I didn't know I was going to have to stay two nights in London. I didn't know it would take so long, but I went to all the wrong places first." Ted squeezed her hand with sudden sympathy, and she looked up at him in surprise. "But do look at it," she said, brushing aside the question of her own meals. "I don't know whether it's any use or what you wanted to know, but it was so extraordinary that I thought you must see it."

"But, my dear," said Mrs. Warrender, taking the wad of typescript out of the envelope, "what a lot! And you've typed it all out! That must have taken a dreadfully long time."

"I had to copy it," Daphne explained, "because I couldn't take the books away. And I'm afraid the drawings aren't very well done, because I'm not at all good at drawing, and the man wouldn't let me trace them. But I thought I'd better have them all, and that was what took the time, because I couldn't finish them yesterday."

"But what is it all?"

"All about Vetturi," Daphne said. "You asked about him." She closed her eyes for a moment as Mrs. Warrender began to turn the typescript over; the room was still showing a tendency to go round and round.

"Let her be," said Mrs. Warrender. "She's tired out—perhaps she'll go to sleep." She began to read; but very soon uttered a startled exclamation which caused the girl on the couch to open her eyes and pull herself to a half-sitting position.

The first part of the typescript was drawn, it stated, from a handbook on *Craftsmen of the Renaissance,* and dealt with the career of Niccolo Vetturi, born in Venice in 1457 or thereabouts, which career for some time apparently followed a perfectly normal course. Mrs. Warrender noted that he received his training from people whom she supposed were very distinguished, though she had never heard their names, that he became a master of his "mistery" at an unusually early age, and that he was specially noted as a maker of trinkets of exceptionally fine glass and fantastic design. So far, it was all what she had expected. Then, however, came the passage which caused her to exclaim.

"It appears," said the somewhat flat-footed compiler of the handbook, "that at some time or other Vetturi became infected with the common trouble among craftsmen of the Renaissance—an acquaintance with crime. It is not quite certain, because most of the evidence comes from the reports of a single trial, but it is at any rate highly probable that he began to dabble in poisons. The story is that he made, for a lady with whom he had questionable relations, a necklace from which depended a pendant or charm in the shape of a heart made of this very fine glass of which he had the secret. By misfortune, the lady, while wearing the pendant beneath her bodice, slipped, and crushed it against her throat. The glass penetrated the skin, in such sort that she nearly bled to death before help could be obtained; whereat the irate husband accused the craftsman of an attempt to kill his wife, and inflicted violent physical chastisement upon him.

"Whereupon Vetturi became very resentful and conceived the idea of taking revenge upon the society which had suffered a mere accident to be so savagely punished; and he then began the manufacture of the objects which were afterwards known as Vetturi's Poison Toys. These were containers of fine glass, white or coloured, generally amulets, but sometimes whole necklaces, bracelets, or even ornaments for the head, which were filled with decoctions of various of the many poisons known to the

Renaissance. Vetturi made these, and sold them, doubtless at a high price, to persons who wished to get rid of enemies or relatives. The purchaser would then present to his victim a poisoned toy, with a request that it be worn next to the skin. Sooner or later, the glass container was bound to break, and the glass to cut a path by which the poison could pass into the body of the victim, who subsequently died in agony.

"There is nothing inherently unlikely in the story, which is borne out by any study of the practices of the Renaissance poisoners such as Benvenuto Cellini. The direct evidence, such as it is, comes from a long trial of a man called Guido Scaparelli, in 1494, for the attempted murder of his wife. It was there alleged, and seems to have been discussed without surprise, that Scaparelli had made use of one of Vetturi's Toys in order to poison her; and it is certainly significant that all mention of Vetturi in Venetian records ceases from that date. Presumably he fled the city, and we have no further knowledge of him or his activities."

"But, my dear!" said Mrs. Warrender, looking up at this point. "Glass beads—and poison! Do I read on?"

"Please. The second book was much harder to get hold of. They didn't want to let me have it."

The book from which the second part of the typescript had been taken was a publication of the late eighteenth century, entitled *An Account of Divers Strange Devyses of Craftsmen and Artificers, by William Hurlingham, Gent.*, and the extract which had been copied was called simply "Vetturi's Poyson Toyes."

"There was a lot at the beginning I left out because I hadn't time to copy it," Daphne said. "About the processes he used and that sort of thing."

But what remained was interesting enough. There

was an account of Vetturi's practices, somewhat amplified and couched in more flowery language, but in essence substantially the same, as that given in the handbook. But more than that, there were descriptions and drawings of the principal "poyson toyes" which Vetturi had made—and it was obvious that the original drawings had been very carefully made to correspond with the descriptions. And it was these pictures that caused Mrs. Warrender's cheeks to flush with excitement. There were amulets and pendants of various shapes and colours; there was a sea-horse, in emerald-green glass, "very featly made"; and there was a necklace of red and white beads, "with one Grate Partie-colored Bead in the Center, the which was alone charged with the Poyson." Following it immediately, however, there was a drawing and a description, which caused her to gasp, and to pass it to the others with a cry. The drawing was of a dagger made of glass, with a round hilt or handle one and three-quarter inches in diameter, of solid glass, and a blade five inches long, hollow and slender, of very thin glass and filled with poison; the hilt, as the book explained, being made heavy and solid in order to provide sufficient weight behind the thrust.

"*Look!*" said Mrs. Warrender. The other two stared, at a loss to account for her excitement. "Oh, I forgot, you haven't seen it."

She opened a drawer, and produced the ball of glass, solid, with the rough edges of fine glass projecting from it. "I found *this*," she said, "in the grass outside Mr. Pleydell's study. And there were scraps of thin glass lying beside his body. Look at it—look at those bits where something has broken off—and then look at the picture!"

"You mean—it was something like that?" Daphne

said, heaving herself upright to look at it, and wishing she did not still feel so sleepy.

"I—I don't quite know what I mean," said Mrs. Warrender. "I wish I could think more clearly. But what I do know," she said firmly, having looked round the room, "is that it's getting late, and you ought to have been in bed hours ago. You've done splendidly, my dear"—as Daphne tried to protest—"but everything can perfectly well wait until the morning. Mr. Fenton, I look to you to see that Miss Gray gets home all right, and that they look after her properly at her rooms."

"You can trust me," said Mr. Fenton. "Come along, Daphne, I'm going to take you home. No, don't you argue. You've been looking after me quite enough; it's my turn now. Good-night, madam."

"Good-night," said Mrs. Warrender, but she did not go to sleep for a long time. She went to bed, it is true, but for nearly half the night she lay awake, tossing from one side to the other, and trying to make sense of the message of William Hurlingham, Gent., and the writer of the handbook. Poison toys—glass beads—glass daggers—and the head of a glass dagger in her own handkerchief drawer—what could it all mean?

At last, and as the clock was striking three, the answer suddenly came to her. "*Of course,*" she whispered to herself, "of course. And—and I believe that was why he gave me the address. He looked kind—he wouldn't want anybody else to suffer."

She slept then; but she was down early to breakfast the next day, and immediately it was over she made her way to the post office, and after a certain amount of difficulty and hesitation, succeeded in sending off a long and expensive telegram to an address in Buenos Aires.

X

It was some weeks before the letter came, and by that time the flutter was all over. The papers were without news, but Ted Fenton was unmolested in Quartermouth, the Murrays had returned to a quiet life in Wembley, and Mrs. Warrender and her son were back again in their home in Hampstead. But the letter had been forwarded from Quartermouth; it was a very fat letter, and it bore a South American stamp but no address.

"Dear Mrs. Warrender," it said,

"You were quite right, of course, and it was clever of you to remember the address. It was just a stroke of genius—one of my few, alas!—to let it slip to you that night on the jetty. I somehow felt I could trust you not to give it away unnecessarily. I hope the cable I sent stopped the police from making serious fools of themselves; but you'd better let them have this letter to satisfy their minds. I'm sorry I made such a bungle of faking the suicide; I thought I'd done it so neatly, remembering to put his fingerprints on the syringe, but I suppose something went wrong.

"I killed him. But it wasn't murder, you know; it was execution, and I still don't see that there was any other way—as I didn't see how to blackmail him into killing himself. You see, you couldn't know C.P. as I did—even if you are rather good at guessing at people. He was just a flaming egotist through and through. I dare say his books are very great art, and all that, but when I think of the price other people have paid for the writing of them it makes my blood boil. Even now. Not always in such big ways, but in little ones, which is meaner, to my mind; squeezing out all their miserable little intimacies and then sticking them down on paper. (He was *damned* good at sucking out confidences. I've seen him do it again and again.) And it wasn't only in connection with his writing, for which, I suppose, he might have claimed some excuse; it was in everything. *Anything* Crampton Pleydell wanted he had to have, like that, and anybody who stood in the way had just got to get out of it. As you'll see.

"Also, anybody who continued to stand in the way and be in the picture when Crampton Pleydell had done with them. Because he couldn't bear to keep anything he was tired of, and he had absolutely no sense of obligation to any human creature. I'm not sure if I'm succeeding in getting him across to you—what a great, greedy, insensate *lump* he was. But he was, and though I think he got more arrogant and more impatient as he got older, the main thing had been there ever since I've known him. I think it's what really accounts for most murderers, don't you? This feeling that they're God Almighty and got to be swatted, like a mosquito. Anyway, that's why Irene Gray was murdered—and why your young friend was probably going to be murdered, too. He was rash enough—C.P., I mean—to use a girl out of the town for his purposes. He was writing about a beauty shop, or some such tripe, and had her up and picked her brains, and made love to her, of course—that went without saying for most of them. And when he'd done with her and wanted her to fade out she wouldn't fade; she stayed in the picture and made a fuss. And he was particularly annoyed because it was in Quartermouth; he'd really begun to feel the place belonged to him, and she looked like spoiling it all.

"I hope you don't think I'm inventing fairy-tales, by the way—he did murder her. Made an appointment with her in the woods, gave her a necklace with a great glass bead in the middle of it, very pretty, embraced her and squashed the glass and the poison into her. Very simple. I know he did, because he told me himself. He was quite satisfied about it—I think he'd been dying to tell somebody how clever he'd been, and it never occurred to him that I'd have dared to do anything about it. I dare say I shouldn't, though I'd come down to Quartermouth with some such idea in my mind—I'm not a person who always does what he means to—only after I'd talked to you that night I felt certain that there was another murder in the offing, so to speak. (By the way, the poison in the necklace was curare; I know, because I put it there.)

"I suppose I'd better tell you how that came about, though you must know most of it, or you wouldn't have cabled. It started not long after we'd come down from Oxford, where we had both got interested in glass processes—we were members of an aesthetic affair called the Guild of St. Joseph, which nobody'll remember nowadays; it didn't last long. And we used to mess about trying to find out about reproductions of old glass of various sorts—Bristol glass, Waterford glass, and eventually Venetian glass. I and a fellow called Harrison did most of the technical side of it; C.P.'s interest was literary and dilettante—I don't mean he wasn't interested, but he liked the idea of it, and to write little imaginative sketches about it better than messing about in workshops himself. However, he gradually got keener and keener, especially after we'd found Vetturi's book—which isn't, as you'll know if you've read it, by any means all about poison toys. The chap was a damn' fine craftsman.

"Anyway, C.P. got so keen that nothing would serve him but to set up in business for himself. He'd a little money, then—not much, but he persuaded two fellows, Lord Twymouth and a man named Osborn (I'm giving you their names, not because they had anything to do with this affair, but so that you can check up if you want to)—and we made a company and bought a small place near Laverstoke in Hampshire, and started away. We had some assistants, of course; but I did most of the work myself at first. C.P. tried to, but he wasn't much good at it; he preferred to be an Inspiration. (There I believe I'm being unfair to him; he certainly did produce a lot of ideas, and he could make me at any rate work like the devil. But he never was any good with his hands.)

"Two of the workmen that we got turned out extremely well, and really, though I say it, we made some pretty good stuff. We followed old Vetturi's instructions and bettered them a bit, and some of the fine glass we made then you'll find in museums and private collections in a lot of places. Of course there wasn't very much of it; but we were getting to be quite a fine little highbrow show.

"Then, however, C.P. got the idea that he'd got to follow it out to the bitter end and make the poison toys with real poison. It was a fool's trick, and I always told him so; but he was dead set on it. (I believe, as a matter of fact, that that was what he had intended to do all along, and that was his chief real interest in the thing; however, I didn't know that at the time.) Anyhow, he *was,* and to cut a long story short, we made them. We made that dagger that I broke and a duplicate of it, and we made lockets and amulets and bangles and a chain of red and white beads, graded in size, of which the big centre one was full of poison. What I can't tell you is how we got the fillings; but you can take it from me that it wasn't too difficult. The laws about sale of poisons weren't as strict then as they are now, and C.P. always had a lot of queer friends who would do funny jobs for him. And, having been a chemist—did I mention I'd taken chemistry at Oxford?—I was able to do a bit of the necessary technical work. We fitted up a small laboratory on the premises. It was rather fascinating, really; one had to be so frightfully careful, what with the poisons and that very thin glass; it gave me a respect for the Renaissance craftsmen that I've never lost.

"Well, after a while—it was in January, 1910, to be exact—I went off for a week to look at an experimental glassworks which somebody'd started near Glasgow, leaving Crampton in charge, in a particularly foul temper, because something he specially wanted done turned out not to be possible, and he was trying to bully Brown, the foreman, into doing it. When I got back I found the village in a perfect ferment and policemen all over the place. Brown had been killed or rather had died by poisoning with cyanide. Crampton's story was that he had been messing around the lab, where he'd no business to be, and had got some of the stuff into him. He was frightfully sorry, and all that; but the chemist (that was me) was away, and he himself didn't know enough about what was and what wasn't in the lab to tell anybody.

"Well, I knew *that* was poppycock. C.P. couldn't handle poisons, but he was always nosing around the lab, and he knew which was which every bit as well as I did. And when I found one of the glass daggers had disappeared, I knew what must have happened just as well as if I'd seen it—that C.P.'d had a row with the chap, and stuck the dagger into him in a fit of rage, or maybe simply to see if it would work. Even then, I remember, it didn't surprise me as much as I expected.

"Nothing happened. The trouble between Brown and C.P. hadn't got about—Brown was a dour sort of chap who didn't talk, and, of course nobody had any idea what we used the poisons for. Everybody supposed it was just an experimental laboratory, and I got censured for not leaving things properly locked up and that was all. Naturally I couldn't say anything. But I told Crampton that the thing had got to stop—anyway, I'd got the offer of a decent job and I wanted to quit, and he couldn't have carried on without me—and that the other lethal objects we'd made had got to be destroyed. He said he'd already destroyed them. So we parted company. I went to my job, and then came the war, and after that I drifted about a good bit, mostly out of England, and never saw C.P., though I heard, of course, about his 'going from strength to strength,'—I suppose that's the way to put it—and he was never one to hide his light under a bushel. And then, when I was just comfortably set up as DeRosas in Buenos Aires, I found in a fellow's house a whole bunch of English newspapers, which happened to contain a full account of the inquest on Irene Gray—and it mentioned the bead necklace.

"I don't know why I jumped to it, but I did—at any rate, enough to make me come over here to have a look as soon as I had got things in shape so that I could leave them—and much good that will do me now. I went straight down to Quartermouth, and called on C.P., who was most affable, asked me to stay and all manner of things—God, what a pompous swine the man had grown in twenty-five years! Pretty soon he took me down to his study, and there, in a glass case all by themselves, were the trinkets we'd made down in the works at Laverstoke—only the necklace of red and white beads was missing. I might have known, of course, that he'd never have thrown the things away. They were *his*—besides, the sense of power in having them, even if he'd never used them, was just what he'd love.

"The rest you know, or nearly. I couldn't say anything, of course, and he knew it. And I hadn't come with any really definite plan in mind; I didn't see anything I could do, until after I had talked to you that evening. I'd had a word or two with C.P. about the girl the night before. Then it just seemed perfectly simple. He'd got to die and I'd got to kill him. I said goodbye the next day, but the morning after I ran the boat into the creek and came up by the holly path. I knew he was going to be working in the study all day, because he'd told me, and I knew it was twenty to one against anybody seeing either me or the boat. I just went up and knocked. I said, 'I've come back for a few minutes; I want to have a look at those things again.' So he gave me his keys and I took the dagger out and stabbed him in his open collar. He didn't take long to become unconscious—I held him so that he shouldn't make a row—and then I put the syringe in his hand and jabbed him with it. I conclude that didn't work properly. Then I collected the other toys—I subsequently bashed them against the side of the boat and threw them into the sea—locked the case and put his keys back, and went out through the window. But somewhere I dropped the hilt of the dagger—I don't know if anybody found it.

"Well, that's that. I'm very sorry about the young photographer—the cyanide was just an unlucky coincidence. But I've no feeling of remorse for anything else, except for having been so slow on the uptake. I'm afraid your police will have to take a chance on believing this, because they'll never be able to check it from me. But you can hint to the lad, if he's still mourning over his girl, that he was much better out of it. Nobody whom C.P. ever had a go at has been good for much afterwards, including

"Yours very sincerely,

"Nigel Herdman.

"P.S.—I wish I'd met you earlier. You'd probably have been able to suggest some quite simple way of doing it, without creating all this fuss."

"Indeed I'm glad he didn't!" Mrs. Warrender said to herself as she folded up the letter. "What a dreadful experience it would have been to be *told* all that. I hope—I hope he feels better about it now, poor fellow."

THE CALICO DOG

by Mignon Eberhart

It was nothing short of an invitation to murder.

"You don't mean to say," Susan Dare said in a small voice, "that both of them—*both* of them are living here?"

Idabelle Lasher—Mrs. Jeremiah Lasher, that is, widow of the patent medicine emperor who died last year (resisting, it is said, his own medicine to the end with the strangest vehemence)—Idabelle Lasher turned large pale blue eyes upon Susan and sighed and said:

"Why, yes. There was nothing else to do. I can't turn my own boy out into the world."

Susan took a long breath. "Always assuming," she said, "that one of them is your own boy."

"Oh, there's no doubt about that, Miss Dare," said Idabelle Lasher simply.

"Let me see," Susan said, "if I have this straight. Your son Derek was lost twenty years ago. Recently he has returned. Rather, two of him has returned."

Mrs. Lasher was leaning forward, tears in her large pale eyes. "Miss Dare," she said, "one of them must be my son. I need him so much." Her large blandness, her artificiality, the padded ease and softness of her life dropped away before the earnestness and honesty of that brief statement. She was all at once pathetic—no, it was on a larger scale; she was tragic in her need for her child.

"And besides," she said suddenly and with an odd naiveté, "besides, there's all that money. Thirty millions."

"*Thirty*—" began Susan and stopped. It was simply

not comprehensible. Half a million, yes; even a million. But thirty millions!

"But if you can't tell yourself which of the two young men is your son, how can I? And with so much money involved—"

"That's just it," said Mrs. Lasher, leaning forward earnestly again. "I'm sure that Papa would have wanted me to be perfectly sure. The last thing he said to me was to warn me. 'Watch out for yourself, Idabelle,' he said. 'People will be after your money. Impostors.' "

"But I don't see how I can help you," Susan repeated firmly.

"You *must* help me," said Mrs. Lasher. "Christabel Frame told me about you. She said you wrote mystery stories and were the only woman who could help me, and that you were right here in Chicago."

Her handkerchief poised, she waited with childlike anxiety to see if the name of Christabel Frame had its expected weight with Susan. But it was not altogether the name of one of her most loved friends that influenced Susan. It was the childlike appeal on the part of this woman.

"How do you feel about the two claimants?" she said. "Do you feel more strongly attracted to one than to the other?"

"That's just the trouble," said Idabelle Lasher. "I like them both."

"Let me have the whole story again, won't you? Try to tell it quite definitely, just as things occurred."

Mrs. Lasher put the handkerchief away and sat up briskly.

"Well," she began. "It was like this: . . . " Two months ago a young man called Dixon March had called on her; he had not gone to her lawyer, he had come to see her. And he had told her a very straight story.

"You must remember something of the story—oh, but, of course, you couldn't. You're far too young. And then, too, we weren't as rich as we are now, when little Derek disappeared. He was four at the time. And his nursemaid disappeared at the same time, and I always thought, Miss Dare, that it was the nursemaid who stole him."

"Ransom?" asked Susan.

"No. That was the queer part of it. There never was any attempt to demand ransom. I always felt the nursemaid simply wanted him for herself—she was a very peculiar woman."

Susan brought her gently back to the present.

"So Dixon March is this claimant's name?"

"Yes. That's another thing. It seemed so likely to me that he could remember his name—Derek—and perhaps in saying Derek in his baby way, the people at the orphanage thought it was Dixon he was trying to say, so they called him Dixon. The only trouble is—"

"Yes," said Susan, as Idabelle Lasher's blue eyes wavered and became troubled.

"Well, you see, the other young man, the other Derek—well, his name is Duane. You see?"

Susan felt a little dizzy. "Just what is Dixon's story?"

"He said that he was taken in at an orphanage at the age of six. That he vaguely remembers a woman, dark, with a mole on her chin, which is an exact description of the nursemaid. Of course, we've had the orphanage records examined, but there's nothing conclusive and no way to identify the woman; she died—under the name of Sarah Gant, which wasn't the nursemaid's name—and she was very poor. A social worker simply arranged for the child's entrance into the orphanage."

"What makes him think he is your son, then?"

"Well, it's this way. He grew up and made as much as he could of the education they gave him and actually was making a nice thing with a construction company when he got to looking into his—his origins, he said— and an account of the description of our Derek, the dates, the fact that he could discover nothing of the woman, Sarah Gant, previous to her life in Ottawa—"

"Ottawa?"

"Yes. That was where he came from. The other one, Duane, from New Orleans. And the fact that Dixon remembered her, she looked very much like the newspaper pictures of the nursemaid, suggested the possibility that he was our lost child."

"So, on the evidence of corresponding dates and the likeness of the woman who was caring for him before he was taken to the orphanage, he comes to you, claiming to be your son. A year after your husband died."

"Yes, and—well——" Mrs. Lasher flushed pinkly. "There are some things he can remember."

"Things—such as what?"

"The—the green curtains in the nursery. There *were* green curtains in the nursery. And a—a calico dog. And—and a few other things. The lawyers say that isn't conclusive. But I think it's very important that he remembers the calico dog."

"You've had lawyers looking into his claims."

"Oh, dear, yes," said Mrs. Lasher. "Exhaustively."

"But can't they trace Sarah Gant?"

"Nothing conclusive, Miss Dare."

"His physical appearance?" suggested Susan.

"Miss Dare," said Mrs. Lasher. "My Derek was blond with gray eyes. He had no marks of any kind. His teeth were still his baby teeth. Any fair young man with gray eyes might be my son. And both of these men—

either of these men might be Derek. I've looked long and wearily, searching every feature and every expression for a likeness to my boy. It is equally there—and not there. I feel sure that one of them is my son. I am absolutely sure that he has—has come home."

"But you don't know which one?" said Susan softly.

"I don't know which one," said Idabelle Lasher. "But one of them *is Derek.*"

She turned suddenly and walked heavily to a window. Her pale green gown of soft crêpe trailed behind her, its hem touching a priceless thin rug that ought to have been in a museum. Behind her, against the gray wall, hung a small Mauve, exquisite. Twenty-one stories below, traffic flowed unceasingly along Lake Shore Drive.

"One of them must be an impostor," Idabelle Lasher was saying presently in a choked voice.

"Is Dixon certain he is your son?"

"He says only that he thinks so. But since Duane has come, too, he is more—more positive—"

"Duane, of course." The rivalry of the two young men must be rather terrible. Susan had a fleeting glimpse again of what it might mean: one of them certainly an impostor, both impostors, perhaps, struggling over Idabelle Lasher's affections and her fortune. The thought opened, really, quite appalling and horrid vistas.

"What is Duane's story?" asked Susan.

"That's what makes it so queer, Miss Dare. Duane's story—is—well, it is exactly the same."

Susan stared at her wide green back, cushiony and bulgy in spite of the finest corseting that money could obtain.

"You don't mean *exactly* the same!" she cried.

"Exactly." The woman turned and faced her. "Exactly the same, Miss Dare, except for the names and places. The name of the woman in Duane's case was Mary Miller, the orphanage was in New Orleans, he was going to art school here in Chicago when—when, he says, just as Dixon said—he began to be more and more interested in his parentage and began investigating. And he, too, remembers things, little things from his boyhood and our house that only Derek could remember."

"Wait, Mrs. Lasher," said Susan, grasping at something firm. "Any servant, any of your friends, would know these details also."

Mrs. Lasher's pale, big eyes became more prominent.

"You mean, of course, a conspiracy. The lawyers have talked nothing else. But, Miss Dare, they authenticated everything possible to authenticate in both statements. I know what has happened to the few servants we had—all, that is, except the nursemaid. And we don't have many close friends, Miss Dare. Not since there was so much money. And none of them—none of them would do this."

"But both young men can't be Derek," said Susan desperately. She clutched at common sense again and said: "How soon after your husband's death did Dixon arrive?"

"Ten months."

"And Duane?"

"Three months after Dixon."

"And they are both living here with you now?"

"Yes." She nodded toward the end of the long room. "They are in the library now."

"Together?" said Susan irresistibly.

"Yes, of course," said Mrs. Lasher. "Playing cribbage."

"I suppose you and your lawyers have tried every possible test?"

"Everything, Miss Dare."

"You have no fingerprints of the baby?"

"No, that was before fingerprints were so important. We tried blood tests, of course. But they are of the same type."

"Resemblances to you or your husband?"

"You'll see for yourself at dinner tonight, Miss Dare. You will help me?"

Susan sighed. "Yes," she said.

The bedroom to which Mrs. Lasher herself took Susan was done in the French manner with much taffeta, inlaid satinwood, and lace cushions. It was very large and overwhelmingly magnificent, and gilt mirrors reflected Susan's small brown figure in unending vistas.

Susan dismissed the maid, thanked fate that the only dinner gown she had brought was a new and handsome one, and felt very awed and faintly dissolute in a great, sunken, black marble pool that she wouldn't have dared call a tub. After all, reflected Susan, finding that she could actually swim a stroke or two, thirty millions was thirty millions.

She had got into a white chiffon dress with silver sandals when Mrs. Lasher knocked.

"It's Derek's baby things," she said in a whisper and with a glance over her fat white shoulder. "Let's move a little farther from the door."

They sat down on a cushioned chaise-longue and between them, incongruous against the suave cream satin, Idabelle Lasher spread out certain small objects, touching them lingeringly.

"His little suit—he looked so sweet in yellow. Some pictures. A pink plush teddy bear. His little nursery-school reports—he was already in nursery school, Miss Dare—pre-kindergarten, you know. It was in an experimental stage then, and so interesting. And the calico dog, Miss Dare."

She stopped there, and Susan looked at the faded, flabby calico dog held so tenderly in those fat diamonded hands. She felt suddenly a wave of cold anger toward the man who was not Derek and who must know that he was not Derek. She took the pictures eagerly.

But they were only pictures. One at about two, made by a photographer; a round baby face without features that were at all distinctive. Two or three pictures of a little boy playing, squinting against the sun.

"Has anyone else seen these things?"

"You mean either of the two boys—either Dixon or Duane? No, Miss Dare."

"Has anyone at all seen them? Servants? Friends?"

Idabelle's blue eyes became vague and clouded.

"Long ago, perhaps," she said. "Oh, many, many years ago. But they've been in the safe in my bedroom for years. Before that in a locked closet."

"How long have they been in the safe?"

"Since we bought this apartment. Ten—no, twelve years."

"And no one—there's never been anything like an attempted robbery of that safe?"

"Never. No, Miss Dare. There's no possible way for either Dixon or Duane to know of the contents of this box except from memory."

"And Dixon remembers the calico dog?"

"Yes." The prominent blue eyes wavered again, and Mrs. Lasher rose and walked toward the door. She paused then and looked at Susan again.

"And Duane remembers the teddy bear and described it to me," she said definitely and went away.

There was a touch of comedy about it, and, like all comedy, it overlay tragedy.

Left to herself, Susan studied the pictures again thoughtfully. The nursery-school reports, written out in beautiful "vertical" handwriting. *Music*: A good ear. *Memory*: Very good. *Adaptability*: Very good. *Sociability*: Inclined to shyness. *Rhythm*: Poor (advise skipping games at home). *Conduct*: (this varied; with at least once a suggestive blank and once a somewhat terse remark to the effect that there had been considerable disturbance during the half hours devoted to naps and a strong suggestion that Derek was at the bottom of it). Susan smiled there and began to like baby Derek. And it was just then that she found the first indication of an identifying trait. And that was after the heading, *Games*. One report said: Quick. Another said: Mentally quick but does not coordinate muscles well. And a third said, definitely pinning the thing down: Tendency to use left hand which we are endeavoring to correct.

Tendency to use left hand. An inborn tendency, cropping out again and again all through life. In those days, of course, it had been rigidly corrected—thereby inducing all manner of ills, according to more recent trends of education. But was it ever altogether conquered?

Presently Susan put the things in the box again and went to Mrs. Lasher's room. And Susan had the somewhat dubious satisfaction of watching Mrs. Lasher open a delicate ivory panel which disclosed a very utilitarian steel safe set in the wall behind it and place the box securely in the safe.

"Did you find anything that will be of help?" asked Mrs. Lasher, closing the panel.

"I don't know," said Susan. "I'm afraid there's nothing very certain. Do Dixon and Duane know why I am here?"

"No," said Mrs. Lasher, revealing unexpected cunning. "I told them you were a dear friend of Christabel's. And that you were very much interested in their— my—our situation. We talk it over, you know, very frankly, Miss Dare. The boys are as anxious as I am to discover the truth of it."

Again, thought Susan feeling baffled, as the true Derek would be. She followed Mrs. Lasher toward the drawing room again, prepared heartily to dislike both men.

But the man sipping a cocktail in the doorway of the library was much too old to be either Dixon or Duane.

"Major Briggs," said Mrs. Lasher. "Christabel's friend, Susan, Tom." She turned to Susan. "Major Briggs is our closest friend. He was like a brother to my husband, and has been to me."

"Never a brother," said Major Briggs with an air of gallantry. "Say, rather, an admirer. So this is Christabel's little friend." He put down his cocktail glass and bowed and took Susan's hand only a fraction too tenderly.

Then Mrs. Lasher drifted across the room where Susan was aware of two pairs of black shoulders rising to greet her, and Major Briggs said beamingly:

"How happy we are to have you with us, my dear. I suppose Idabelle has told you of our—our problem."

He was about Susan's height; white-haired, rather puffy under the eyes, and a bit too pink, with hands that were inclined to shake. He adjusted his gold-rimmed eyeglasses, then let them drop the length of their black ribbon and said:

"What do you think of it, my dear?"

"I don't know," said Susan. "What do you think?"

"Well, my dear, it's a bit difficult, you know. When Idabelle herself doesn't know. When the most rigid—yes, the most rigid and searching investigation on the part of highly trained and experienced investigators has failed to discover—ah—the identity of the lost heir, how may my own poor powers avail!" He finished his cocktail, gulped, and said blandly: "But it's Duane."

"What—" said Susan.

"I said, it's Duane. He is the heir. Anybody could see it with half an eye. Spittin' image of his dad. Here they come now."

They were alike and yet not alike at all. Both were rather tall, slender, and well made. Both had medium-brown hair. Both had grayish-blue eyes. Neither was particularly handsome. Neither was exactly unhandsome. Their features were not at all alike in bone structure, yet neither had features that were in any way distinctive. Their description on a passport would not have varied by a single word. Actually they were altogether unlike each other.

With the salad Major Briggs roused to point out a portrait that hung on the opposite wall.

"Jeremiah Lasher," he said, waving a pink hand in that direction. He glanced meaningly at Susan and added: "Do you see any resemblance, Miss Susan? I mean between my old friend and one of these lads here."

One of the lads—it was Dixon—wriggled perceptibly, but Duane smiled.

"We are not at all embarrassed, Miss Susan," he said pleasantly. "We are both quite accustomed to this sort of scrutiny." He laughed lightly, and Idabelle smiled, and Dixon said:

"Does Miss Dare know about this?"

"Oh, yes," said Idabelle, turning as quickly and attentively to him as she had turned to Duane. "There's no secret about it."

"No," said Dixon somewhat crisply. "There's certainly no secret about it."

There was, however, no further mention of the problem of identity during the rest of the evening. Indeed, it was a very calm and slightly dull evening except for the affair of Major Briggs and the draft.

That happened just after dinner. Susan and Mrs. Lasher were sitting over coffee in the drawing room, and the three men were presumably lingering in the dining room.

It had been altogether quiet in the drawing room, yet there had not been audible even the distant murmur of the men's voices. Thus the queer, choked shout that arose in the dining room came as a definite shock to the two women.

It all happened in an instant. They hadn't themselves time to move or inquire before Duane appeared in the doorway. He was laughing but looked pale.

"It's all right," he said. "Nothing's wrong."

"*Duane,*" said Idabelle Lasher gaspingly. "*What—*"

"Don't be alarmed," he said swiftly. "It's nothing." He turned to look down the hall at someone approaching and added: "Here he is, safe and sound."

He stood aside, and Major Briggs appeared in the doorway. He looked so shocked and purple that both women moved hurriedly forward, and Idabelle Lasher said: "Here—on the divan. Ring for brandy, Duane. Lie down here, Major."

"Oh, no—no," said Major Briggs stertorously. "No. I'm quite all right."

Duane, however, supported him to the divan, and Dixon appeared in the doorway.

"What happened?" he said.

Major Briggs waved his hands feebly. Duane said:

"The Major nearly went out of the window."

"O-h-h—" it was Idabelle in a thin, long scream.

"Oh, it's all right," said Major Briggs shakenly. "I caught hold of the curtain. By God, I'm glad you had heavy curtain rods at that window, Idabelle."

She was fussing around him, her hands shaking, her face ghastly under its make-up.

"But how could you—" she was saying jerkily— "what on earth—how could it have happened—"

"It's the draft," said the Major irascibly. "The confounded draft on my neck. I got up to close the window and—I nearly went out!"

"But how could you—" began Idabelle again.

"I don't know how it happened," said the Major. "Just all at once—" A look of perplexity came slowly over his face. "Queer," said Major Briggs suddenly, "I suppose it was the draft. But it was exactly as if—" He stopped, and Idabelle cried:

"As if what?"

"As if someone had pushed me," said the Major.

Perhaps it was fortunate that the butler arrived just then, and there was the slight diversion of getting the Major to stretch out full length on the divan and sip a restorative.

And somehow in the conversation it emerged that neither Dixon nor Duane had been in the dining room when the thing had happened.

"There'd been a disagreement over—well, it was over inheritance tax," said Dixon, flushing. "Duane had gone to the library to look in an encyclopedia, and I had gone to the room to get the evening paper which had some reference to it. So the Major was alone when it happened. I knew nothing of it until I heard the commotion in here."

"I," said Duane, watching Dixon, "heard the Major's

shout from the library and hurried across."

That night, late, after Major Briggs had gone home, and Susan was again alone in the paralyzing magnificence of the French bedroom, she still kept thinking of the window and Major Briggs. And she put up her own window so circumspectly that she didn't get enough air during the night and woke struggling with a silk-covered eiderdown under the impression that she herself was being thrust out the window.

It was only a nightmare, of course, induced as much as anything by her own hatred of heights. But it gave an impulse to the course she proposed to Mrs. Lasher that very morning.

It was true, of course, that the thing may have been exactly what it appeared to be, and that was, an accident. But if it was not accident, there were only two possibilities.

"Do you mean," cried Mrs. Lasher incredulously when Susan had finished her brief suggestion, "that I'm to say openly that Duane is my son! But you don't understand, Miss Dare. I'm not sure. It may be Dixon."

"I know," said Susan. "And I may be wrong. But I think it might help if you will announce to—oh, only to Major Briggs and the two men—that you are convinced that it is Duane and are taking steps for legal recognition of the fact."

"Why? What do you think will happen? How will it help things to do that?"

"I'm not sure it will help," said Susan wearily. "But it's the only thing I see to do. And I think that you may as well do it right away."

"Today?" said Mrs. Lasher reluctantly.

"At lunch," said Susan inexorably. "Telephone to invite Major Briggs now."

"Oh, very well," said Idabelle Lasher. "After all, it will please Tom Briggs. He has been urging me to make a decision. He seems certain that it is Duane."

But Susan, present and watching closely, could detect nothing except that Idabelle Lasher, once she was committed to a course, undertook it with thoroughness. Her fondness for Duane, her kindness to Dixon, her air of relief at having settled so momentous a question, left nothing to be desired. Susan was sure that the men were convinced. There was, to be sure, a shade of triumph in Duane's demeanor, and he was magnanimous with Dixon—as, indeed, he could well afford to be. Dixon was silent and rather pale and looked as if he had not expected the decision and was a bit stunned by it. Major Briggs was incredulous at first, and then openly jubilant, and toasted all of them.

Indeed, what with toasts and speeches on the part of Major Briggs, the lunch rather prolonged itself, and it was late afternoon before the Major had gone and Susan and Mrs. Lasher met alone for a moment in the library.

Idabelle was flushed and worried.

"Was it all right, Miss Dare?" she asked in a stage whisper.

"Perfectly," said Susan.

"Then—then do you know——"

"Not yet," said Susan. "But keep Dixon here."

"Very well," said Idabelle.

The rest of the day passed quietly and not, from Susan's point of view, at all valuably, although Susan tried to prove something about the possible left-handedness of the real Derek. Badminton and several games of billiards resulted only in displaying the more perfectly a consistent right-handedness on the part of both the claimants.

Dressing again for dinner, Susan looked at herself ruefully in the great mirror.

She had never in her life felt so utterly helpless, and the thought of Idabelle Lasher's faith in her hurt. After all, she ought to have realized her own limits: the problem that Mrs. Lasher had set her was one that would have baffled—that, indeed, had baffled—experts. Who was she, Susan Dare, to attempt its solution?

The course of action she had laid out for Idabelle Lasher had certainly, thus far, had no development beyond heightening an already tense situation. It was quite possible that she was mistaken and that nothing at all would come of it. And if not, what then?

Idabelle Lasher's pale eyes and anxious, beseeching hands hovered again before Susan, and she jerked her satin slip savagely over her head—thereby pulling loose a shoulder strap and being obliged to ring for the maid who sewed the strap neatly and rearranged Susan's hair.

"You'll be going to the party tonight, ma'am?" said the maid in a pleasant Irish accent.

"Party?"

"Oh, yes, ma'am. Didn't you know? It's the Charity Ball. At the Dycke Hotel. In the Chandelier Ballroom. A grand, big party, ma'am. Madame is wearing her pearls. Will you bend your head, please, ma'am."

Susan bent her head and felt her white chiffon being slipped over it. When she emerged she said:

"Is the entire family going?"

"Oh, yes, ma'am. And Major Briggs. There you are, ma'am—and I do say you look beautiful. There's orchids, ma'am, from Mr. Duane. And gardenias from Mr. Dixon. I believe," said the maid thoughtfully, "that I could put them all together. That's what I'm doing for Madame."

"Very well," said Susan recklessly. "Put them all together."

It made a somewhat staggering decoration—staggering, thought Susan, but positively abandoned in luxuriousness. So, too, was the long town car which waited for them promptly at ten when they emerged from the towering apartment house. Susan, leaning back in her seat between Major Briggs and Idabelle Lasher, was always afterward to remember that short ride through crowded, lighted streets to the Dycke Hotel.

No one spoke. Perhaps only Susan was aware (and suddenly realized that she was aware) of the surging desires and needs and feelings that were bottled up together in the tonneau of that long, gliding car. She was aware of it quite suddenly and tinglingly.

Nothing had happened. Nothing, all through that long dinner from which they had just come, had been said that was at all provocative.

Yet all at once Susan was aware of a queer kind of excitement.

She looked at the black shoulders of the two men, Duane and Dixon, riding along beside each other. Dixon sat stiff and straight; his shoulders looked rigid and unmoving. He had taken it rather well, she thought; did he guess Idabelle's decision was not the true one? Or was he still stunned by it?

Or was there something back of that silence? Had she underestimated the force and possible violence of Dixon's reaction? Susan frowned: it was dangerous enough without that.

They arrived at the hotel. Their sudden emergence from the silence of the car, with its undercurrent of emotion, into brilliant lights and crowds and the gay lilt of an orchestra somewhere, had its customary tonic effect. Even Dixon shook off his air of brooding and, as they finally strolled into the Chandelier Room, and Duane and Mrs. Lasher danced smoothly into the revolving colors, asked Susan to dance.

They left the Major smiling approval and buying

cigarettes from a girl in blue pantaloons.

The momentary gayety with which Dixon had asked Susan to dance faded at once. He danced conscientiously but without much spirit and said nothing. Susan glanced up at his face once or twice; his direct, dark blue eyes looked straight ahead, and his face was rather pale and set.

Presently Susan said: "Oh, there's Idabelle!"

At once Dixon lost step. Susan recovered herself and her small silver sandals rather deftly, and Idabelle, large and pink and jewel-laden, danced past them in Duane's arms. She smiled at Dixon anxiously and looked, above her pearls, rather worried.

Dixon's eyebrows were a straight dark line, and he was white around the mouth.

"I'm sorry, Dixon," said Susan. She tried to catch step with him, for the moment, and added: "Please don't mind my speaking about it. We are all thinking of it. I do think you behave very well."

He looked straight over her head, danced several somewhat erratic steps, and said suddenly:

"It was so—unexpected. And you see, I was so sure of it."

"Why were you so sure?" asked Susan.

He hesitated, then burst out again:

"Because of the dog," he said savagely, stepping on one of Susan's silver toes. She removed it with Spartan composure, and he said: "The calico dog, you know. And the green curtains. If I had known there was so much money involved, I don't think I'd have come to—Idabelle. But then, when I did know, and this other—fellow turned up, why, of course, I felt like sticking it out!"

He paused, and Susan felt his arm tighten around her waist. She looked up, and his face was suddenly chalk white and his eyes blazing.

"Duane!" he said hoarsely. "I hate him. I could kill him with my own hands."

The next dance was a tango, and Susan danced it with Duane. His eyes were shining, and his face flushed with excitement and gayety.

He was a born dancer, and Susan relaxed in the perfect ease of his steps. He held her very closely, complimented her gracefully, and talked all the time, and for a few moments Susan merely enjoyed the fast swirl of the lovely Argentine dance. Then Idabelle and Dixon went past, and Susan saw again the expression of Dixon's set white face as he looked at Duane, and Idabelle's swimmimg eyes above her pink face and bare pink neck.

The rest of what was probably a perfect dance was lost on Susan, busy about certain concerns of her own, which involved some adjusting of the flowers on her shoulder. And the moment the dance was over she slipped away.

White chiffon billowed around her, and her gardenias sent up a warm fragrance as she huddled into a telephone booth. She made sure the flowers were secure and unrevealing upon her shoulder, steadied her breath, and smiled a little tremulously as she dialed a number she very well knew. It was getting to be a habit—calling Jim Byrne, her newspaper friend, when she herself had reached an impasse. But she needed him. Needed him at once.

"Jim—Jim," she said. "It's Susan. Listen. Get into a white tie and come as fast as you can to the Dycke Hotel. The Chandelier Room."

"What's wrong?"

"Well," said Susan in a small voice. "I've set something going that—that I'm afraid is going to be more than I meant——"

"You're good at stirring up things, Sue," he said. "What's the trouble now?"

"Hurry, Jim," said Susan. "I mean it." She caught her breath. "I—I'm afraid," she said.

His voice changed.

"I'll be right there. Watch for me at the door." The telephone clicked, and Susan leaned rather weakly against the wall of the telephone booth.

She went back to the Chandelier Room. Idabelle Lasher, pink and worried-looking, and Major Briggs and the two younger men made a little group standing together, talking. She breathed a little sigh of relief. So long as they remained together, and remained in that room surrounded by hundreds of witnesses, it was all right. Surely it was all right. People didn't murder in cold blood when other people were looking on.

It was Idabelle who remembered her duties as hostess and suggested the fortune teller.

"She's very good, they say," said Idabelle. "She's a professional, not just doing it for a stunt, you know. She's got a booth in one of the rooms."

"By all means, my dear," said Major Briggs at once. "This way?" She put her hand on his arm and, with Duane at her other side, moved away, and Dixon and Susan followed. Susan cast a worried look toward the entrance. But Jim couldn't possibly get there in less than thirty minutes, and by that time they would have returned.

Dixon said: "Was it the Major that convinced Idabelle that Duane is her son?"

Susan hesitated.

"I don't know," she said cautiously, "how strong the Major's influence has been."

Her caution was not successful. As they left the ballroom and turned down a corridor, he whirled toward her.

"This thing isn't over yet," he said with the sudden savagery that had blazed out in him while they were dancing.

She said nothing, however, for Major Briggs was beckoning jauntily from a doorway.

"Here it is," he said in a stage whisper as they approached him. "Idabelle has already gone in. And would you believe it, the fortune teller charges twenty dollars a throw!"

The room was small: a dining room, probably, for small parties. Across the end of it a kind of tent had been arranged with many gayly striped curtains.

Possibly due to her fees, the fortune teller did not appear to be very popular; at least, there were no others waiting, and no one came to the door except a bellboy with a tray in his hand who looked them over searchingly, murmured something that sounded very much like Mr. Haymow, and wandered away. Duane sat nonchalantly on the small of his back, smoking. The Major seemed a bit nervous and moved restlessly about. Dixon stood just behind Susan. Odd that she could feel his hatred for the man lolling there in the armchair almost as if it were a palpable, living thing flowing outward in waves. Susan's sense of danger was growing sharper. But surely it was safe—so long as they were together.

The draperies of the tent moved confusedly and opened, and Idabelle stood there, smiling and beckoning to Susan.

"Come inside, my dear," she said. "She wants you, too."

Susan hesitated. But, after all, so long as the three men were together, nothing could happen. Dixon gave her a sharp look, and Susan moved across the room. She felt a slight added qualm when she discovered that in an effort probably to add mystery to the fortune teller's trade, the swatching curtains had been arranged so that one entered a kind of narrow passage among them, which one followed with several turns before arriving at the looped-up curtain which made an entrance to the center of the maze and faced the fortune teller herself.

Susan stifled her uneasiness and sat down on some

cushions beside Idabelle. The fortune teller, in Egyptian costume, with French accent and a Sibylline manner, began to talk. Beyond the curtains and the drone of her voice Susan could hear little, although once she thought there were voices.

But the thing, when it happened, gave no warning.

There was only, suddenly, a great dull shock of sound that brought Susan taut and upright and left the fortune teller gasping and still and turned Idabelle Lasher's broad pinkness to a queer pale mauve.

"*What was that?*" whispered Idabelle in a choked way.

And the fortune teller cried: "It's a gunshot—out there!"

Susan stumbled and groped through the folds of draperies, trying to find the way through the entangling maze of curtains and out of the tent. Then all at once they were outside the curtains and staring at a figure that lay huddled on the floor, and confusion everywhere.

It was Major Briggs. And he'd been shot and was dead, and there was no revolver anywhere.

Susan felt ill and faint and after one long look backed away to the window. Idabelle was weeping, her face blotched. Dixon was beside her, and then suddenly someone from the hotel had closed the door into the corridor. And a bellboy's voice, the one who'd wandered into the room looking for Mr. Haymow, rose shrilly above the tumult.

"Nobody at all, " he was saying. "Nobody came out of the room. I was at the end of the corridor when I heard the shot and this is the only room on this side that's unlocked and in use tonight. So I ran down here, and I can swear that nobody came out of the room after the shot was fired. Not before I reached it."

"Was anybody here when you came in? What did you

see?" It was the manager, fat, worried, but competently keeping the door behind him closed against further intrusion.

"Just this man on the floor. He was dead already."

"And nobody in the room?"

"Nobody. Nobody then. But I'd hardly got to him before there was people running into the room. And these three women came out of this tent."

The manager looked at Idabelle—at Susan.

"He was with you?" he asked Idabelle.

"Oh, yes, yes," sobbed Idabelle. "It's Major Briggs."

The manager started to speak, stopped, began again:

"I've sent for the police," he said. "You folks that were in his party—how many of you are there?"

"Just Miss Dare and me," sobbed Idabelle. "And"— she singled out Dixon and Duane—"these two men."

"All right. You folks stay right here, will you? And you, too, miss"—indicating the fortune teller—"and the bellboy. The rest of you will go to a room across the hall. Sorry, but I'll have to hold you till the police get here."

It was not well received. There were murmurs of outrage and horrified looks over slender bare backs and the indignant rustle of trailing gowns, but the scattered groups that had pressed into the room did file slowly out again under the firm look of the manager.

The manager closed the door and said briskly:

"Now, if you folks will be good enough to stay right here, it won't be long till the police arrive."

"A doctor," faltered Idabelle. "Can't we have a doctor?"

The manager looked at the sodden, lifeless body.

"You don't want a doctor, ma'am," he said. "What you want is an under—" He stopped abruptly and reverted to his professional suavity. "We'll do everything in our power to save your feelings, Mrs. Lasher," he said. "At the same time we would much appreciate your—er—

assistance. You see, the Charity Ball being what it is, we've got to keep this thing quiet." He was obviously distressed but still suave and competent. "Now, then," he said. "I've got to make some arrangements—if you'll just stay here." He put his hand on the door knob and then turned toward them again and said quite definitely, looking at the floor: "It would be just as well if none of you were to try to leave."

With that he was gone.

The fortune teller sank down into a chair and said, "Good gracious me," with some emphasis and a Middle-Western accent. The bellboy retired nonchalantly to a corner and stood there, looking very childish in his smart white uniform, but very knowing. And Idabelle Lasher looked at the man at her feet and began to sob again, and Duane tried to comfort her, while Dixon shoved his hands in his pockets and glowered at nothing.

"But I don't see," wailed Idabelle, "how it could have happened!" Odd, thought Susan, that she didn't ask who did it. That would be the natural question. Or why? Why had a man who was—as she had said, like a brother to her—been murdered?

Duane patted Idabelle's heaving bare shoulders and said something soothing, and Idabelle wrung her hands and cried again: "How could it have happened! We were all together—he was not alone a moment——"

Dixon stirred.

"Oh, yes, he was alone," he said. "He wanted a drink, and I'd gone to hunt a waiter."

"And you forget to mention," said Duane icily, "that I had gone with you."

"You left this room at the same time, but that's all I know."

"I went at the same time you did. I stopped to buy cigarettes, and you vanished. I don't know where you went, but I didn't see you again. Not till I came back with the crowd into this room. Came back to find you already here."

"What do you mean by that?" Dixon's eyes were blazing in his white face, and his hands were working. "If you are accusing me of murder, say so straight out like a man instead of an insolent little puppy."

Duane was white, too, but composed.

"All right," he said. "You know whether you murdered him or not. All I know is when I got back I found him dead and you already here."

"*You——*"

"*Dixon!*" cried Idabelle sharply, her laces swirling as she moved hurriedly between the two men. "Stop this! I won't have it. There'll be time enough for questions when the police come. When the police—" She dabbed at her mouth, which was still trembling, and at her chin, and her fingers went on to her throat, groped, closed convulsively, and she screamed: "*My pearls!*"

"Pearls?" asked Dixon staring, and Duane darted forward.

"Pearls—they're gone!"

The fortune teller had started upward defensively, and the bellboy's eyes were like two saucers. Susan said:

"They are certainly somewhere in the room, Mrs. Lasher. And the police will find them for you. There's no need to search for them, now."

Susan pushed a chair toward her, and she sank helplessly into it.

"Tom murdered—and now my pearls gone—and I don't know which is Derek, and I—*I don't know what to do——*" Her shoulders heaved, and her face was hidden in her handkerchief, and her corseted fat body collapsed into lines of utter despair.

Susan said deliberately:

"The room will be searched, Mrs. Lasher, every square inch of it—ourselves included. There is nothing," said Susan with soft emphasis, "nothing that they will miss."

Then Dixon stepped forward. His face was set, and there was an ominous flare of light in his eyes.

He put his hand upon Idabelle's shoulder to force her to look up into his face, and brushed aside Duane, who had moved quickly forward, too, as if his defeated rival had threatened Idabelle.

"Why—why, Dixon," faltered Idabelle Lasher, "you look so strange. What is it? Don't, my dear, you are hurting my shoulder—"

Duane cried: "Let her alone. Let her alone." And then to Idabelle: "Don't pay any attention to him. He's out of his mind. He's—" He clutched at Dixon's arm, but Dixon turned, gave him one black look, and thrust him away so forcefully that Duane staggered backward against the walls of the tent and clutched at the curtains to save himself from falling.

"Look here," said Dixon grimly to Idabelle, "what do you mean when you say as you did just now, that you don't know which is Derek? What do you mean? You must tell me. It isn't fair. *What do you mean?*"

His fingers sank into her bulging flesh. She stared upward as if hypnotized, choking. "I meant just that, Dixon. I don't know yet. I only said I had decided in order to—"

"In order to what?" said Dixon inexorably.

A queer little tingle ran along Susan's nerves, and she edged toward the door. She must get help. Duane's eyes were strange and terribly bright. He still clutched the garishly striped curtains behind him. Susan took another silent step and another toward the door without removing her gaze from the tableau, and Idabelle Lasher looked up into

Dixon's face, and her lips moved flabbily, and she said the strangest thing:

"*How like your father you are, Derek.*"

Susan's heart got up into her throat and left a very curious empty place in the pit of her stomach. She probably moved a little farther toward the door, but was never sure, for all at once, while mother and son stared revealingly and certainly at each other, Duane's white face and queer bright eyes vanished.

Susan was going to run. She was going to fling herself out the door and shriek for help. For there was going to be another murder in that room. There was going to be another murder, and she couldn't stop it, she couldn't do anything, she couldn't even scream a warning. Then Duane's black figure was outlined against the tent again. And he held a revolver in his hand. The fortune teller said: "Oh, my God!" and the white streak that had been the bellboy dissolved rapidly behind a chair.

"Call him your son if you want to," Duane said in an odd jerky way, addressing Mrs. Lasher and Derek confusedly. "Then your son's a murderer. He killed Briggs. He hid in the folds of this curtain till—the room was full of people—and then he came out again. He left his revolver there. And here it is. *Don't move.* One word or move out of any of you, and I'll shoot." He stopped to take a breath. He was smiling a little and panting. "Don't move," he said again sharply. "I'm going to hand you over to the police, Mr. *Derek.* You won't be so anxious to say he's your son then, perhaps. It's his revolver. He killed Briggs with it because Briggs favored me. He knew it, and he did it for revenge."

He was crossing the room with smooth steps, holding the revolver poised threateningly, and his eyes were rapidly shifting from one to another. Susan hadn't the slightest doubt that the smallest move would bring a revolver shot crashing through someone's brain. He's going to escape, she thought, he's going to escape. I can't do a thing. And he's mad with rage. Mad with the terrible excitement of having already killed once.

Duane caught the flicker of Susan's eyes. He was near her now, so near that he could have touched her. He cried:

"It's you that's done this! You that advised her! You were on his side! Well—" He'd reached the door now, and there was nothing they could do. He was gloating openly, the way of escape before him. In an excess of dreadful triumphant excitement, he cried: "I'll shoot you first—it's too bad, when you are so pretty. But I'm going to do it." It's the certainty, thought Susan numbly; Idabelle is so certain that Derek is the other one that Duane knows it, too. He knows there's no use in going on with it. And he knew, when I said what I said about the pearls, that I know.

She felt oddly dizzy. Something was moving. Was she going to faint—was she—something *was* moving, and it was the door behind Duane. It was moving silently, very slowly.

Susan steeled her eyes not to reveal that knowledge. If only Idabelle and Derek would not move—would not see those panels move and betray what they had seen.

Duane laughed.

And Derek moved again, and Idabelle tried to thrust him away from her, and Duane's revolver jerked and jerked again, and the door pushed Duane suddenly to one side and there was a crash of glass, and voices and flashing movement. Susan knew only that someone had pinioned Duane from behind and was holding his arms close to his side. Duane gasped, his hand writhed and dropped the revolver.

Then somebody at the door dragged Duane away; Susan realized confusedly that there were police there. And Jim Byrne stood at her elbow. He looked unwontedly handsome in white tie and tails, but very angry. He said:

"Go home, Sue. Get out of here."

It was literally impossible for Susan to speak or move. Jim stared at her as if nothing else was in the room, got out a handkerchief and wiped his forehead with it.

"I've aged ten years in the last five minutes," he said. He glanced around. Saw Major Briggs's body there on the floor—saw Idabelle Lasher and Derek—saw the fortune teller and the bellboy.

"Is that Mrs. Jeremiah Lasher over there?" he said to Susan.

Mrs. Lasher opened her eyes, looked at him, and closed them again.

Jim looked meditatively at a revolver in his hand, put it in his pocket, and said briskly:

"You can stay for a while, Susan. Until I hear the whole story. Who shot Major Briggs?"

Susan's lips moved and Derek straightened up and cried:

"Oh, it's my revolver all right. But I didn't kill Major Briggs—I don't expect anyone to believe me, but I didn't."

"He didn't," said Susan wearily. "Duane killed Major Briggs. He killed him with Derek's revolver, perhaps, but it was Duane who did the murder."

Jim did not question her statement, but Derek said eagerly:

"How do you know? Can you prove it?"

"I think so," said Susan. "You see, Duane had a revolver when I danced with him. It was in his pocket. That's when I phoned for you, Jim. But I was too late."

"But how—" said Jim.

"Oh, when Duane accused Derek, he actually described the way he himself murdered Major Briggs and concealed himself and the revolver in the folds of the tent until the room was full of people and he could quietly mingle with them as if he had come from the hall. We were all staring at Major Briggs. It was very simple. Duane had got hold of Derek's revolver and knew it would be traced to Derek and the blame put on him, since Derek had every reason to wish to revenge himself upon Major Briggs."

Idabelle had opened her eyes. They looked a bit glassy but were more sensible.

"Why—" she said, "—why did Duane kill Major Briggs?"

"I suppose because Major Briggs had backed him. You see," said Susan gently, "one of the claimants had to be an impostor and a deliberate one. And the attack upon Major Briggs last night suggested either that he knew too much or was a conspirator himself. The exact coinciding of the stories (particularly clever on Major Briggs's part) and the fact that Duane turned up after Major Briggs had had time to search for someone who would fulfill the requirements necessary to make a claim to being your son, seemed to me an indication of conspiracy; besides, the very nature of the case involved imposture. But there had to be a conspiracy; someone had to tell one of the claimants about the things upon which to base his claim, especially about the memories of the baby things—the calico dog," said Susan with a little smile, "and the plush teddy bear. It had to be someone who had known you long ago and could have seen those things before you put them away in the safe. Someone who knew all your circumstances."

"You mean that Major Briggs planned Duane's claim—planned the whole thing? But why—" Idabelle's eyes were full of tears again.

"There's only one possible reason," said Susan. "He must have needed money very badly, and Duane, coming into thirty millions of dollars, would have been obliged to share his spoils."

"Then Derek—I mean Dixon—I mean," said Idabelle confusedly, clutching at Derek, "this one. He really is my son?"

"You know he is," said Susan. "You realized it yourself when you were under emotional stress and obliged to feel instead of reason about it. However, there's reason for it, too. *He is Derek.*"

"He—is—Derek," said Idabelle, catching at Susan's words. "You are sure?"

"Yes," said Susan quietly. "He is Derek. You see, I'd forgotten something. Something physical that never changes all through life. That is, a sense of rhythm. Derek has no sense of rhythm and has never had. Duane was a born dancer."

Idabelle said: "Thank God!" She looked at Susan, looked at Derek, and quite suddenly became herself again. She got up briskly, glanced at Major Briggs's body, said calmly: "We'll try to keep some of this quiet. I'll see that things are done decently—after all, poor old fellow, he did love his comforts. Now, then. Oh, yes, if someone will just see the manager of the hotel about my pearls—"

Susan put a startled hand to her gardenias.

"I'd forgotten your pearls, too. Here they are." She fumbled a moment among the flowers, detached a string of flowing beauty, and held it toward Idabelle. "I took them from Duane while we were dancing."

"Duane," said Idabelle. "But—" She took the pearls and said incredulously: "They *are* mine!"

"He had taken them while he danced with you. During the next dance you passed me, and I saw that your neck was bare."

Jim turned to Susan.

"Are you sure about that, Susan?" he said. "I've managed to get the outline of the story, you know. And I don't think the false claimant would have taken such a risk. Not with thirty millions in his pocket, so to speak."

"Oh, they were for the Major," said Susan. "At least, I think that was the reason. I don't know yet, but I think we'll find that he was pretty hard pressed for cash and had to have some right away. Immediately. Duane probably balked at demanding money of Mrs. Lasher so soon, so the Major suggested the pearls. And Duane was in no position to refuse the Major's demands. Then, you see, he had no pearls because I took them; he and the Major must have quarreled, and Duane, who had already foreseen that he would be at Major Briggs's mercy as long as the Major lived, was already prepared for any opportunity to kill him. After he had once got to Idabelle, he no longer needed the Major. He had armed himself with Derek's revolver after what must have seemed to him a heaven-sent chance to stage an accident had failed. Mrs. Lasher's decision removed any remaining small value that the Major was to him and made Major Briggs only a menace. But I think he wasn't sure just what he would do or how—he acceded to the Major's demand for the pearls because it was at the moment the simplest course. But he was ready and anxious to kill him, and when he knew that the pearls had gone from his pocket he must have guessed that I had taken them. And he decided to get rid of Major Briggs at once, before he could possibly tell anything, for any story the Major chose to tell would have been believed by Mrs. Lasher. Later, when I said that the police would search the room, he knew that I knew. And that I knew the revolver was still here."

"Is that why you advised me to announce my decision that Duane was my son?" demanded Idabelle Lasher.

Susan shuddered and tried not to look at that black heap across the room.

"No," she said steadily. "I didn't dream of—murder. I only thought that it might bring the conspiracy that evidently existed somewhere into the open."

Jim said: "Here are the police."

Queer, thought Susan much later, riding along the Drive in Jim's car, with her white chiffon flounces tucked in carefully, and her green velvet wrap pulled tightly about her throat against the chill night breeze, and the scent of gardenias mingling with the scent of Jim's cigarette—queer how often her adventures ended like this: driving silently homeward in Jim's car.

She glanced at the irregular profile behind the wheel and said: "I suppose you know you saved my life tonight."

His mouth tightened in the little glow from the dashlight. Presently he said:

"How did you know he had the pearls in his pocket?"

"Felt 'em," said Susan. "And you can't imagine how terribly easy it was to take them. In all probability a really brilliant career in picking pockets was sacrificed when I was provided with moral scruples."

The light went to yellow and then red, and Jim stopped. He turned and gave Susan a long look through the dusk, and then slowly took her hand in his own warm fingers for a second or two before the light went to green again.

THE BOOK THAT SQUEALED
by Cornell Woolrich

The outside world never intruded into the sanctum where
Prudence Roberts worked. Nothing violent or exciting ever
happened there, or was ever likely to. Voices were never
raised above a whisper, or at the most a discreet murmur. The most untoward thing that could possibly occur
would be that some gentleman browser became so
engrossed he forgot to remove his hat and had to be tact-
fully reminded. Once, it is true, a car backfired violently
somewhere outside in the street and the whole staff gave
a nervous start, including Prudence, who dropped her
date stamp all the way out in the aisle in front of her
desk; but that had never happened again after that one
time.

Things that the papers printed, holdups, gang warfare,
kidnappings, murders, remained just things that the papers
printed. They never came past these portals behind which
she worked.

Just books came in and went out again. Harmless, silent
books.

Until, one bright June day—

The Book showed up around noon, shortly before Prudence Roberts was due to go off duty for lunch. She was on
the Returned Books desk. She turned up her nose with
unqualified inner disapproval at first sight of the volume.
Her taste was severely classical; she had nothing against
light reading in itself, but to her, light reading meant
Dumas, Scott, Dickens. She could tell this thing before
her was trash by the title alone, and the author's pen
name: "Manuela Gets Her Man," by Orchid Ollivant.

Furthermore it had a lurid orange dust cover that showed just what kind of claptrap might be expected within. She was surprised a city library had added such worthless tripe to its stock; it belonged more in a candy-store lending library than here. She supposed there had been a great many requests for it among a certain class of readers; that was why.

Date stamp poised in hand, she glanced up, expecting to see one of these modern young hussies, all paint and boldness, or else a faded middle-aged blonde of the type that lounged around all day in a wrapper, reading such stuff and eating marshmallows. To her surprise the woman before her was drab, looked hard-working and anything but frivolous. She didn't seem to go with the book at all.

Prudence Roberts didn't say anything, looked down again, took the book's reference card out of the filing drawer just below her desk, compared them.

"You're two days overdue with this," she said. "It's a one-week book. That'll be four cents."

The woman fumbled timidly in an old-fashioned handbag, placed a nickel on the desk.

"My daughter's been reading it to me at nights," she explained, "but she goes to night school and some nights she couldn't; that's what delayed me. Oh, it was grand." She sighed. "It brings back all your dreams of romance."

"Humph," said Prudence Roberts, still disapproving as much as ever. She returned a penny change to the borrower, stamped both cards. That should have ended the trivial little transaction.

But the woman had lingered there by the desk, as though trying to summon up courage to ask something. "Please," she faltered timidly when Prudence had glanced up a second time, "I was wondering, could you tell me what happens on Page 42? You know, that time when the rich man lures her on his yasht?"

"Yacht," Prudence corrected her firmly. "Didn't you

read the book yourself?"

"Yes, my daughter read it to me, but Pages 41 and 42 are missing, and we were wondering, we'd give anything to know, if Ronald got there in time to save her from that awful—"

Prudence had pricked up her official ears at that. "Just a minute," she interrupted, and retrieved the book from where she had just discarded it. She thumbed through it rapidly. At first glance it seemed in perfect condition; it was hard to tell anything was the matter with it. If the borrower hadn't given her the exact page number—but Pages 41 and 42 were missing, as she had said. A telltale scalloping of torn paper ran down the seam between Pages 40 and 43. The leaf had been plucked out bodily, torn out like a sheet in a notebook, not just become loosened and fallen out. Moreover, the condition of the book's spine showed that this could not have happened from wear and tear; it was still too new and firm. It was a case of out-and-out vandalism. Inexcusable destruction of the city's property.

"This book's been damaged," said Prudence ominously. "It's only been in use six weeks, it's still a new book, and this page was deliberately ripped out along its entire length. I'll have to ask you for your reader's card back. Wait here, please."

She took the book over to Miss Everett, the head librarian, and showed it to her. The latter was Prudence twenty years from now, if nothing happened in between to snap her out of it. She sailed back toward the culprit, steel-rimmed spectacles glittering balefully.

The woman was standing there cringing, her face as white as though she expected to be executed on the spot. She had the humble person's typical fear of anyone in authority. "Please, lady, I didn't do it," she whined.

"You should have reported it before taking it out," said the inexorable Miss Everett. "I'm sorry, but as the last borrower, we'll have to hold you responsible. Do you realize you could go to jail for this?"

The woman quailed. "It was that way when I took it home," she pleaded; "I didn't do it."

Prudence relented a little. "She did call my attention to it herself, Miss Everett," she remarked. "I wouldn't have noticed it otherwise."

"You know the rules as well as I do, Miss Roberts," said her flinty superior. She turned to the terrified drudge. "You will lose your card and all library privileges until you have paid the fine assessed against you for damaging this book." She turned and went careening off again.

The poor woman still hovered there, pathetically anxious. "Please don't make me do without my reading," she pleaded. "That's the only pleasure I got. I work hard all day. How much is it? Maybe I can pay a little something each week."

"Are you sure you didn't do it?" Prudence asked her searchingly. The lack of esteem in which she held this book was now beginning to incline her in the woman's favor. Of course, it was the principle of the thing, it didn't matter how trashy the book in question was. On the other hand, how could the woman have been expected to notice that a page was gone, in time to report it, *before* she had begun to read it?

"I swear I didn't," the woman protested. "I love books, I wouldn't want to hurt one of them."

"Tell you what I'll do," said Prudence, lowering her voice and looking around to make sure she wasn't overheard. "I'll pay the fine for you out of my own pocket, so you can go ahead using the library meanwhile. I think it's likely this was done by one of the former borrowers, ahead of you. If such proves not to be the case, however, then you'll simply have to repay me a little at a time."

The poor woman actually tried to take hold of her hand to kiss it. Prudence hastily withdrew it, marked the fine paid, and returned the card to her.

"And I suggest you try to read something a little more worthwhile in future," she couldn't help adding.

She didn't discover the additional damage until she had gone upstairs with the book, when she was relieved for lunch. It was no use sending it back to be rebound or repaired; with one entire page gone like that, there was nothing could be done with it; the book was worthless. Well, it had been that to begin with, she thought tartly.

She happened to flutter the leaves scornfully and light filtered through one of the pages, in dashes of varying length, like a sort of Morse code. She looked more closely, and it was the forty-third page, the one immediately after the missing leaf. It bore innumerable horizontal slashes scattered all over it from top to bottom, as though some moron had underlined the words on it, but with some sharp-edged instrument rather than the point of a pencil. They were so fine they were almost invisible when the leaf was lying flat against the others, white on white; it was only when it was up against the light that they stood revealed. The leaf was almost threadbare with them. The one after it had some too, but not nearly so distinct; they hadn't pierced the thickness of the paper, were just scratches on it.

She had heard of books being defaced with pencil, with ink, with crayon, something visible at least—but with an improvised stylus that just left slits? On the other hand, what was there in this junky novel important enough to be emphasized—if that was why it had been done?

She began to read the page, to try to get some connected meaning out of the words that had been underscored. It was just a lot of senseless drivel about the heroine who was being entertained on the villain's yacht. It couldn't have been done for emphasis, then, of that Prudence was positive.

But she had the type of mind that, once something aroused its curiosity, couldn't rest again until the matter had been solved. If she couldn't remember a certain name, for instance, the agonizing feeling of having it on the tip of her tongue but being unable to bring it out would keep her from getting any sleep until the name had come back to her.

This now took hold of her in the same way. Failing to get anything out of the entire text, she began to see if she could get something out of the gashed words in themselves. Maybe that was where the explanation lay. She took a pencil and paper and began to transcribe them one by one, in the same order in which they came in the book. She got:

hardly anyone going invited merrily

Before she could go any farther than that, the lunch period was over, it was time to report down to her desk again.

She decided she was going to take the book home with her that night and keep working on it until she got something out of it. This was simply a matter of self-defense; she wouldn't be getting any sleep until she did. She put it away in her locker, returned downstairs to duty, and put the money with which she was paying Mrs. Trasker's fine into the till. That was the woman's name, Mrs. Trasker.

The afternoon passed as uneventfully as a hundred others had before it, but her mind kept returning to the enigma at intervals. "There's a reason for everything in this world," she insisted to herself, "and I want to know the reason for this: why were certain words in this utterly un-memorable novel underscored by slashes as though they were Holy Writ or something? And I'm going to find out if it takes me all the rest of this summer!"

She smuggled the book out with her when she left for home, trying to keep it hidden so the other members of the staff wouldn't notice. Not that she would have been refused permission if she had asked for it, but she would have had to give her reasons for wanting to take it, and she was afraid they would all laugh at her or think she was becoming touched in the head if she told them. After all, she excused herself, if she could find out the meaning of what had been done, that might help the library to discover who the guilty party really was and recover damages, and she could get back her own money that she had put in for poor Mrs. Trasker.

Prudence hurried up her meal as much as possible, and returned to her room. She took a soft pencil and lightly went over the slits in the paper, to make them stand out more clearly. It would be easy enough to erase the pencil marks later. But almost as soon as she had finished and could get a comprehensive view of the whole page at a glance, she saw there was something wrong. The underscorings weren't flush with some of the words. Sometimes they only took in half a word, carried across the intervening space, and then took in half of the next. One of them even fell where there was absolutely no word at all over it, in the blank space between two paragraphs.

That gave her the answer; she saw in a flash what her mistake was. She'd been wasting her time on the wrong page. It was the leaf before, the missing Page 41, that had held the real meaning of the slashed words. The sharp instrument used on it had simply carried through to the leaf under it, and even, very lightly, to the third one following. No wonder the scorings overlapped and she hadn't been able to make sense out of them! Their real sense, if any, lay on the page that had been removed.

Well, she'd wasted enough time on it. It probably wasn't anything anyway. She tossed the book contemp-

tuously aside, made up her mind that was the end of it.
A moment or so later her eyes strayed irresistibly, long-
ingly over to it again. "I know how I *could* find out for
sure," she tempted herself.

Suddenly she was putting on her things again to go
out. To go out and do something she had never done before: buy a trashy, frothy novel. Her courage almost
failed her outside the bookstore window, where she finally located a copy, along with bridge sets, ash trays,
statuettes of Dopey, and other gew-gaws. If it had only
had a less . . . er . . . compromising title. She set her
chin, took a deep breath, and plunged in.

"I want a copy of *Manuela Gets Her Man*, please," she
said, flushing a little.

The clerk was one of these brazen blondes painted up
like an Iroquois. She took in Prudence's shell-rimmed
glasses, knot of hair, drab clothing. She smirked a little,
as if to say, "So you're finally getting wise to yourself?"
Prudence Roberts gave her two dollars, almost ran out of
the store with her purchase, cheeks flaming with embar-
rassment.

She opened it the minute she got in and avidly scanned
Page 41. There wasn't anything on it, in itself, of more
consequence than there had been on any of the other pages,
but that wasn't stopping her this time. This thing had
now cost her over three dollars of her hard-earned
money, and she was going to get something out of it.

She committed an act of vandalism for the first time in
her life, even though the book was her own property and not
the city's. She ripped Pages 41 and 42 neatly out of the
binding, just as the leaf had been torn from the other book.
Then she inserted it in the first book, the original one.
Not *over* Page 43, where it belonged, but under it. She
found a piece of carbon paper, cut it down to size, and
slipped that between the two. Then she fastened the

three sheets together with paper clips, carefully seeing to it that the borders of the two printed pages didn't vary by a hair's breadth. Then she took her pencil and once more traced the gashes on Page 43, but this time bore down heavily on them. When she had finished, she withdrew the loose Page 41 from under the carbon and she had a haphazard array of underlined words sprinkled over the page. The original ones from the missing page. Her eye traveled over them excitedly. Then her face dropped again. They didn't make sense any more than before. She opened the lower half of the window, balanced the book in her hand, resisted an impulse to toss it out then and there. She gave herself a fight talk instead. "I'm a librarian. I have more brains than whoever did this to this book, I don't care who they are! I can get out whatever meaning they put into it, if I just keep cool and keep at it." She closed the window, sat down once more.

She studied the carbon-scored page intently, and presently a belated flash of enlightenment followed. The very arrangement of the dashes showed her what her mistake had been this time. They were too symmetrical, each one had its complement one line directly under it. In other words they were really double, not single lines. Their vertical alignment didn't vary in the slightest. She should have noticed that right away. She saw what it was now. The words hadn't been merely underlined, they had been cut out of the page bodily by four gashes around each required one, two vertical, two horizontal, forming an oblong that contained the wanted word. What she had mistaken for dashes had been the top and bottom lines of these "boxes." The faint side lines she had overlooked entirely.

She canceled out every alternate line, beginning with the top one, and that should have given her the real kernel of the message. But again she was confronted with a meaningless jumble, scant as the residue of words was. She held her head distractedly as she took it in:

> cure
>   wait
>   poor
>   honey   to
>   grand
>   her
>   health
>   your
>   fifty
>
>   instructions

"The text around them is what's distracting me," she decided after a futile five or ten minutes of poring over them. "Subconsciously I keep trying to read them in the order in which they appear on the page. Since they were taken bodily out of it, that arrangement was almost certainly not meant to be observed. It is, after all, the same principle as a jig-saw puzzle. I have the pieces now, all that remains is to put each one in the right place."

She took a small pair of nail scissors and carefully clipped out each boxed word, just as the unkown predecessor had whose footsteps she was trying to unearth. That done, she discarded the book entirely, in order to be hampered by it no longer. Then she took a blank piece of paper, placed all the little paper cut-outs on it, careful that they remained right side up, and milled them about with her finger, to be able to start from scratch.

"I'll begin with the word 'fifty' as the easiest entering wedge," she breathed absorbedly. "It is a numerical adjective, and therefore simply must modify one of those three nouns, according to all the rules of grammar." She separated it from the rest, set to work. Fifty health—no, the noun is in the singular. Fifty honey—no, again singular. Fifty instructions—yes, but it was an awkward combination, something about it didn't ring true, she wasn't quite satisfied with it. Fifty grand? That was it! It was grammatically incorrect, it wasn't a noun at all, but in slang it was used as one. She had often heard it herself, used by people who were slovenly in their speech. She set the two words apart, satisfied they belonged together.

"Now a noun, in any kind of sentence at all," she murmured to herself, "has to be followed by a verb." There were only two to choose from. She tried them both. Fifty grand wait. Fifty grand cure. Elliptical, both. But that form of the verb had to take a preposition, and there was one there at hand: "to." She tried it that way. Fifty grand to wait. Fifty grand to cure. She chose the latter, and the personal pronoun fell into place almost automatically after it. Fifty grand to cure her. That was almost certainly it.

She had five out of the eleven words now. She had a verb, two adjectives, and three nouns left: wait, your, poor, honey, health, instructions. But that personal pronoun already in place was a stumbling block, kept baffling her. It seemed to refer to some preceding proper name, it demanded one to make sense, and she didn't have any in her six remaining words. And then suddenly she saw that she did have. Honey. It was to be read as a term of endearment, not a substance made by bees.

The remaining words paired off almost as if magnetically drawn toward one another. Your honey, poor health, wait instructions. She shifted them about the basic nucleus she already had, trying them out before and after it, until, with a little minor rearranging, she had them satisfactorily in place.

your honey poor health fifty grand to cure her wait instructions

There it was at last. It couldn't be any more lucid than that. She had no mucilage at hand to paste the little paper oblongs down flat and hold them fast in the position she had so laboriously achieved. Instead she took a number of pins and skewered them to the blank sheets of paper. Then she sat back looking at them.

It was a ransom note. Even she, unworldly as she was, could tell that at a glance. Printed words cut bodily out of a book, to avoid the use of handwriting or typewriting that might be traced later. Then the telltale leaf with the gaps had been torn out and destroyed. But in their hurry they had overlooked one little thing, the slits had carried through to the next page. Or else they had thought it didn't matter, no one would be able to reconstruct the thing once the original page was gone. Well, she had.

There were still numerous questions left unanswered. To whom had the note been addressed? By whom? Whose "honey" was it? And why, with a heinous crime like kidnapping for ransom involved, had they taken the trouble to return the book at all? Why not just destroy it entirely and be done with it? The answer to that could very well be that the actual borrower—one of those names on the book's reference card—was someone who knew them, but wasn't aware what they were doing, what the book had been used for, hadn't been present when the message was concocted; had all unwittingly returned the book.

There was of course a question as to whether the message was genuine or simply some adolescent's practical joke, yet the trouble taken to evade the use of handwriting argued that it was anything but a joke. And the most important question of all was: Should she go to the police about it? She answered that then and there, with a slow but determined *yes!*

It was well after eleven by now, and the thought of

venturing out on the streets alone at such an hour, especially to and from a place like a police station, filled her timid soul with misgivings. She could ring up from here, but then they'd send someone around to question her most likely, and that would be even worse. What would the landlady and the rest of the roomers think of her, receiving a gentleman caller at such an hour, even if he was from the police? It looked so . . . er . . . rowdy.

She steeled herself to go to them in person, and it required a good deal of steeling and even a cup of hot tea, but finally she set out, book and transcribed message under her arm, also a large umbrella with which to defend herself if she were insulted on the way.

She was ashamed to ask anyone where the nearest precinct house was, but luckily she saw a pair of policemen walking along as if they were going off duty, and by following them at a discreet distance, she finally saw them turn and go into a building that had a pair of green lights outside the entrance. She walked past it four times, twice in each direction, before she finally got up nerve enough to go in.

There was a uniformed man sitting at a desk near the entrance and she edged over and stood waiting for him to look up at her. He didn't, he was busy with some kind of report, so after standing there a minute or two, she cleared her throat timidly.

"Well, lady?" he said in a stentorian voice that made her jump and draw back.

"Could I speak to a . . . a detective, please?" she faltered.

"Any particular one?"

"A good one."

He said to a cop standing over by the door: "Go in and tell Murph there's a young lady out here wants to see him."

A square-shouldered, husky young man came out a

minute later, hopefully straightening the knot of his tie and looking around as if he expected to see a Fifth Avenue model at the very least. His gaze fell on Prudence, skipped over her, came up against the blank walls beyond her, and then had to return to her again.

"You the one?" he asked.

"Could I talk to you privately?" she said. "I believe I have made a discovery of the greatest importance."

"Why . . . uh . . . sure," he said, without too much enthusiasm. "Right this way." But as he turned to follow her inside, he slurred something out of the corner of his mouth at the smirking desk sergeant that sounded suspiciously like "I'll fix you for this, kibitzer. It couldn't have been Dolan instead, could it?"

He snapped on a cone light in a small office toward the back, motioned Prudence to a chair, leaned against the edge of the desk.

She was slightly flustered; she had never been in a police station before. "Has . . . er . . . anyone been kidnapped lately, that is to say within the past six weeks?" she blurted out.

He folded his arms, flipped his hands up and down against his own sides. "Why?" he asked noncommittally.

"Well, one of our books came back damaged today, and I think I've deciphered a kidnap message from its pages."

Put baldly like that, it did sound sort of farfetched, she had to admit that herself. Still, he should have at least given her time to explain more fully, not acted like a jackass just because she was prim-looking and wore thick-lensed glasses.

His face reddened and his mouth started to quiver treacherously. He put one hand up over it to hide it from her, but he couldn't keep his shoulders from shaking. Finally he had to turn away altogether and stand in front of the water cooler a minute. Something that sounded like a strangled cough came from him.

"You're laughing at me!" she snapped accusingly. "I

come here to help you, and that's the thanks I get!"

He turned around again with a carefully straightened face. "No, ma'am," he lied cheerfully right to her face, "I'm not laughing at you. I . . . . we . . . appreciate your co-operation. You leave this here and we . . . we'll check on it."

But Prudence Roberts was nobody's fool. Besides, he had ruffled her plumage now, and once that was done, it took a great deal to smooth it down again. She had a highly developed sense of her own dignity. "You haven't the slightest idea of doing anything of the kind!" she let him know. "I can tell that just by looking at you! I must say I'm very surprised that a member of the police department of this city—"

She was so steamed up and exasperated at his facetious attitude, that she removed her glasses, in order to be able to give him a piece of her mind more clearly. A little thing like that shouldn't have made the slightest difference—after all this was police business, not a beauty contest—but to her surprise it seemed to.

He looked at her, blinked, looked at her again, suddenly began to show a great deal more interest in what she had come here to tell him. "What'd you say your name was again, miss?" he asked, and absently made that gesture to the knot of his tie again.

She hadn't said what it was in the first place. Why, this man was just a common—a common masher; he was a disgrace to the shield he wore. "I am Miss Roberts of the Hillcrest Branch of the Public Library," she said stiffly. "What has that to do with this?"

"Well . . . er . . . we have to know the source of our information," he told her lamely. He picked up the book, thumbed through it, then he scanned the message she had deciphered. "Yeah"—Murphy nodded slowly—"that does read like a ransom note."

Mollified, she explained rapidly the process by which

she had built up from the gashes on the succeeding leaf of the book.

"Just a minute, Miss Roberts," he said, when she had finished. "I'll take this in and show it to the lieutenant."

But when he came back, she could tell by his attitude that his superior didn't take any more stock in it than he had himself. "I tried to explain to him the process by which you extracted it out of the book, but. . .er. . .in his opinion it's just a coincidence, I mean the gashes may not have any meaning at all. For instance, someone may have been just cutting something out on top of the book, cookies or pie crust and—"

She snorted in outrage. "Cookies or pie crust! I got a coherent message. If you men can't see it there in front of your eyes—"

"But here's the thing, Miss Roberts," he tried to soothe her. "We haven't any case on deck right now that this could possibly fit into. No one's been reported missing. And we'd know, wouldn't we? I've heard of kidnap cases without ransom notes, but I never heard of a ransom note without a kidnap case to go with it."

"As a police officer doesn't it occur to you that in some instances a kidnapped person's relatives would purposely refrain from notifying the authorities to avoid jeopardizing their loved ones? That may have happened in this case."

"I mentioned that to the lieutenant myself, but he claims it can't be done. There are cases where we purposely hold off at the request of the family until after the victim's been returned, but it's never because we haven't been informed about what's going on. You see, a certain length of time always elapses between the snatch itself and the first contact between the kidnappers and the family, and no matter how short that is, the family has almost always reported the person missing in the meantime, before they know what's up themselves. I can check with Missing Persons if you want, but if it's anything more than just a straight disappearance, they always turn it over to us right away, anyway."

But Prudence didn't intend urging or begging them to look into it as a personal favor to her. She considered she'd done more than her duty. If they discredited it, they discredited it. *She* didn't, and she made up her mind to pursue the investigation, single-handed and without their help if necessary, until she had settled it one way or the other. "Very well," she said coldly, "I'll leave the transcribed message and the extra copy of the book here with you. I'm sorry I bothered you. Good evening." She stalked out, still having forgotten to replace her glasses.

Her indignation carried her as far as the station-house steps, and then her courage began to falter. It was past midnight by now, and the streets looked so lonely; suppose—suppose she met a drunk? While she was standing there trying to get up her nerve, this same Murphy came out behind her, evidently on his way home himself. She had put her glasses on again by now.

"You look a lot different without them," he remarked lamely, stopping a step below her and hanging around.

"Indeed," she said forbiddingly.

"I'm going off duty now. Could I . . . uh . . . see you to where you live?"

She would have preferred not to have to accept the offer, but those shadows down the street looked awfully deep and the light posts awfully far apart. "I *am* a little nervous about being out alone so late," she admitted, starting out beside him. "Once I met a drunk and he said, 'H'lo, babe.' I had to drink a cup of hot tea when I got home, I was so upset."

"Did you have your glasses on?" he asked cryptically.

"No. Come to think of it, that was the time I'd left them to be repaired."

He just nodded knowingly, as though that explained everything.

When they got to her door, he said: "Well, I'll do some

more digging through the files on that thing, just to make sure. If I turn up anything . . . uh . . . suppose I drop around tomorrow night and let you know. And if I don't, I'll drop around and let you know that too. Just so you'll know what's what."

"That's very considerate of you."

"Gee, you're refined," he said wistfully. "You talk such good English."

He seemed not averse to lingering on here talking to her, but someone might have looked out of one of the windows and it would appear so unrefined to be seen dallying there at that hour, so she turned and hurried inside.

When she got to her room, she looked at herself in the mirror. Then she took her glasses off and tried it that way. "How peculiar," she murmured. "How very unaccountable!"

The following day at the library she got out the reference card on *Manuela Gets Her Man* and studied it carefully. It had been out six times in the six weeks it had been in stock. The record went like this:

Doyle, Helen (address)	Apr. 15–Apr. 22
Caine, Rose	Apr. 22–Apr. 29
Dermuth, Alvin	Apr. 29–May 6
Turner, Florence	May 6–May 18
Baumgarten, Lucille	May 18–May 25
Trasker, Sophie	May 25–June 3

Being a new book, it had had a quick turnover, had been taken out again each time the same day it had been brought back. Twice it had been kept out overtime, the first time nearly a whole week beyond the return limit. There might be something in that. All the borrowers but one, so far, were women; that was another noticeable fact. It was, after all, a woman's book. Her library experience had taught her that what is called a "man's book" will often be read by women, but a "woman's book" is absolutely never, and there are few exceptions to this rule, read by men. That might mean something, that one male borrower. She must have seen him at the time, but so many faces passed her desk daily she couldn't remember what he was like any more, if she had. However, she decided not to jump to hasty conclusions, but investigate the list one by one in reverse order. She'd show that ignorant, skirt-chasing Murphy person that where there's smoke there's fire, if you only take the trouble to look for it!

At about eight thirty, just as she was about to start out on her quest—she could only pursue it in the evenings, of course, after library hours—the doorbell rang and she found him standing there. He looked disappointed when he saw that she had her glasses on. He came in rather shyly and clumsily, tripping over the threshold and careening several steps down the hall.

"Were you able to find out anything?" she asked eagerly.

"Nope, I checked again, I went all the way back six months, and I also got in touch with Missing Persons. Nothing doing, I'm afraid it isn't a genuine message, Miss Roberts; just a fluke, like the lieutenant says."

"I'm sorry, but I don't agree with you. I've copied a list of the borrowers and I intend to investigate each one of them in turn. That message was not intended to be readily deciphered, or for that matter deciphered at all; therefore it is not a practical joke of some adolescent's prank. Yet it has a terrible coherence; therefore it is not a fluke or a haphazard scarring of the page, your lieutenant to the contrary. What remains? It is a genuine ransom note, sent in deadly earnest, and I should think you and your superiors would be the first to—"

"Miss Roberts," he said soulfully, "you're too refined to

. . . to dabble in crime like this. Somehow it don't seem right for you to be talking shop, about kidnappings and—" He eased his collar. "I . . . uh . . . it's my night off and I was wondering if you'd like to go to the movies."

"So that's why you took the trouble of coming around!" she said indignantly. "I'm afraid your interest is entirely too personal and not nearly official enough!"

"Gee, even when you talk fast," he said admiringly, "you pronounce every word clear, like in a po-em."

"Well, you don't. It's poem, not po-em. I intend going ahead with this until I can find out just what the meaning of that message is, and who sent it! And I *don't* go to movies with people the second time I've met them!"

He didn't seem at all fazed. "Could I drop around sometime and find out how you're getting along?" he wanted to know, as he edged through the door backward.

"That will be entirely superfluous," she said icily. "If I uncover anything suspicious, I shall of course report it promptly. It is not my job, after all, but . . . ahem . . . other people's."

"Movies! The idea!" She frowned after she had closed the door on him. Then she dropped her eyes and pondered a minute. "It would have been sort of frisky, at that." She smiled.

She took the book along with her as an excuse for calling, and set out, very determined on the surface, as timid as usual underneath. However, she found it easier to get started because the first name on the list, the meek Mrs. Trasker, held no terror even for her. She was almost sure she was innocent, because it was she herself who had called the library's attention to the missing page in the first place, and a guilty person would hardly do that. Still there was always a possibility it was someone else in her family or household, and she meant to be thorough about this if nothing else.

Mrs. Trasker's address was a small old-fashioned

apartment building of the pre-War variety. It was not expensive by any means, but still it did seem beyond the means of a person who had been unable to pay even a two-dollar fine, and for a moment Prudence thought she scented suspicion in this. But as soon as she entered the lobby and asked for Mrs. Trasker, the mystery was explained.

"You'll have to go to the basement for her," the elevator boy told her, "she's the janitress."

A young girl of seventeen admitted her at the basement entrance and led her down a bare brick passage past rows of empty trash cans to the living quarters in the back.

Mrs. Trasker was sitting propped up in bed, and again showed a little alarm at sight of the librarian, a person in authority. An open book on a chair beside her showed that her daughter had been reading aloud to her when they were interrrupted.

"Don't be afraid," Prudence reassured them. "I just want to ask a few questions."

"Sure, anything, missis," said the janitress, clasping and unclasping her hands placatingly.

"Just the two of you live here? No father or brothers?"

"Just mom and me, nobody else," the girl answered.

"Now tell me, are you sure you didn't take the book out with you anywhere, to some friend's house, or lend it to someone else?"

"No, no, it stayed right here!" They both said it together and vehemently.

"Well, then, did anyone call on you down here, while it was in the rooms?"

The mother answered this. "No, no one. When the tenants want me for anything, they ring down for me from upstairs. And when I'm working around the house, I keep our place locked just like anyone does their apartment. So I know no one was near the book while we had it."

"I feel pretty sure of that myself," Prudence said, as she got up to go. She patted Mrs. Trasker's toil-worn hand reassuringly. "Just forget about my coming here like this. Your fine is paid and there's nothing to worry about. See you at the library."

The next name on the reference card was Lucille Baumgarten. Prudence was emboldened to stop in there because she noticed the address, though fairly nearby, in the same branch-library district, was in a higher-class neighborhood. Besides, she was beginning to forget her timidity in the newly awakened interest her quest was arousing in her. It occurred to her for the first time that detectives must lead fairly interesting lives.

A glance at the imposing, almost palatial apartment building Borrower Baumgarten lived in told her this place could probably be crossed off her list of suspects as well. Though she had heard vaguely somewhere or other that gangsters and criminals sometimes lived in luxurious surroundings, these were more than that. These spelled solid, substantial wealth and respectability that couldn't be faked. She had to state her name and business to a uniformed houseman in the lobby before she was even allowed to go up.

"Just tell Miss Baumgarten the librarian from her branch library would like to talk to her a minute."

A maid opened the upstairs door, but before she could open her mouth, a girl slightly younger than Mrs. Trasker's daughter had come skidding down the parquet hall, swept her aside, and displaced her. She was about fifteen at the most and really had no business borrowing from the adult department yet. Prudence vaguely recalled seeing her face before, although then it had been liberally rouged and lipsticked, whereas now it was properly without cosmetics.

She put a finger to her lips and whispered conspiratorially, "Sh! Don't tell my—"

Before she could get any further, there was a firm tread behind her and she was displaced in turn by a stout matronly lady wearing more diamonds than Prudence had ever seen before outside of a jewelry-store window.

"I've just come to check up on this book which was returned to us in a damaged condition," Prudence explained. "Our record shows that Miss Lucille Baumgarten had it out between—"

"Lucille?" gasped the bediamonded lady. "Lucille? There's no Lucille—" She broke off short and glanced at her daughter, who vainly tried to duck out between the two of them and shrink away unnoticed. "Oh, so that's it!" she said, suddenly enlightened. "So Leah isn't good enough for you any more!"

Prudence addressed her offspring, since it was obvious that the mother was in the dark about more things than just the book. "Miss Baumgarten, I'd like you to tell me whether there was a page missing when you brought the book home with you." And then she added craftily: "It was borrowed again afterward by several other subscribers, but I haven't got around to them yet." If the girl was guilty, she would use this as an out and claim the page had still been in, implying it had been taken out afterward by someone else. Prudence knew it hadn't, of course.

But Lucille-Leah admitted unhesitatingly: "Yes, there was a page or two missing, but it didn't spoil the fun much, because I could tell what happened after I read on a little bit." Nothing seemed to hold any terrors for her, compared to the parental wrath brewing in the heaving bosom that wedged her in inextricably.

"Did you lend it to anyone else, or take it out of the house with you at any time, while you were in possession of it?"

The girl rolled her eyes meaningly. "I should say not! I kept it hidden in the bottom drawer of my bureau the whole time; and now you had to come around here and give me away!"

"Thank you," said Prudence, and turned to go. This place was definitely off her list too, as she had felt it would be even before the interview. People who lived in such surroundings didn't send kidnap notes or associate with people who did.

The door had closed, but Mrs. Baumgarten's shrill, punitive tones sounded all too clearly through it while Prudence stood there waiting for the elevator to take her down. "I'll *give* you Lucille! Wait'll your father hears about this! I'll give you such a *frass*, you won't know whether you're Lucille or Gwendolyn!" punctuated by a loud, popping slap on youthful epidermis.

The next name on the list was Florence Turner. It was already well after ten by now, and for a moment Prudence was tempted to go home, and put off the next interview until the following night. She discarded the temptation resolutely. "Don't be such a 'fraid-cat,' " she lectured herself. "Nothing's happened to you so far, and nothing's likely to happen hereafter either." And then too, without knowing it, she was already prejudiced; in the back of her mind all along there lurked the suspicion that the lone male borrower, Dermuth, was the one to watch out for. He was next but one on the list, in reverse order. As long as she was out, she would interview Florence Turner, who was probably harmless, and then tackle Dermuth good and early tomorrow night—and see to it that a policeman waited for her outside his door so she'd be sure of getting out again unharmed.

The address listed for Library Member Turner was not at first sight exactly prepossessing, when she located it. It was a rooming house, or rather that newer variation of one called a "residence club," which has sprung up in the larger cities within the past few years, in which the rooms are grouped into detached little apartments. Possibly it was the sight of the chop-suey place that occupied the ground floor that gave it its unsavory aspect in her eyes; she had peculiar notions about some things.

Nevertheless, now that she had come this far, she wasn't going to let a chop-suey restaurant frighten her away without completing her mission. She tightened the book under her arm, took a good deep breath to ward off possible hatchet men and opium smokers, and marched into the building, whose entrance adjoined that of the restaurant.

She rang the manager's bell and a blowsy-looking, middle-aged woman came out and met her at the foot of the stairs. "Yes?" she said gruffly.

"Have you a Florence Turner living here?"

"No. We did have, but she left."

"Have you any idea where I could reach her?"

"She left very suddenly, didn't say where she was going."

"About how long ago did she leave, could you tell me?"

"Let's see now." The woman did some complicated mental calculation. "Two weeks ago Monday, I think it was. That would bring it to the 17th. Yes, that's it, May 17th."

Here was a small mystery already. The book hadn't been returned until the 18th. The woman's memory might be at fault, of course. "If you say she left in a hurry, how is it she found time to return this book to us?"

The woman glanced at it. "Oh, no, I was the one returned that for her," she explained. "My cleaning maid found it in her room the next morning after she was gone, along with a lot of other stuff she left behind her. I saw it was a library book, so I sent Beulah over with it, so's it wouldn't roll up a big fine for her. I'm economical that way. How'd you happen to get hold of it?" she asked in surprise.

"I work at the library," Prudence explained. "I wanted to see her about this book. One of the pages was torn out."

She knew enough not to confide any more than that about what her real object was.

"Gee, aren't you people fussy," marveled the manager.

"Well, you see, it's taken out of my salary," prevaricated Prudence, trying to strike a note she felt the other might understand.

"Oh, that's different. No wonder you're anxious to locate her. Well, all I know is she didn't expect to go when she did; she even paid for her room ahead, I been holding it for her ever since, till the time's up. I'm conshenshus that way."

"That's strange," Prudence mused aloud. "I wonder what could have—"

"I think someone got took sick in her family," confided the manager. "Some friends or relatives, I don't know who they was, called for her in a car late at night and off she went in a rush. I just wanted to be sure it wasn't no one who hadn't paid up yet, so I opened my door and looked out."

Prudence pricked up her ears. The fatal curiosity of hers was driving her on like a spur. She had suddenly forgotten all about being leery of the nefarious chop-suey den on the premises. She was starting to tingle all over, and tried not to show it. Had she unearthed something at last, or wasn't it anything at all? "You say she left some belongings behind? Do you think she'll be back for them?"

"No, she won't be back herself, I don't believe. But she did ask me to keep them for her; she said she'd send someone around to get them as soon as she was able."

Prudence suddenly decided she'd give almost anything to be able to get a look at the things this Turner girl had left behind her; why, she wasn't quite sure herself. They might help her to form an idea of what their owner was like. She couldn't ask openly; the woman might suspect her of trying to steal something. "When will her room be available?" she asked offhandedly. "I'm thinking of moving, and as long as I'm here, I was wondering—"

"Come on up and I'll show it to you right now," offered the manager with alacrity. She evidently considered librarians superior to the average run of tenants she got.

Prudence followed her up the stairs, incredulous at her own effrontery. This didn't seem a bit like her; she wondered what had come over her.

"Murphy should see me now!" she gloated.

The manager unlocked a door on the second floor.

"It's real nice in the daytime," she said. "And I can turn it over to you day after tomorrow."

"Is the closet good and deep?" asked Prudence, noting its locked doors.

"I'll show you." The woman took out a key, opened it unsuspectingly for her approval.

"My," said the subtle Prudence, "she left lots of things behind!"

"And some of them are real good too," agreed the landlady. "I don't know how they do it, on just a hat check girl's tips. And she even gave that up six months ago."

"Hm-m-m," said Prudence absently, deftly edging a silver slipper she noted standing on the floor up against one of another pair, with the tip of her own foot. She looked down covertly; with their heels in true with one another, there was an inch difference in the toes. Two different sizes! She absently fingered the lining of one of the frocks hanging up, noted its size tag. A 34. "Such exquisite things," she murmured, to cover up what she was doing. Three hangers over there was another frock. Size 28.

"Did she have anyone else living here with her?" she asked.

The manager locked the closet, pocketed the key once more.

"No. These two men friends or relatives of hers used to visit with her a good deal, but they never made a sound and they never came one at a time, so I didn't raise any objections. Now, I have another room, nearly as nice, just down the hall I could show you."

"I wish there were some way in which you could notify me when someone does call for her things," said Prudence, who was getting better as she went along. "I'm terribly anxious to get in touch with her. You see, it's not only the fine, it might even cost me my job."

"Sure I know how it is," said the manager sympathetically. "Well, I could ask whoever she sends to leave word where you can reach her."

"No, don't do that!" said Prudence hastily. "I'm afraid they . . . er . . . I'd prefer if you didn't mention I was here asking about her at all."

"Anything you say," said the manager amenably. "If you'll leave your number with me, I could give you a ring and let you know whenever the person shows up."

"I'm afraid I wouldn't get over here in time; they might be gone by the time I got here."

The manager tapped her teeth helpfully. "Why don't you take one of my rooms then? That way you'd be right on the spot when they do show up."

"Yes, but suppose they come in the daytime? I'd be at the library, and I can't leave my job."

"I don't think they'll come in the daytime. Most of her friends and the people she went with were up and around at night, more than in the daytime."

The idea appealed to Prudence, although only a short while before she would have been aghast at the thought of moving into such a place. She made up her mind quickly without giving herself time to stop and get cold feet. It might be a wild-goose chase, but she'd never yet heard of a woman who wore two different sizes in dresses like this Florence Turner seemed to. "All right, I will," she decided, "if you'll promise two things. To let me know without fail the minute someone comes to get her things, and not to say a word to them about my coming here and asking about her."

"Why not?" said the manager accommodatingly. "Anything to earn an honest dollar."

But when the door of her new abode closed on her, a good deal of her new-found courage evaporated. She sat down limply on the edge of the bed and stared in bewilderment at her reflection in the cheap dresser mirror. "I must be crazy to do a thing like this!" she gasped. "What's come over me anyway?" She didn't even have her teapot with her to brew a cup of the fortifying liquid. There was nothing the matter with the room itself, but that sinister Oriental den downstairs had a lurid red tube sign just under her window and its glare winked malevolently in at her. She imagined felt-slippered hirelings of some Fu-Manchu creeping up the stairs to snatch her bodily from her bed. It was nearly daylight before she could close her eyes. But so far as the room across the hall was concerned, as might have been expected no one showed up.

Next day at the library, between book returns, Prudence took out the reference card on *Manuela* and placed a neat red check next to Mrs. Trasker's name and Lucille Baumgarten's, to mark the progress of her investigation so far. But she didn't need this; it was easy enough to remember whom she had been to see and whom she hadn't, but she had the precise type of mind that liked everything neatly docketed and in order. Next to Florence Turner's name she placed a small red question mark.

She was strongly tempted to call up Murphy on her way home that evening, and tell him she already felt she was on the trail of something, But for one thing, nothing definite enough had developed yet. If he'd laughed at her about the original message itself, imagine how he'd roar if she told him the sum total of her suspicions was based on the fact that a certain party had two different-sized dresses in her clothes closet. And secondly, even in her new state of emancipation, it still seemed awfully forward to call a man up, even a detective. She would track down this Florence Turner first, and then she'd call Murphy up if her findings warranted it. "And if he says I'm good, and asks me to go to the movies with him," she threatened, "I'll . . . I'll make him ask two or three times before I do!"

She met the manager on her way in. "Did anyone come yet?" she asked in an undertone.

"No. I'll keep my promise. I'll let you know; don't worry."

A lot of the strangeness had already worn off her new surroundings, even after sleeping there just one night, and it occurred to her that maybe she had been in a rut, should have changed living quarters more often in the past. She went to bed shortly after ten, and even the Chinese restaurant sign had no power to keep her awake tonight; she fell asleep almost at once, tired from the night before.

About an hour or so later, she had no way of telling how long afterward it was, a surreptitious tapping outside her door woke her. "Yes?" she called out forgetfully, in a loud voice.

The manager stuck her tousled head in.

'Shh!" she warned. "Somebody's come for her things. You asked me to tell you, and I've been coughing out there in the hall, trying to attract your attention. He just went down with the first armful; he'll be up again in a minute. You'd better hurry if you want to catch him before he goes; he's working fast.'

"Don't say anything to him," Prudence whispered

back. "See if you can delay him a minute or two, give me time to get downstairs."

"Are you sure it's just a library book this is all about?" the manager asked searchingly. "Here he comes up again." She pulled her head back and swiftly closed the door.

Prudence had never dressed so fast in her life before. Even so, she managed to find time to dart a glance down at the street from her window. There was a black sedan drawn up in front of the house. "How am I ever going to—" she thought in dismay. She didn't let that hold her up any. She made sure she had shoes on and a coat over her and let the rest go hang. There was no time to phone Murphy, even if she had wanted to, but the thought didn't occur to her.

She eased her room door open, flitted out into the hall and down the stairs, glimpsing the open door of Florence Turner's room as she sneaked by. She couldn't see the man, whoever he was, but she could hear the landlady saying, "Wait a minute, until I make sure you haven't left anything behind."

Prudence slipped out of the street door downstairs, looked hopelessly up and down the street. He had evidently come alone in the car; there was no one else in it. He had piled the clothing on the back seat. For a moment she even thought of smuggling herself in and hiding under it, but that was too harebrained to be seriously considered. Then, just as she heard his tread start down the inside stairs behind her, the much-maligned chop-suey joint came to her aid. A cab drove up to it, stopped directly behind the first machine, and a young couple got out.

Prudence darted over, climbed in almost before they were out of the way.

"Where to, lady?" asked the driver.

She found it hard to come out with it, it sounded so unrespectable and fly-by-nightish. Detectives, she supposed, didn't think twice about giving an order like that, but with her it was different. "Er . . . would you mind just waiting a minute until the car in front of us leaves?" she said constrainedly. "Then take me wherever it goes."

He shot her a glance in his rear-sight mirror, but didn't say anything. He was probably used to getting stranger orders than that. A man came out of the same doorway she had just left herself. She couldn't get a very good look at his face, but he had a batch of clothing slung over his arm. He dumped the apparel in the back of the sedan, got in himself, slammed the door closed, and started off. A moment later the cab was in motion as well.

"Moving out on ya, huh?" said the driver knowingly. "I don't blame ya for follying him."

"That will do," she said primly. This night life got you into more embarrassing situations! "Do you think you can manage it so he won't notice you coming after him?" she asked after a block or two.

"Leave it to me, lady," he promised, waving his hand at her. "I know this game backwards."

Presently they had turned into one of the circumferential express highways leading out of the city. "Now it's gonna be pie!" he exulted. "He won't be able to tell us from anyone else on here. Everyone going the same direction and no turning off."

The stream of traffic was fairly heavy for that hour of the night; homeward-bound suburbanites for the most part. But then, as the city limits were passed and branch road after branch road drained it off, it thinned to a mere trickle. The lead car finally turned off itself, and onto a practically deserted secondary highway.

"Now it's gonna be ticklish," the cabman admitted. "I'm gonna have to hang back as far as I can from him, or he'll tumble to us."

He let the other car pull away until it was merely a red dot in the distance. "You sure must be carryin' some torch,"

he said presently with a baffled shake of his head, "to come all
the way out this far after him."

"Please confine yourself to your driving," was the
haughty reproof.

The distant red pin point had suddenly snuffed out.
"He must've turned off up ahead some place," said the
driver, alarmed. "I better step it up!"

When they had reached the approximate place, minutes
later, an even less-traveled bypass than the one they were on
was revealed, not only lightless but even unsurfaced. It
obviously didn't lead anywhere that the general public
would have wanted to go, or it would have been better
maintained. They braked forthwith.

"What a lonely-looking road." Prudence shuddered in-
voluntarily.

"Y'wanna chuck it and turn back?" he suggested, as
though he would have been only too willing to himself.

She probably would have if she'd been alone, but she
hated to admit defeat in his presence. He'd probably laugh at
her all the way back. "No, now that I've come this far, I'm
not going back until I find out exactly where he went. Don't
stand here like this: you won't be able to catch up with him
again!"

The driver gave his cap a defiant hitch. "The time has
come to tell you I've got you clocked at seven bucks and
eighty-five cents, and I didn't notice any pockybook in your
hand when you got in. Where's it coming from?" He tapped
his fingers sardonically on the rim of his wheel.

Prudence froze. Her handbag was exactly twenty or
thirty miles away, back in her room at the residence club.
She didn't have to answer; the driver was an old experienced
hand at this sort of thing; he could read the signs.

"I thought so," he said, almost resigned. He got
down, opened the door. "Outside," he said. "If you was a
man, I'd take it out of your jaw. Or if there was a cop

anywhere within five miles, I'd have you run in. Take off that coat." He looked it over, slung it over his arm. "It'll have to do. Now if you want it back, you know what to do; just look me up with seven-eighty-five in your mitt. And for being so smart, you're gonna walk all the way back from here on your two little puppies."

"Don't leave me all alone, in the dark, in this God-forsaken place! I don't even know where I am!" she wailed after him.

"I'll tell you where you are," he called back remorse-lessly. "You're on your own!" The cab's taillight went streaking obliviously back the way they had just come.

She held the side of her head and looked helplessly all around her. Real detectives didn't run into these predica-ments, she felt sure. It only happened to her! "Oh, why didn't I just mind my own business back at the library!" she lamented.

It was too cool out here in the wilds to stand still without a coat on, even though it was June. She might stand waiting here all night and no other machine would come along. The only thing to do was to keep walking until she came to a house, and then ask to use the telephone. There must be a house somewhere around here.

She started in along the bypath the first car had taken, gloomy and forbidding as it was, because it seemed more likely there was a house some place farther along it, than out on this other one. They hadn't passed a single dwelling the whole time the cab was on the road, and she didn't want to walk still farther out along it; no telling where it led to. The man she'd been following must have had *some* destination. Even if she struck the very house he had gone to, there wouldn't really be much harm to it, because he didn't know who she was, he'd never seen her before. Neither had this Florence Turner, if she was there with him. She could just say she'd lost her way or something. Anyone would have looked good to her just then, out here alone in the dark the way she was.

If she'd been skittish of shadows on the city streets, there was reason enough for her to have St. Vitus' dance here; it was nothing *but* shadows. Once she came in sight of a little clearing, with a scarecrow fluttering at the far side of it, and nearly had heart failure for a minute. Another time an owl went "Who-o-o" up in a tree over her, and she ran about twenty yards before she could pull herself together and stop again. "Oh, if I ever get back to the nice safe library after tonight, I'll never—" she sobbed nervously.

The only reason she kept going on now was because she was afraid to turn back any more. Maybe that hadn't been a scarecrow after all—

The place was so set back from the road, so half hidden amidst the shrubbery, that she had almost passed it by before she even saw it there. She happened to glance to her right as she came to a break in the trees, and there was the unmistakable shadowy outline of a decrepit house. Not a chink of a light showed from it, at least from where she was. Wheel ruts unmistakably led in toward it over the grass and weeds, but she wasn't much of a hand at this sort of lore, couldn't tell if they'd been made recently or long ago. The whole place had an appearance of not being lived in.

It took nearly as much courage to turn aside and start over toward it as it would have to continue on the road. It was anything but what she'd been hoping for, and she knew already it was useless to expect to find a telephone in such a ramshackle wreck.

The closer she got to it, the less inviting it became. True, it was two or three in the morning by now, and even if anyone had been living in it, they probably would have been fast asleep by this time, but it didn't seem possible such a forlorn, neglected-looking place could be inhabited. Going up onto that ink-black porch and knocking for admittance took more nerve than she could muster. Heaven knows what she was liable to bring out on her; bats or rats or maybe some horrible hobos.

She decided she'd walk all around the outside of it just once, and if it didn't look any better from the sides and rear than it did from the front, she'd go back to the road and take her own chances on that some more. The side was no better than the front when she picked her way cautiously along it. Twigs snapped under her feet and little stones shifted, and made her heart miss a beat each time. But when she got around to the back, she saw two things at once that showed her she had been mistaken, there was someone in there after all. One was the car, the same car that had driven away in front of the residence club, standing at a little distance behind the house, under some kind of warped toolshed or something. The other was a slit of light showing around three sides of a ground-floor window. It wasn't a brightly lighted pane by any means; the whole window still showed black under some kind of sacking or heavy covering; there was just this telltale yellow seam outlining three sides of it if you looked closely enough.

Before she could decide what to do about it, if anything, her gaze traveled a little higher up the side of the house and she saw something else that brought her heart up into her throat. She choked back an inadvertent scream just in time. It was a face. A round white face staring down at her from one of the upper windows, dimly visible behind the dusty pane.

Prudence Roberts started to back away apprehensively a step at a time, staring up at it spellbound as she did so, and ready at any moment to turn and run for her life, away from whomever or whatever that was up there. But before she could carry out the impulse, she saw something else that changed her mind, rooted her to the spot. Two wavering white hands had appeared, just under the ghost-like face. They were making signs to her, desperate, pleading signs. They beckoned her nearer, then they clasped together imploringly, as if trying to say, "Don't go away, don't leave me."

Prudence drew a little nearer again. The hands were warning her to silence now, one pointing downward toward the floor below, the other holding a cautioning finger to their owner's mouth.

It was a young girl; Prudence could make out that much, but most of the pantomime was lost through the blurred dust-caked pane. She gestured back to her with upcurved fingers, meaning, "Open the window so I can hear you."

It took the girl a long time. The window was either fastened in some way or warped from lack of use, or else it stuck just because she was trying to do it without making any noise. The sash finally jarred up a short distance, with an alarming creaking and grating in spite of her best efforts. Or at least it seemed so in the preternatural stillness that reigned about the place. They both held their breaths for a wary moment, as if by mutual understanding.

Then as Prudence moved in still closer under the window, a faint sibilance came down to her from the narrow opening.

"Please take me away from here. Oh, please help me to get away from here."

"What's the matter?" Prudence whispered back.

Both alike were afraid to use too much breath even to whisper, it was so quiet outside the house. It was hard for them to make themselves understood. She missed most of the other's answer, all but:

"They won't let me go. I think they're going to kill me. They haven't given me anything to eat in two whole days now."

Prudence inhaled fearfully. "Can you climb out through there and let yourself drop from the sill? I'll get a seat cover from that car and put it under you."

"I'm chained to the bed up here. I've pulled it over little by little to the window. Oh, please hurry and bring someone back with you; that's the only way—"

Prudence nodded in agreement, made hasty encouraging signs as she started to draw away. "I'll run all the way back to where the two roads meet, and stop the first car that comes al—"

Suddenly she froze, and at the same instant seemed to light up yellowly from head to foot, like a sort of living torch. A great fan of light spread out from the doorway before her, and in the middle of it a wavering shadow began to lengthen toward her along the ground.

"Come in, sweetheart and stay a while," a man's voice said slurringly. He sauntered out toward her with lithe, springy determination. Behind him in the doorway were another man and woman.

"Naw, don't be bashful," he went on, moving around in back of her and prodding her toward the house with his gun. "You ain't going on nowheres else from here. You've reached your final destination."

A well-dressed, middle-aged man was sitting beside the lieutenant's desk, forearm supporting his head, shading his eyes with outstretched fingers, when Murphy and every other man jack available came piling in, responding to the urgent summons.

The lieutenant had three desk phones going at once, and still found time to say, "Close that door, I don't want a word of this to get out," to the last man in. He hung up—*click, click, clack*—speared a shaking finger at the operatives forming into line before him.

"This is Mr. Martin Rapf, men," he said tensely. "I won't ask him to repeat what he's just said to me; he's not in any condition to talk right now. His young daughter, Virginia, left home on the night of May 17th and she hasn't been seen since. He and Mrs. Rapf received an anonymous telephone call that same night, before they'd even had time to become alarmed at her absence, informing them not to expect her back and warning them above all not to report her missing to us. Late the next day Mr. Rapf received a ransom note demanding fifty thousand dollars. This is it here."

Everyone in the room fastened their eyes on it as he spun it around on his desk to face them. At first sight it seemed to be a telegram. It was an actual telegraph blank form, taken from some office pad, with strips of paper containing printed words pasted on it.

"It wasn't filed, of course; it was slipped under the front door in an unaddressed envelope," the lieutenant went on. "The instructions didn't come for two more days, by telephone again. Mr. Rapf had raised the amount and was waiting for them. They were rather amateurish, to say the least. And amateurs are more to be dreaded than professionals at this sort of thing, as you men well know. He was to bring the money along in a cigar box, he was to go all the way out to a certain seldom-used suburban crossroads, and wait there. Then when a closed car with its rear windows down drove slowly by and sounded its horn three times, two short ones and a long one, he was to pitch the cigar box in the back of it through the open window and go home.

"In about a quarter of an hour a closed car with its windows down came along fairly slowly. Mr. Rapf was too concerned about his daughter's safety even to risk memorizing the numerals on its license plates, which were plainly exposed to view. A truck going crosswise to it threatened to block it at the intersection, and it gave three blasts of its horn, two short ones and a long one. Mr. Rapf threw the cigar box in through its rear window and watched it pick up speed and drive away. He was too excited and overwrought to start back immediately, and in less than five minutes, while he was still there, a second car came along with its windows down and its license plates removed. It gave three blasts of its horn, without there being any obstruction ahead. He ran out toward it to try and explain, but only succeeded in frightening it off. It put on speed and got away from him. I don't know whether it was actually a ghastly coincidence, or whether an unspeakable trick was perpetrated on him, to get twice the amount they had originally asked. Probably just a hideous coincidence, though, because he would have been just as willing to give them one hundred thousand from the beginning.

"At any rate, what it succeeded in doing was to throw a hitch into the negotiations, make them nervous and skittish. They contacted him again several days later, refused to believe his explanation, and breathed dire threats against the girl. He pleaded with them for another chance, and asked for more time to raise a second fifty thousand. He's been holding it in readiness for some time now, and they're apparently suffering from a bad case of fright; they cancel each set of new instructions as fast as they issue them to him. Wait'll I get through, please, will you, Murphy? It's five days since Mr. Rapf last heard from them, and he is convinced that—" He didn't finish it, out of consideration for the agonized man sitting there. Then he went ahead briskly: "Now here's Miss Rapf's description, and here's what our first move is going to be. Twenty years old, weight so-and-so, height so-and-so, light-brown hair—"

"She was wearing a pale-pink party dress and dancing shoes when she left the house," Rapf supplied forlornly.

"We don't pin any reliance on items of apparel in

matters of this kind," the lieutenant explained to him in a kindly aside. "That's for amnesia cases or straight disappearances. They almost invariably discard the victim's clothes, to make accidental recognition harder. Some woman in the outfit will usually supply her with her own things."

"It's too late, lieutenant; it's too late," the man who sat facing him murmured, grief-stricken. "I know it; I'm sure of it."

"We have no proof that it is," the lieutenant replied reassuringly. "But if it is, Mr. Rapf, you have only yourself to blame for waiting this long to come to us. If you'd come to us sooner, you might have your daughter back by now—"

He broke off short. "What's the matter, Murphy?" he snapped. "What are you climbing halfway across the desk at me like that for?"

"Will you let me get a word in and tell you, lieutenant?" Murphy exclaimed with a fine show of exasperated insubordination. "I been trying to for the last five minutes! That librarian, that Miss Roberts that came in here the other night—It was this thing she stumbled over accidentally then already. It must have been! It's the same message."

The lieutenant's jaw dropped well below his collar button. "Ho-ly smoke!" he exhaled. "Say, she's a smart young woman all right!"

"Yeah, she's so smart we laughed her out of the place, book and all," Murphy said bitterly. "She practically hands it to us on a silver platter, and you and me, both, we think it's the funniest thing we ever heard of."

"Never mind that now! Go out and get hold of her! Bring her in here fast!"

"She's practically standing in front of you!" The door swung closed after Murphy.

Miss Everett, the hatchet-faced librarian, felt called

upon to interfere at the commotion that started up less than five minutes later at the usually placid new-membership desk, which happened to be closest to the front door.

"Will you *kindly* keep your voice down, young man?" she said severely, sailing over. "This is a library, not a—"

"I haven't got time to keep my voice down! Where's Prudence Roberts? She's wanted at headquarters right away."

"She didn't come to work this morning. It's the first time she's ever missed a day since she's been with the library. What is it she's wanted—" But there was just a rush of outgoing air where he'd been standing until then. Miss Everett looked startled at the other librarian. "What was that he just said?"

"It sounded to me like 'Skip it, toots'!"

Miss Everett looked blankly over her shoulder to see if anyone else was standing there, but no one was.

In a matter of minutes Murphy had burst in on them again, looking a good deal more harried than the first time. "Something's happened to her. She hasn't been at her rooming house all night either, and that's the first time *that* happened too! Listen. There was a card went with that book she brought to us, showing who had it out and all that. Get it out quick; let me have it!"

He couldn't have remembered its name just then to save his life, and it might have taken them until closing time and after to wade through the library's filing system. But no matter how much of a battle-ax this Miss Everett both looked and was, one thing must be said in her favor: she had an uncanny memory when it came to damaged library property. "The reference card on *Manuela Gets Her Man*, by Ollivant," she snapped succinctly to her helpers. And in no time it was in his hands.

His face lighted. He brought his fist down on the counter with a bang that brought every nose in the place up out of its book, and for once Miss Everett forgot to remonstrate or even frown. "Thank God for her methodical mind!" he exulted. "Trasker, check; Baumgarten, check; Turner, question mark. It's as good as though she left full directions behind her!"

"What was it he said *that* time?" puzzled Miss Everett, as the doors flapped hectically to and fro behind him.

"It sounded to me like 'Keep your fingers crossed.' Only, I'm not sure if it was 'fingers' or—"

"It's getting dark again," Virginia Rapf whimpered dragging herself along the floor toward her fellow captive. "Each time night comes, I think they're going to . . . *you* know! Maybe tonight they *will*."

Prudence Roberts was fully as frightened as the other girl, but simply because one of them had to keep the other's courage up, she wouldn't let herself show it. "No, they won't; they wouldn't dare!" she said with a confidence she was far from feeling.

She went ahead tinkering futilely with the small padlock and chain that secured her to the foot of the bed. It was the same type that is used to fasten bicycles to something in the owner's absence, only of course the chain had not been left in an open loop or she could simply have withdrawn her hand. It was fastened tight around her wrist by passing the clasp of the lock through two of the small links at once. It permitted her a radius of action of not more than three or four yards around the foot of the bed at most. Virginia Rapf was similarly attached to the opposite side.

"In books you read," Prudence remarked, "women

prisoners always seem to be able to open anything from a strong box to a cell door with just a hairpin. I don't seem to have the knack, somehow. This is the last one I have left."

"If you couldn't do it before, while it was light, you'll never be able to do it in the dark."

"I guess you're right," Prudence sighed. "There it goes, out of shape like all the rest, anyway." She tossed it away with a little *plink*.

"Oh, if you'd only moved away from under that window a minute sooner, they wouldn't have seen you out there, you might have been able to—"

"No use crying over spilt milk," Prudence said briskly.

Sounds reached them from outside presently, after they'd been lying silent on the floor for a while.

"Listen," Virginia Rapf breathed. "There's someone moving around down there, under the window. You can hear the ground crunch every once in a while."

Something crashed violently, and they both gave a start.

"What was that, their car?" asked Virginia Rapf.

"No, it sounded like a tin can of some kind; something he threw away."

A voice called out of the back door: "Have you got enough?"

The answer seemed to come from around the side of the house. "No, gimme the other one too."

A few moments later a second tinny clash reached their tense ears. They waited, hearts pounding furiously under their ribs. A sense of impending danger assailed Prudence.

"What's that funny smell?" Virginia Rapf whispered fearfully. "Do you notice it? Like—"

Prudence supplied the word before she realized its

portent. "Gasoline." The frightful implication hit the two of them at once. The other girl gave a sob of convulsive terror, cringed against her. Prudence threw her arms about her, tried to calm her. "Shh! Don't be frightened. No, they wouldn't do that, they couldn't be that inhuman." But her own terror was half stifling her.

One of their captors' voices sounded directly under them, with a terrible clarity. "All right, get in the car, Flo. You too, Duke, I'm about ready."

They heard the woman answer him, and there was unmistakable horror even in her tones. "Oh, not *that* way, Eddie. You're going to finish them first, aren't you?"

He laughed coarsely. "What's the difference? The smoke'll finish them in a minute or two; they won't suffer none. All right, soft-hearted, have it your own way. I'll go up and give 'em a clip on the head apiece, if it makes you feel any better." His tread started up the rickety stairs.

They were almost crazed with fear. Prudence fought to keep her presence of mind.

"Get under the bed, quick!" she panted hoarsely.

But the other girl gave a convulsive heave in her arms, then fell limp. She'd fainted dead away. The oncoming tread was halfway up the stairs now. He was taking his time, no hurry. Outside in the open she heard the woman's voice once more, in sharp remonstrance.

"Wait a minute, you dope; not yet! Wait'll Eddie gets out first!"

The man with her must have struck a match. "He can make it; let's see him run for it," he answered jeeringly. "I still owe him something for that hot-foot he gave me one time, remember?"

Prudence had let the other girl roll lifelessly out of her arms, and squirmed under the bed herself, not to try to save her own skin but to do the little that could be done to try to save both of them, futile as she knew it to be. She twisted like a caterpillar, clawed at her own foot, got her right shoe off. She'd never gone in for these stylish featherweight sandals with spindly heels, and she was glad of that now. It was a good strong substantial Oxford, nearly as heavy as a man's, with a club heel. She got a grasp on it by the toe, then twisted her body around so that her legs were toward the side the room door gave onto. She reared one at the knee, held it poised, backed up as far as the height of the bed would allow it to be.

The door opened and he came in, lightless. He didn't need a light for a simple little job like this— stunning two helpless girls chained to a bed. He started around toward the foot of it, evidently thinking they were crouched there hiding from him. Her left leg suddenly shot out between his two, like a spoke, tripping him neatly.

He went floundering forward on his face with a muffled curse. She had hoped he might hit his head, be dazed by the impact if only for a second or two. He wasn't; he must have broken the fall with his arm. She threshed her body madly around the other way again, to get her free arm in play with the shoe for a weapon. She began to rain blows on him with it, trying to get his head with the heel. That went wrong too. He'd fallen too far out along the floor, the chain wouldn't let her come out any farther after him. She couldn't reach any higher up than his muscular shoulders with the shoe, and its blows fell ineffectively there.

Raucous laughter was coming from somewhere outside, topped by warning screams. "Eddie, hurry up and get out, you fool! Duke's started it already!" They held no meaning for Prudence; she was too absorbed in this last despairing attempt to save herself and her fellow prisoner.

But he must have heard and understood them. The room was no longer as inky black as before. A strange wan light was beginning to peer up below the window, like a satanic moonrise. He jumped to his feet with a snarl, turned and fired down pointblank at Prudence as she tried to writhe hastily back under cover. The bullet hit the iron rim of the bedstead directly over her eyes and glanced inside. He was too yellow to linger and try again. Spurred by the screamed warnings and the increasing brightness, he bolted from the room and went crashing down the stairs three at a time.

A second shot went off just as he reached the back doorway, and she mistakenly thought he had fired at his fellow kidnapper in retaliation for the ghastly practical joke played on him. Then there was a whole volley of shots, more than just one gun could have fired. The car engine started up with an abortive flurry, then died down again where it was without moving. But her mind was too full of horror at the imminent doom that threatened to engulf both herself and Virginia Rapf, to realize the meaning of anything she dimly heard going on below. Anything but that sullen hungry crackle, like bundles of twigs snapping, that kept growing louder from minute to minute. They had been left hopelessly chained, to be cremated alive!

She screamed her lungs out, and at the same time knew that screaming wasn't going to save her or the other girl. She began to hammer futilely with her shoe at the chain holding her, so slender yet so strong, and knew that wasn't going to save her either.

Heavy steps pounded up the staircase again, and for a moment she thought he'd come back to finish the two of them after all, and was glad of it. Anything was better than being roasted alive. She wouldn't try to hide this time.

The figure that came tearing through the thickening smoke haze toward her was already bending down above her before she looked and saw that it was Murphy. She'd seen some beautiful pictures in art galleries in her time, but he was more beautiful to her eyes than a Rubens portrait.

"All right, chin up, keep cool," he said briefly, so she wouldn't lose her head and impede him.

"Get the key to these locks! The short dark one has them."

"He's dead and there's no time. Lean back. Stretch it out tight and lean out of the way!" He fired and the small chain snapped in two. "Jump! You can't get down the stairs any more." His second shot, freeing Virginia Rapf, punctuated the order.

Prudence flung up the window, climbed awkwardly across the sill, feet first. Then clung there terrified as an intolerable haze of heat rose up under her from below. She glimpsed two men running up under her with a blanket or lap robe from the car stretched out between them.

"I can't; it's. . .it's right under me!"

He gave her an unceremonious shove in the middle of the back and she went hurtling out into space with a screech. The two with the blanket got there just about the same time she did. Murphy hadn't waited to make sure; a broken leg was preferable to being incinerated. She hit the ground through the lap robe and all, but at least it broke the direct force of the fall.

They cleared it for the next arrival by rolling her out at one side, and by the time she had picked herself, dazed, to her feet, Virginia Rapf was already lying in it, thrown there by him from above.

"Hurry it up, Murph!" she heard one of them shout and instinctively caught at the other girl, dragged her off it to clear the way for him. He crouched with both feet on the sill, came sailing down, and even before he'd hit the blanket, there was a dull roar behind him as the roof caved in, and a great gush of sparks went shooting straight up into the dark night sky.

They were still too close; they all had to draw hurriedly back away from the unbearable heat beginning to radiate from it. Murphy came last, as might have been expected, dragging a very dead kidnapper—the one called Eddie—along the ground after him by the collar of his coat. Prudence saw the other one, Duke, slumped inertly over the wheel of the car he had never had time to make his getaway in, either already dead or rapidly dying. A disheveled blond scarecrow that had been Florence Turner was apparently the only survivor of the trio. She kept whimpering placatingly, "I didn't want to do *that* to them! I didn't want to do *that* to them!" over and over, as though she still didn't realize they had been saved in time.

Virginia Rapf was coming out of her long faint. It was kinder, Prudence thought, that she had been spared those last few horrible moments; she had been through enough without that.

"Rush her downtown with you, fellow!" Murphy said. "Her dad's waiting for her; he doesn't know yet, I shot out here so fast the minute I located that taxi driver outside the residence club, who remembered driving Miss Roberts out to this vicinity, that I didn't even have time to notify headquarters, just picked up whoever I could on the way."

He came over to where Prudence was standing, staring at the fire with horrified fascination.

"How do you feel? Are you O.K.?" he murmured, brow furrowed with a proprietary anxiety.

"Strange as it may be," she admitted in surprise, "I seem to feel perfectly all right; can't find a thing the matter with me."

Back at the library the following day—and what a world away it seemed from the scenes of violence she had just lived through—the acidulous Miss Everett came up to her just before closing time with, of all things, a twinkle in her eyes. Either that or there was a flaw in her glasses.

"You don't have to stay to the very last minute . . . er . . . toots," she confided. "Your boy friend's waiting for you outside; I just saw him through the window."

There he was holding up the front of the library when Prudence Roberts emerged a moment or two later.

"The lieutenant would like to see you to personally convey his thanks on behalf of the department," he said. "And afterward I . . . uh . . .know where there's a real high-brow pitcher showing, awful refined."

Prudence pondered the invitation. "No," she said finally. "Make it a nice snappy gangster movie and you're on. I've got so used to excitement in the last few days, I'd feel sort of lost without it."

THE BROKEN MEN

by Marcia Muller

I

Dawn was breaking when I returned to the Diablo Valley Pavilion. The softly rounded hills that encircled the amphitheater were edged with pinkish gold, but their slopes were still dark and forbidding. They reminded me of a herd of humpbacked creatures huddling together while they waited for the warmth of the morning sun; I could imagine them stretching and sighing with relief when its rays finally touched them.

I would have given a lot to have daylight bring me that same sense of relief, but I doubted that would happen. It had been a long, anxious night since I'd arrived here the first time, over twelve hours before. Returning was a last-ditch measure, and a long shot at best.

I drove up the blacktop road to where it was blocked by a row of posts and got out of the car. The air was chill; I could see my breath. Somewhere in the distance a lone bird called, and there was a faint, monotonous whine that must have had something to do with the security lights that topped the chain-link fence at intervals, but the overall silence was heavy, oppressive. I stuffed my hands into the pockets of my too-light suede jacket and started toward the main entrance next to the box office.

As I reached the fence, a stocky, dark-haired man stepped out of the adjacent security shack and began unlocking the gate. Roy Canfield, night supervisor for the pavilion. He'd been dubious about what I'd suggested when I'd called him from San Francisco three quarters of an hour ago, but had said he'd be glad to cooperate if I came back out here. Canfield swung the gate open and motioned me through one of the turnstiles that had admitted thousands to the Diablo Valley Clown Festival the night before.

He said, "You made good time from the city."

"There's no traffic at five a.m. I could set my own speed limit."

The security man's eyes moved over me appraisingly, reminding me of how rumpled and tired I must look. Canfield himself seemed as fresh and alert as when I'd met him before last night's performance. But then, *he* hadn't been chasing over half the Bay Area all night, hunting for a missing client.

"Of course," I added, "I was anxious to get here and see if Gary Fitzgerald might still be somewhere on the premises. Shall we take a look around?"

Canfield looked as dubious as he'd sounded on the phone. He shrugged and said, "Sure we can, but I don't think you'll find him. We check every inch of the place after the crowd leaves. No way anybody could still be inside when we lock up."

There had been a note of reproach in his words, as if he thought I was questioning his ability to do his job. Quickly I said, "It's not that I don't believe you, Mr. Canfield. I just don't have any place else left to look."

He merely grunted and motioned for me to proceed up the wide concrete steps. They led uphill from the entrance to a promenade whose arms curved out in opposite directions around the edge of the amphitheater. As I recalled from the night before, from the promenade the lawn sloped gently down to the starkly modernistic concert shell. Its stage was wide—roughly ninety degrees of the circle—with wings and dressing rooms built back into the hill behind it. The concrete roof, held aloft by two giant pillars, was a curving slab shaped like a warped arrowhead, its tip pointing to the northeast, slightly off center. Formal seating was limited to a few dozen rows in a semi-circle in front of the stage; the pavilion had been designed mainly for the casual type of concert-goer who prefers to lounge on a blanket on the lawn.

I reached the top of the steps and crossed the promenade to the edge of the bowl, then stopped in surprise.

The formerly pristine lawn was now mounded with trash. Paper bags, cups and plates, beer cans and wine bottles, wrappers and crumpled programs and other indefinable debris were scattered in a crazy-quilt pattern. Trash receptacles placed at strategic intervals along the promenade had overflowed, their contents cascading to the ground. On the low wall between the formal seating and the lawn stood a monumental pyramid of Budweiser cans. In some places the debris was only thinly scattered, but in others it lay deep, like dirty drifted snow.

Canfield came up behind me, breathing heavily from the climb. "A mess, isn't it?" he said.

"Yes. Is it always like this after a performance?"

"Depends. Shows like last night, where you get a lot of young people, families, picnickers, it gets pretty bad. A symphony concert, that's different."

"And your maintenance crew doesn't come on until morning?" I tried not to sound disapproving, but allowing such debris to lie there all night was faintly scandalous to a person like me, who had been raised to believe that not washing the supper dishes before going to bed just might constitute a cardinal sin.

"Cheaper that way—we'd have to pay overtime otherwise. And the job's easier when it's light anyhow."

As if in response to Canfield's words, daylight—more gold than pink now—spilled over the hills in the distance, slightly to the left of the stage. It disturbed the shadows on the lawn below us, making them assume different, distorted forms. Black became gray, gray became white; short shapes elongated, others were truncated; fuzzy lines came into sharp focus. And with the light a cold wind came gusting across the promenade.

I pulled my jacket closer, shivering. The wind rattled the fall-dry leaves of the young poplar trees—little more than saplings—planted along the edge of the promenade. It stirred the trash heaped around the receptacles, then swept down the lawn, scattering debris in its wake. Plastic bags and wads of paper rose in an eerie dance, settled again as the breeze passed. I watched the undulation—a paper wave upon a paper sea—as it rolled toward the windbreak of cypress trees to the east.

Somewhere in the roiling refuse down by the barrier between the lawn and the formal seating I spotted a splash of yellow. I leaned forward, peering toward it. Again I saw the yellow, then a blur of blue and then a flicker of white. The colors were there, then gone as the trash settled.

Had my eyes been playing tricks on me in the halflight? I didn't think so, because while I couldn't be sure of the colors, I was distinctly aware of a shape that the wind's passage had uncovered—long, angular, solid-looking. The debris had fallen in a way that didn't completely obscure it.

The dread that I had held in check all night spread through me. After a frozen moment, I began to scramble down the slope toward the spot I'd been staring at. Behind me, Canfield called out, but I ignored him.

The trash was deep down by the barrier, almost to my knees. I waded through bottles, cans, and papers, pushing their insubstantial mass aside, shoveling with my hands to clear a path. Shoveled until my fingers encountered something more solid . . .

I dropped to my knees and scooped up the last few layers of debris, hurling it over my shoulder.

He lay on his back, wrapped in his bright yellow cape, his baggy blue plaid pants and black patent leather shoes sticking out from underneath it. His black beret was pulled halfway down over his white clown's face hiding his eyes. I couldn't see the red vest that made up the rest of the costume because the cape covered it, but there were faint red stains on the irridescent fabric that draped across his chest.

I yanked the cape aside and touched the vest. It felt sticky, and when I pulled my hand away it was red too. I stared at it, wiped it off on a scrap of newspaper. Then I felt for a pulse in his carotid artery, knowing all the time what a futile exercise it was.

"Oh, Jesus!" I said. For a moment my vision blurred and there was a faint buzzing in my ears.

Roy Canfield came thrashing up behind me, puffing with exertion. "What . . .Oh, my God!"

I continued staring down at the clown; he looked broken, an object that had been used up and tossed on a trash heap. After a moment, I touched my thumb to his cold cheek, brushed at the white makeup. I pushed the beret back, looked at the theatrically blackened eyes. Then I tugged off the flaxen wig. Finally I pulled the fake bulbous nose away.

"Gary Fitzgerald?" Canfield asked.

I looked up at him. His moonlike face creased in concern. Apparently the shock and bewilderment I was experiencing showed.

"Mr. Canfield," I said, "this man is wearing Gary's costume, but it's not him. I've never seen him before in my life."

II

The man I *was* looking for was half of an internationally famous clown act, Fitzgerald and Tilby. The world of clowning, like any other artistic realm, has its various levels—from the lowly rodeo clown whose chief function is to keep bull riders from being stomped on, to circus clowns such as Emmett Kelly and universally acclaimed mimes like Marcel Marceau. Fitzgerald and Tilby were not far below Kelly and Marceau in that hierarchy and gaining on them every day. Instead of merely employing the mute body language of the typical clown, the two Britishers combined it with a subtle and sophisticated verbal comedy routine. Their fame had spread beyond aficionados of clowning in the late seventies when they had made a series of artful and entertaining television commercials for one of the Japanese auto makers, and subsequent ads for, among others, a major U.S. airline, one of the big insurance companies, and a computer firm had assured them of a place in the hearts of humor-loving Americans.

My involvement with Fitzgerald and Tilby came about when they agreed to perform at the Diablo Valley Clown Festival, a charity benefit co-sponsored by the Contra Costa County Chamber of Commerce and KSUN, the radio station where my friend Don Del Boccio works as a disc jockey. The team's manager, Wayne Kabalka, had stipulated only two conditions to their performing for free: that they be given star billing, and that they be provided with a bodyguard. Since Don was to be emcee of the show, he was in on all the planning, and when he heard of Kabalka's second stipulation, he suggested me for the job.

As had been the case ever since I'd bought a house near the Glen Park district of San Francisco the spring

before, I was short of money at the time. And All Souls
Legal Cooperative, where I am staff investigator, had no
qualms about me moonlighting provided it didn't interfere with any of the co-op's cases. Since things had been
slack at All Souls during September, I felt free to accept.
Bodyguarding isn't my idea of challenging work, but I
had always enjoyed Fitzgerald and Tilby, and the idea of
meeting them intrigued me. Besides, I'd be part of the
festival and get paid for my time, rather than attending
on the free pass Don had promised me.

So on that hot Friday afternoon in late September, I
met with Wayne Kabalka in the lounge at KSUN's San
Francisco studios. As radio stations go, KSUN is a casual
operation, and the lounge gives full expression to this
orientation. It is full of mismatched Salvation Army re-
ject furniture, the posters on the walls are torn and tattered, and the big coffee table is always littered with
rumpled newspapers, empty Coke cans and coffee cups,
and overflowing ashtrays. On this particular occasion, it
was also graced with someone's half-eaten Big Mac.

When Don and I came in, Wayne Kabalka was seated on the very edge of one of the lumpy chairs, looking
as if he were afraid it might have fleas. He saw us and
jumped as if one had just bitten him. *His* orientation was
anything but casual: in spite of the heat, he wore a tan
three-piece suit that almost matched his mane of tawny
hair, and a brown striped tie peeked over the V of his
vest. Kabalka and his clients might be based in L.A., but
he sported none of the usual Hollywoodish ac-
coutrements—gold chains, diamond rings, or Adidas
running shoes. Perhaps his very correct appearance was
designed to be in keeping with his clients, Englishmen
with rumored connections to the aristocracy.

Don introduced us and we all sat down, Kabalka
again doing his balancing act on the edge of his chair. Ig-

noring me, he said to Don, "I didn't realize the body-guard you promised would be female."

Don shot me a look, his shaggy black eyebrows raised a fraction of an inch.

I said, "Please don't let my gender worry you, Mr. Kabalka. I've been a private investigator for nine years, and before that I worked for a security firm. I'm fully qualified for the job."

To Don he said, "But has she done this kind of work before?"

Again Don looked at me.

I said, "Bodyguarding is only one of any number of types of assignments I've carried out. And one of the most routine."

Kabalka continued looking at Don. "Is she licensed to carry firearms?"

Don ran his fingers over his thick black mustache, trying to hide the beginnings of a grin. "I think," he said, "that I'd better let the two of you talk alone."

Kabalka put out a hand as if to stay his departure, but Don stood. "I'll be in the editing room if you need me."

I watched him walk down the hall, his gait surpris-ingly graceful for such a tall, stocky man. Then I turned back to Kabalka. "To answer your question, sir, yes, I'm firearms qualified."

He made a sound halfway between clearing his throat and a grunt. "Uh . . . then you have no objection to carrying a gun on this assignment?"

"Not if it's necessary. But before I can agree to that, I'll have to know why you feel your clients require an armed bodyguard."

"I'm sorry?"

"Is there some threat to them that indicates the guard should be armed?"

"Threat. Oh . . . no."

"Extraordinary circumstances, then?"

"Extraordinary circumstances. Well, they're quite famous, you know. The TV commercials—you've seen them?"

I nodded.

"Then you know what a gold mine we have here. We're due to sign for three more within the month. Bank of America, no less. General Foods is getting into the act. Mobil Oil is hedging, but they'll sign. Fitzgerald and Tilby are important properties; they must be protected."

Properties, I thought, not people. "That still doesn't tell me what I need to know."

Kabalka laced his well-manicured fingers together, flexing them rhythmically. Beads of perspiration stood out on his high forehead; no wonder, wearing that suit in this heat. Finally he said, "In the past couple of years we've experienced difficulty with fans when the boys have been on tour. In a few instances, the crowds got a little too rough."

"Why haven't you hired a permanent bodyguard, then? Put one on staff?"

"The boys were opposed to that. In spite of their aristocratic connections, they're men of the people. They didn't want to put any more distance between them and their public than necessary."

The words rang false. I suspected the truth of the matter was that Kabalka was too cheap to hire a permanent guard. "In a place like the Diablo Valley Pavilion, the security is excellent, and I'm sure that's been explained to you. It hardly seems necessary to hire an armed guard when the pavilion personnel—"

He made a gesture of impatience. "Their security force will have dozens of performers to protect, including a number who will be wandering throughout the audience during the show. My clients need extra protection."

I was silent, watching him. He shifted his gaze from mine, looking around with disproportionate interest at the tattered wall posters. Finally I said, "Mr. Kabalka, I don't feel you're being quite frank with me. And I'm afraid I can't take on this assignment unless you are."

He looked back at me. His eyes were a pale blue, washed out—and worried. "The people here at the station speak highly of you," he said after a moment.

"I hope so. They—especially Mr. Del Boccio— know me well." Especially Don; we'd been lovers for more than six months now.

"When they told me they had a bodyguard lined up, all they said was that you were a first-rate investigator. If I was rude earlier because I was surprised by your being a woman, I apologize."

"Apology accepted."

"I assume by first-rate, one of the things they mean is that you are discreet."

"I don't talk about my cases, if that's what you want to know."

He nodded. "All right, I'm going to entrust you with some information. It's not common knowledge, and you're not to pass it on, gossip about it to your friends—"

Kabalka was beginning to annoy me. "Get on with it, Mr. Kabalka. Or find yourself another bodyguard." Not easy to do, when the performers needed to arrive at the pavilion in about three hours.

His face reddened, and he started to retort, but bit back the words. He looked down at his fingers, still laced together and pressing against one another in a feverish rhythm. "All right. Once again I apologize. In my profession you get used to dealing with such scumbags that you lose perspective—"

"You were about to tell me . . .?"

He looked up, squared his shoulders as if he were about to deliver a state secret to an enemy agent. "All right. There *is* a reason why my clients require special security precautions at the Diablo Valley Pavilion. They—Gary Fitzgerald and John Tilby—are originally from Contra Costa County."

"What? I thought they were British."

"Yes, of course you did. And so does almost everyone else. It's part of the mystique, the selling power."

"I don't understand."

"When I discovered the young men in the early seventies, they were performing in a cheap club in San Bernardino, in the valley east of L.A. They were cousins, fresh off the farm—the ranch, in their case. Tilby's father was a dairy rancher in the Contra Costa hills, near Clayton; he raised both boys—Gary's parents had died. When old Tilby died, the ranch was sold and the boys ran off to seek fortune and fame. Old story. And they'd found the glitter doesn't come easy. Another old story. But when I spotted them in that club, I could see they were good. Damned good. So I took them on and made them stars."

"The oldest story of all."

"Perhaps. But now and then it does come true."

"Why the British background?"

"It was the early seventies. The mystique still surrounded such singing groups as the Rolling Stones and the Beatles. What could be better than a British clown act with aristocratic origins? Besides, they were already doing the British bit in their act when I discovered them, and it worked."

I nodded, amused by the machinations of show business. "So you're afraid someone who once knew them might get too close out at the pavilion tonight and recognize them?"

"Yes."

"Don't you think it's a long shot—after all these years?"

"They left there in sixty-nine. People don't change all that much in sixteen years."

That depended, but I wasn't about to debate the point with him. "But what about makeup? Won't that disguise them?" Fitzgerald and Tilby wore traditional clown white-face.

"They can't apply the makeup until they're about to go on—in other circumstances, it might be possible to put it on earlier, but not in this heat."

I nodded. It all made sense. But why did I feel there was something Kabalka wasn't telling me about his need for an armed guard? Perhaps it was the way his eyes had once again shifted from mine to the posters on the walls. Perhaps it was the nervous pressing of his laced fingers. Or maybe it was only that sixth sense that sometimes worked for me: what I called a detective's instinct and others—usually men—labeled woman's intuition.

"All right, Mr. Kabalka," I said, "I'll take the job."

III

I checked in with Don to find out when I should be back at the studios, then went home to change clothing. We would arrive at the pavilion around four; the show—an early one because of its appeal for children—would begin at six. And I was certain that the high temperature—sure to have topped 100 in the Diablo

Valley—would not drop until long after dark. Chambray pants and an abbreviated tank top, with my suede jacket to put on in case of a late evening chill were all I would need. That, and my .38 special, tucked in the outer compartment of my leather shoulderbag.

By three o'clock I was back at the KSUN studios. Don met me in the lobby and ushered me to the lounge where Kabalka, Gary Fitzgerald, and John Tilby waited.

The two clowns were about my age—a little over thirty. Their British accents might once have been a put-on, but they sounded as natural now as if they'd been born and raised in London. Gary Fitzgerald was tall and lanky, with straight dark hair, angular features that stopped just short of being homely, and a direct way of meeting one's eye. John Tilby was shorter, sandy haired—the type we used to refer to in high school as "cute." His shy demeanor was in sharp contrast to his cousin's straightforward greeting and handshake. They didn't really seem like relatives, but then neither do I in comparison to my four siblings and numerous cousins. All of them resemble one another—typical Scotch-Irish towheads—but I have inherited all the characteristics of our one-eighth Shoshone Indian blood. And none of us are similar in personality or outlook, save for the fact we care a great deal about one another.

Wayne Kabalka hovered in the background while the introductions were made. The first thing he said to me was, "Did you bring your gun?"

"Yes, I did. Everything's under control."

Kabalka wrung his hands together as if he only wished it were true. Then he said, "Do you have a car, Ms. McCone?"

"Yes."

"Then I suggest we take both yours and mine. I have to swing by the hotel and pick up my wife and

John's girlfriend."

"All right. I have room for one passenger in mine. Don, what about you? How are you getting out there?"

"I'm going in the Wonder Bus."

I rolled my eyes. The Wonder Bus was a KSUN publicity ploy—a former schoolbus painted in rainbow hues and emblazoned with the station call letters. It traveled to all KSUN-sponsored events, plus to anything else where management deemed its presence might be beneficial. As far as I was concerned, it was the most outrageous in a panoply of the station's brazen efforts at self-promotion, and I took every opportunity to expound this viewpoint to Don. Surprisingly, Don—a quiet classical musician who hated rock-and-roll and the notoriety that went with being a D.J.—never cringed at riding the Wonder Bus. If anything, he took an almost perverse pleasure in the motorized monstrosity.

Secretly, I had a shameful desire to hitch a ride on the Wonder Bus myself.

Wayne Kabalka looked somewhat puzzled at Don's statement. "Wonder Bus?" he said to himself. Then, "Well, if everyone's ready, let's go."

I turned to Don and smiled in a superior fashion. "Enjoy your ride."

We trooped out into the parking lot. Heat shimmered off the concrete paving. Kabalka pulled a handkerchief from his pocket and wiped his brow. "Is it always this hot here in September?"

"This is the month we have our true summer in the city, but no, this is unusual." I went over and placed my bag carefully behind the driver's seat of my MG convertible.

When John Tilby saw the car, his eyes brightened; he came over to it, running a hand along one of its battle-scarred flanks as if it were a brand new Porsche. "I used to have one of these."

"I'll bet it was in better shape than this one."

"Not really." A shadow passed over his face and he continued to caress the car in spite of the fact that the metal must be burning hot to the touch.

"Look," I said, "if you want to drive it out to the pavilion, I wouldn't mind being a passenger for a change."

He hesitated, then said wistfully, "That's nice of you, but I can't . . . I don't drive. But I'd like to ride along—"

"John!" Kabalka's voice was impatient behind us. "Come on, we're keeping Corinne and Nicole waiting."

Tilby gave the car a last longing glance, then shrugged. "I guess I'd better ride out with Wayne and the girls." He turned and walked off to Kabalka's new-looking Seville that was parked at the other side of the lot.

Gary Fitzgerald appeared next to me, a small canvas bag in one hand, garment bag in the other. "I guess you're stuck with me," he said, smiling easily.

"That's not such a bad deal."

He glanced back at Tilby and Kabalka, who were climbing into the Cadillac. "Wayne's right to make John go with him. Nicole would be jealous if she saw him drive up with another woman." His tone was slightly resentful. Of Nicole? I wondered. Perhaps the girlfriend has caused dissension between the cousins.

"Corinne is Wayne's wife?" I asked as we got into the MG.

"Yes. You'll meet both of them at the performance; they're never very far away." Again I heard the undertone of annoyance.

We got onto the freeway and crossed the Bay Bridge. Commute traffic out of the city was already getting heavy; people left their offices early on hot Fridays in September. I wheeled the little car in and out from lane to lane, bypassing trucks and A.C. Transit buses. Fitzgerald didn't speak. I glanced at him a couple of times to see if my maneuvering bothered him, but he sat slumped against the door, his almost-homely features shadowed with thought. Pre-performance nerves, possibly.

From the bridge, I took Highway 24 east toward Walnut Creek. We passed through the outskirts of Oakland, smog-hazed and sprawling—ugly duckling of the Bay Area. Sophisticates from San Francisco scorned Oakland, repeating Gertrude Stein's overused phrase, "There is no there there," but lately there had been a current of unease in their mockery. Oakland's thriving port had stolen much of the shipping business from her sister city across the Bay; her politics were alive and spirited; and on the site of former slums, sleek new buildings had been put up. Oakland was at last shedding her pinfeathers, and it made many of my fellow San Franciscans nervous.

From there we began the long ascent through the Berkeley Hills to the Caldecott Tunnel. The MG's aged engine strained as we passed lumbering trucks and slower cars, and when we reached the tunnel—three tunnels, actually, two of them now open to accommodate the eastbound commuter rush—I shot into the far lane. At the top of the grade midway through the tunnel, I shifted into neutral to give the engine a rest. Arid heat assailed us as we emerged; the temperature in San Francisco had been nothing compared to this.

The freeway continued to descend, past brown sun-baked hills covered with live oak and eucalyptus. Then houses began to appear, tucked back among the trees. The air was scented with dry leaves and grass and dust.

Fire danger, I thought. One spark and those houses become tinderboxes.

The town of Orinda appeared on the right. On the left, in the center of the freeway, a BART train was pulling out of the station. I accelerated and tried to outrace it, giving up when my speedometer hit eighty and waving at some schoolkids who were watching from the train. Then I dropped back to sixty and glanced at Fitzgerald, suddenly embarrassed by my childish display. He was sitting up straighter and grinning.

I said, "The temptation was overwhelming."

"I know the feeling."

Feeling more comfortable now that he seemed willing to talk, I said, "Did Mr. Kabalka tell you that he let me in on where you're really from?"

For a moment he looked startled, then nodded.

"Is this the first time you've been back here in Contra Costa County?"

"Yes."

"You'll find it changed."

"I guess so."

"Mainly there are more people. Places like Walnut Creek and Concord have grown by leaps and bounds in the last ten years."

The county stretched east from the ridge of hills we'd just passed over, toward Mount Diablo, a nearly 4,000-foot peak which had been developed into a 15,000-acre state park. On the north side of the county was the Carquinez Strait, with its oil refineries, Suisun Bay, and the San Joaquin River which separated Contra Costa from Sacramento County and the Delta. The city of Richmond and environs, to the west, were also part of the county, and their inclusion had always struck me as odd. Besides being geographically separated by the expanse of Tilden Regional Park and San Pablo Reservoir, the mostly black industrial city was culturally light years away from the rest of the suburban, upwardly mobile county. With the exception of a few towns like Pittsburgh or Antioch, this was affluent, fast-developing land; I supposed one day even those north-county backwaters would fall victim to expensive residential tracts and shopping centers full of upscale boutiques.

When Fitzgerald didn't comment, I said, "Does it look different to you?"

"Not really."

"Wait till we get to Walnut Creek. The area around the BART station is all highrise buildings now. They're predicting it will become an urban center that will eventually rival San Francisco."

He grunted in disapproval.

"About the only thing they've managed to preserve out here is the area around Mount Diablo. I suppose you know it from when you were a kid."

"Yes."

"I went hiking in the park last spring, during wildflower season. It was really beautiful that time of year. They say if you climb high enough you can see thirty-five counties from the mountain."

"This pavilion," Fitzgerald said, "is it part of the state park?"

For a moment I was surprised, then realized the pavilion hadn't been in existence in 1969, when he'd left home. "No, but near it. The land around it is relatively unspoiled. Horse and cattle ranches, mostly. They built it about eight years ago, after the Concord Pavilion became such a success. I guess that's one index of how this part of the Bay Area has grown, that it can support two concert pavilions."

He nodded. "Do they ever have concerts going at the same time at both?"

"Sure."

"It must really echo off these hills."

"I imagine you can hear it all the way to Port Chicago." Port Chicago was where the Naval Weapons Station was located, on the edge of Suisun Bay.

"Well, maybe not all the way to Chicago."

I smiled at the feeble joke, thinking that for a clown, Fitzgerald really didn't have much of a sense of humor, then allowed him to lapse back into his moody silence.

IV

When we arrived at the pavilion, the parking lot was already crowded, the gates having opened early so people could picnic before the show started. An orange-jacketed attendant directed us to a far corner of the lot which had been cordoned off for official parking near the performers' gate. Fitzgerald and I waited in the car for about fifteen minutes, the late afternoon sun beating down on us, until Wayne Kabalka's Seville pulled up alongside. With the manager and John Tilby were two women: a chic, fortyish redhead, and a small, dark-haired woman in her twenties. Fitzgerald and I got out and went to greet them.

The redhead was Corinne Kabalka; her strong handshake and level gaze made me like her immediately. I was less sure about Nicole Leland; the younger woman was beautiful, with short black hair sculpted close to her head and exotic features, but her manner was very cold. She nodded curtly when introduced to me, then took Tilby's arm and led him off toward the performers' gate. The rest of us trailed behind.

Security was tight at the gate. We met Roy Canfield, who was personally superintending the check-in, and each of us was issued a pass. No one, Canfield told us, would be permitted backstage or through the gate without showing his pass. Security personnel would also be stationed in the audience to protect those clowns who, as part of the show, would be performing out on the lawn.

We were then shown to a large dressing room equipped with a couch, a folding card table and chairs. After everyone was settled there I took Kabalka aside and asked him if he would take charge of the group for about fifteen minutes while I checked the layout of the pavilion. He nodded distractedly and I went out front.

Stage personnel were scurrying around, setting up sound equipment and checking the lights. Don had already arrived, but he was conferring with one of the other KSUN jocks and didn't look as if he could be disturbed. The formal seating was empty, but the lawn was already crowded. People lounged on blankets, passing around food, drink and an occasional joint. Some of the picnics were elaborate—fine china, crystal wineglasses, ice buckets, and in one case, a set of lighted silver candelabra; others were of the paper-plate and plastic-cup variety. I spotted the familiar logos of Kentucky Fried Chicken and Jack-in-the-Box here and there. People called to friends, climbed up and down the hill to the restroom and refreshment facilities, dropped by other groups' blankets to see what goodies they had to trade. Children ran through the crowd, an occasional Frisbee sailed through the air. I noticed a wafting trail of iridescent soap bubbles, and my eyes followed it to a young woman in a red halter top who was blowing them, her face aglow with childlike pleasure.

For a moment I felt a stab of envy, realizng that if I hadn't taken on this job I could be out front, courtesy of the free pass Don had promised me. I could have packed a picnic, perhaps brought along a woman friend, and Don could have dropped by to join us when he had time. But instead, I was bodyguarding a pair of clowns who—given the pavilion's elaborate security measures—probably didn't need me. And in addition to Fitzgerald and Tilby, I seemed to be responsible for an entire group. I could see why Kabalka might want to stick close to his clients, but why did the wife and girlfriend have to crowd into what was already a stuffy, hot dressing room? Why couldn't they go out front and enjoy the performance? It complicated my assignment, having to contend with an entourage, and the thought of those complications made me grumpy.

The grumpiness was probably due to the heat, I decided. Shrugging it off, I familiarized myself with the layout of the stage and the points at which someone could gain access. Satisfied that pavilion security could deal with any problems that might arise there, I made my way through the crowd—turning down two beers, a glass of wine, and a pretzel—and climbed to the promenade. From there I studied the stage once more, then raised my eyes to the sun-scorched hills to the east.

The slopes were barren, save for an occasional outcropping of rock and live oak trees, and on them a number of horses with riders stood. They clustered together in groups of two, four, six and even at this distance, I sensed they shared the same camaraderie as the people on the lawn. They leaned toward one another, gestured, and occasionally passed objects—perhaps they were picnicking too—back and forth.

What a great way to enjoy a free concert, I

thought. The sound, in this natural echo chamber, would easily carry to where the watchers were stationed. How much more peaceful it must be on the hill, free of crowds and security measures. Visibility, however, would not be very good . . .

And then I saw a flare of reddish light and glanced over to where a lone horseman stood under the sheltering branches of a live oak. The light flashed again, and I realized he was holding binoculars which had caught the setting sun. Of course—with binoculars or opera glasses, visibility would not be bad at all. In fact, from such a high vantage point it might even be better than from many points on the lawn. My grumpiness returned; I'd have loved to be mounted on a horse on that hillside.

Reminding myself that I was here on business that would pay for part of the new bathroom tile, I turned back toward the stage, then started when I saw Gary Fitzgerald. He was standing on the lawn not more than six feet from me, looking around with one hand forming a visor over his eyes. When he saw me he started too, and then waved.

I rushed over to him and grabbed his arm. "What are you doing out here? You're supposed to stay backstage!"

"I just wanted to see what the place looks like."

"Are you out of your mind? Your manager is paying good money for me to see that people stay away from you. And here you are, wandering through the crowd—"

He looked away, at a family on a blanket next to us. The father was wiping catsup from the smallest child's hands. "No one's bothering me."

"That's not the point." Still gripping his arm, I began steering him toward the stage. "Someone might recognize you, and that's precisely what Kabalka hired me to prevent."

"Oh, Wayne's just being a worrywart about that. No one's going to recognize anybody after all this time. Besides, it's common knowledge in the trade that we're not what we're made out to be."

"In the trade, yes. But your manager's worried about the public." We got to the stage, showed our passes to the security guard, and went back to the dressing room.

At the door Fitzgerald stopped. "Sharon, would you mind not mentioning my going out there to Wayne?"

"Why shouldn't I?"

"Because it would only upset him, and he's nervous enough before a performance. Nothing happened— except that I was guilty of using bad judgment."

His smile was disarming, and I took the words as an apology. "All right. But you'd better go get into costume. There's only half an hour before the grand procession begins."

V

The next few hours were uneventful. The grand procession––a parade through the crowd in which all the performers participated—went off smoothly. After they returned to the dressing room, Fitzgerald and Tilby removed their makeup—which was already running in the intense heat—and the Kabalkas fetched supper from the car—deli food packed in hampers by their hotel. There was a great deal of grumbling about the quality of the meal, which was not what one would have expected of the St. Francis, and Fitzgerald teased the others because he was staying at a small bed-and-breakfast establishment in the Haight-Ashbury which had better food at half the price.

Nicole said, "Yes, but your hotel probably has bed-bugs."

Fitzgerald glared at her, and I was reminded of the disapproving tone of voice in which he'd first spoken of her. "Don't be ignorant. Urban chic has come to the Haight-Ashbury."

"Making it difficult for you to recapture your mis-spent youth there, no doubt."

"Nicole," Kabalka said.

"That *was* your intention in separating from the rest of us, wasn't it, Gary?" Nicole added.

Fitzgerald was silent.

"Well, Gary?"

He glanced at me. "You'll have to excuse us for let-ting our hostilities show."

Nicole smiled nastily. "Yes, when a man gets to a certain age, he must try to recapture—"

"Shut up, Nicole," Kabalka said.

She looked at him in surprise, then picked up her sandwich and nibbled daintily at it. I could understand why she had backed off; there was something in Kabal-ka's tone that said he would put up with no more from her.

After the remains of supper were packed up, everyone settled down. None of them displayed the slightest inclination to go out front and watch the show. Kabalka read—one of those slim volumes that claim you can make a financial killing in spite of the world eco-nomic crisis. Corinne crocheted—granny squares. Fitzgerald brooded. Tilby played solitaire. Nicole fid-geted. And while they engaged in these activities, they also seemed to be watching one another. The covert vigilant atmosphere puzzled me; after a while I concluded that maybe the reason they all stuck together was that each was afraid to leave the others alone. But why?

Time crawled. Outside, the show was going on; I could hear music, laughter, and—occasionally—Don's enthusiastic voice as he introduced the acts. Once more I began to regret taking this job.

After a while Tilby reshuffled the cards and slapped them on the table. "Sharon, do you play gin rummy?"

"Yes."

"Good. Let's have a few hands."

Nicole frowned and made a small sound of protest.

Tilby said to her, "I offered to teach you. It's not my fault you refused."

I moved my chair over to the table and we played in silence for a while. Tilby was good, but I was better. After about half an hour, there was a roar from the crowd and Tilby raised his head. "Casey O'Connell must be going on."

"Who?" I said.

"One of our more famous circus clowns."

"There really is quite a variety among the performers in your profession, isn't there?"

"Yes, and quite a history: clowning is an old and honored art. They had clowns back in ancient Greece. Wandering entertainers, actually, who'd show up at a wealthy household and tell jokes, do acrobatics, or juggle for the price of a meal. Then in the Middle Ages, mimes appeared on the scene."

"That long ago?"

"Uh-huh. They were the cream of the crop back then. Most of the humor in the Middle Ages was kind of basic; they loved buffoons, jesters, simpletons, that sort of thing. But they served the purpose of making people see how silly we really are."

I took the deuce he'd just discarded, then lay down my hand to show I had gin. Tilby frowned and slapped down his cards; nothing matched. Then he grinned. "See what I mean—I'm silly to take this game so seriously."

I swept the cards together and began to shuffle. "You seem to know a good bit about the history of clowning."

"Well, I've done some reading along those lines. You've heard the term *commedia dell'arte?*"

"Yes."

"It appeared in the late 1500s, an Italian brand of the traveling comedy troupe. The comedians always played the same role—a Harlequin or a Pulcinella or a Pantalone. Easy for the audience to recognize."

"I know what a Harlequin is, but what are the other two?"

"Pantalone is a personification of the overbearing father figure. A stubborn, temperamental old geezer. Pulcinella was costumed all in white, usually with a dunce's cap; he assumed various roles in the comedy— lawyer, doctor, servant, whatever—and was usually greedy, sometimes pretty coarse. One of his favorite tricks was urinating onstage."

"Good Lord!"

"Fortunately we've become more refined since then. The British contributed a lot, further developing the Harlequin, creating the Punch and Judy shows. And of course, the French had their Figaro. The Indians created the *vidushaka*—a form of court jester. The entertainers at the Chinese court were known as *Chous*, after the dynasty in which they originated. And Japan has a huge range of comic figures appearing in their *Kyogen* plays—the humorous counterpart of the *Noh* play."

"You really have done your homework."

"Well, clowning's my profession. Don't you know about the history of yours?"

"What I know is mostly fictional; private investigation is more interesting in books than in real life, I'm afraid."

"Gin." Tilby spread his cards on the table. "Your deal. But back to what I was saying, it's the more contemporary clowns that interest me. And I use the term 'clown' loosely."

"How so?"

"Well, do you think of Will Rogers as a clown?"

"No."

"I do. And Laurel and Hardy, Flip Wilson, Mae West, Woody Allen, Lucille Ball. As well as the more traditional figures like Emmett Kelly, Charlie Chaplin, and Marceau. There's a common denominator among all those people; they're funny and, more important, they all make the audience take a look at humanity's foibles. They're as much descended from those historical clowns as the whiteface circus performer."

"The whiteface is the typical circus clown, right?"

"Well, there are three basic types; whiteface is your basic slaphappy fellow. The Auguste—who was created almost simultaneously in Germany and France—usually wears pink- or blackface and is the one you see falling all over himself in the ring, often sopping wet from having buckets of water thrown at him. The Grotesque is usually a midget or a dwarf, or has some other distorted feature. And there are performers whom you can't classify because they've created something unique, such as Kelly's Weary Willie, or Russia's Popov, who is such an artist that he doesn't even need to wear makeup."

"It's fascinating. I never realized there was such variety. Or artistry."

"Most people don't. They think clowning is easy,

but a lot of the time it's just plain hard work. Especially when you have to go on when you aren't feeling particularly funny." Tilby's mouth drooped as he spoke, and I wondered if tonight was one of those occasions for him.

I picked up a trey and said, "Gin," then tossed my hand on the table and watched as he shuffled and dealt. We fell silent once more. The sounds of the show went on, but the only noise in the dressing room was the slap of the cards on the table. It was still uncomfortably hot. Moths fluttered around the glaring bare bulbs of the dressing tables. At about ten-thirty, Fitzgerald stood up.

"Where are you going?" Kabalka said.

"The men's room. Do you mind?"

I said, "I'll go with you."

Fitzgerald smiled faintly. "Really, Sharon, that's above and beyond the call of duty."

"I mean, just to the door."

He started to protest, then shrugged and picked up his canvas bag.

Kabalka said, "Why are you taking that?"

"There's something in it I need."

"What?"

"For Christ's sake, Wayne!" He snatched up his yellow cape, flung it over one shoulder.

Kabalka hesitated. "All right, go. But Sharon goes with you."

Fitzgerald went out into the hall and I followed. Behind me, Nicole said, "Probably Maalox or something like that for his queasy stomach. You can always count on Gary to puke at least once before a performance."

Kabalka said, "Shut up, Nicole."

Fitzgerald started off, muttering, "Yes, we're one big happy family."

I followed him and took up a position next to the men's room door. It was ten minutes before I realized he was taking too long a time, and when I did I asked one of the security guards to go in after him. Fitzgerald had vanished, apparently through an open window high off the floor—a trash receptacle had been moved beneath it, which would have allowed him to climb up there. The window opened onto the pavilion grounds rather than outside of the fence, but from there he could have gone in any one of a number of directions—including out the performers' gate.

From then on, all was confusion. I told Kabalka what had happened and again left him in charge of the others. With the help of the security personnel, I combed the backstage area—questioning the performers, stage personnel, Don, and the other people from KSUN. No one had seen Fitzgerald. The guards in the audience were alerted, but no one in baggy plaid pants, a red vest, and a yellow cape was spotted. The security man on the performers' gate knew nothing; he'd only come on minutes ago, and the man he had relieved had left the grounds on a break.

Fitzgerald and Tilby were to be the last act to go on—at midnight, as the star attraction. As the hour approached, the others in their party grew frantic and Don and the KSUN people grew grim. I continued to search systematically. Finally I returned to the performers' gate; the guard had returned from his break and Kabalka had buttonholed him. I took over the questioning. Yes, he remembered Gary Fitzgerald. He'd left at about ten thirty, carrying his yellow cape and a small canvas bag. But wait—hadn't he returned just a few minutes ago, before Kabalka had come up and started asking questions? But maybe that wasn't the same man, there had been something different . . .

Kabalka was on the edge of hysterical collapse. He yelled at the guard and only confused him further.

Maybe the man who had just come in had been wearing a red cape . . . maybe the pants were green rather than blue . . . no, it wasn't the same man after all . . .

Kabalka yelled louder, until one of the stage personnel told him to shut up, he could be heard out front. Corinne appeared and momentarily succeeded in quieting her husband. I left her to deal with him and went back to the dressing room. Tilby and Nicole were there. His face was pinched, white around the mouth. Nicole was pale and —oddly enough—had been crying. I told them what the security guard had said, cautioned them not to leave the dressing room.

As I turned to go, Tilby said, "Sharon, will you ask Wayne to come in here?"

"I don't think he's in any shape—"

"Please, it's important."

"All right. But why?"

Tilby looked at Nicole. She turned her tear-streaked face away toward the wall.

He said, "We have a decision to make about the act."

"I hardly think so. It's pretty clear cut. If Gary doesn't turn up, you simply can't go on."

He stared bleakly at me. "Just ask Wayne to come in here."

Of course the act didn't go on. The audience was disappointed, the KSUN people were irate, and the Fitzgerald and Tilby entourage were grim—a grimness that held a faint undercurrent of tightly-reined panic. No one could shed any light on where Fitzgerald might have gone, or why—at least, if anyone had suspicions, he was keeping it to himself. The one thing everyone agreed on was that his disappearance wasn't my fault; I hadn't been hired to prevent treachery within the ranks. I myself wasn't so sure of my lack of culpability.

So I'd spent the night chasing around, trying to find a trace of him. I'd gone to San Francisco: to Fitzgerald's hotel in the Haight-Ashbury, to the St. Francis where the rest of the party were staying, even to the KSUN studios. Finally I went back to the Haight, to a number of the after-hours places I knew of, in the hopes Fitzgerald was there recapturing his youth, as Nicole had termed it earlier. And I still hadn't found a single clue to his whereabouts.

Until now. I hadn't located Gary Fitzgerald, but I'd found his clown costume. On another man. A dead man.

VI

After the county sheriff's men had finished questioning me and said I could go, I decided to return to the St. Francis and talk to my clients once more. I wasn't sure if Kabalka would want me to keep searching for Fitzgerald now, but he—and the others—deserved to hear from me about the dead man in Gary's costume, before the authorities contacted them. Besides, there were things bothering me about Fitzgerald's disappearance, some of them obvious, some vague. I hoped talking to Kabalka and company once more would help me bring the vague ones into more clear focus.

It was after seven by the time I had parked under Union Square and entered the hotel's elegant, dark-paneled lobby. The few early risers who clustered there seemed to be tourists, equipped with cameras and anxious to get on with the day's adventures. A dissipated-looking couple in evening clothes stood waiting for an elevator, and a few yards away in front of the first row of expensive shops, a maid in the hotel uniform was pushing a vacuum cleaner with desultory strokes. When the elevator came, the couple and I rode up in silence; they got off at the floor before I did.

Corinne Kabalka answered my knock on the door of the suite almost immediately. Her eyes were deeply shadowed, she wore the same white linen pantsuit—now severely rumpled—that she'd had on the night before, and in her hand she clutched her crocheting. When she saw me, her face registered disappointment.

"Oh," she said, "I thought . . ."

"You hoped it would be Gary."

"Yes. Well, any of them, really."

"Them? Are you alone?"

She nodded and crossed the sitting room to a couch under the heavily-draped windows, dropping onto it with a sigh and setting down the crocheting.

"Where did they go?"

"Wayne's out looking for Gary. He refuses to believe he's just . . . vanished. I don't know where John is, but I suspect he's looking for Nicole."

"And Nicole?"

Anger flashed in her tired eyes. "Who knows?"

I was about to ask her more about Tilby's unpleasant girlfriend when a key rattled in the lock, and John and Nicole came in. His face was pulled into taut lines, reflecting a rage more sustained than Corinne's brief flare-up. Nicole looked haughty, tight-lipped, and a little defensive.

Corinne stood. "Where have you two been?"

Tilby said, "*I* was looking for Nicole. It occurred to me that we didn't want to lose another member of this happy party."

Corinne turned to Nicole. "And you?"

The younger woman sat on a spindly chair, studiously examining her plum-colored fingernails. "I was having breakfast."

"Breakfast?"

"I was hungry, after that disgusting supper last night. So I went around the corner to a coffee shop—"

"You could have ordered from room service. Or eaten downstairs where John could have found you more easily."

"I needed some air."

Now Corinne drew herself erect. "Always thinking of Nicole, aren't you?"

"Well, what of it? Someone around here has to act sensibly."

In their heated bickering, they all seemed to have forgotten I was there. I remained silent, taking advantage of the situation; one could learn very instructive things by listening to people's unguarded conversations.

Tilby said, "Nicole's right, Corinne. We can't all run around like Wayne, looking for Gary when we have no idea where to start."

"Yes, *you* would say that. You never did give a damn about him, or anyone. Look how you stole Nicole from your own cousin—"

"Good God, Corinne! You can't *steal* one person from another."

"You did. You stole her and then you wrecked—"

"Let's not go into this, Corinne. Especially in front of an outsider." Tilby motioned at me.

Corinne glanced my way and colored. "I'm sorry, Sharon. This must be embarrassing for you."

On the contrary, I wished they would go on. After all, if John had taken Nicole from his cousin, Gary would have had reason to resent him—perhaps even to want to destroy their act.

I said to Tilby, "Is that the reason Gary was staying at a different hotel—because of you and Nicole?"

He looked startled.

"How long have you two been together?" I asked.

"Long enough." He turned to Corinne. "Wayne hasn't come back or called, I take it?"

"I've heard nothing. He was terribly worried about Gary when he left."

Nicole said, "He's terribly worried about the TV commercials and his cut of them."

"Nicole!" Corinne whirled on her.

Nicole looked up, her delicate little face all innocence. "You know it's true. All Wayne cares about is money. I don't know why he's worried, though. He can always get someone to replace Gary, Wayne's good at doing that sort of thing—"

Corinne stepped forward and her hand lashed out at Nicole's face, connecting with a loud smack. Nicole put a hand to the reddening stain on her cheekbone, eyes widening; then she got up and ran from the room. Corinne watched her go, satisfaction spreading over her handsome features. When I glanced at Tilby, I was surprised to see he was smiling.

"Round one to Corinne," he said.

"She had it coming." The older woman went back to the couch and sat, smoothing her rumpled pantsuit. "Well, Sharon, once more you must excuse us. I assume you came here for a reason?"

"Yes." I sat down in the chair Nicole had vacated and told them about the dead man at the pavilion. As I spoke, the two exchanged glances that were at first puzzled, then worried, and finally panicky.

When I had finished, Corinne said, "But who on earth can the man in Gary's costume be?" The words sounded theatrical, false.

"The sheriff's department is trying to make an identification. Probably his fingerprints will be on file somewhere. In the meantime, there are a few distinctive things about him which may mean something to you or John."

John sat down next to Corinne. "Such as?"

"The man had been crippled, probably a number of years ago, according to the man from the medical examiner's office. One arm was bent badly, and he wore a lift to compensate for a shortened leg. He would have walked with a limp."

The two of them looked at each other, and then Tilby said—too quickly—"I don't know anyone like that."

Corinne also shook her head, but she didn't meet my eyes.

I said, "Are you sure?"

"Of course we're sure." There was an edge of annoyance in Tilby's voice.

I hesitated, then went on, "The sheriff's man who examined the body theorizes that the dead man may have been from the countryside around there, because he had fragments of madrone and chapparal leaves caught in his shoes, as well as foxtails in the weave of his pants. Perhaps he's someone you knew when you lived in the area?"

"No, I don't remember anyone like that."

"He was about Gary's height and age, but with sandy hair. He must have been handsome once, in an elfin way, but his face was badly scarred."

"I said, I don't know who he is."

I was fairly certain he was lying, but accusing him would get me nowhere.

Corinne said, "Are you sure the costume was Gary's? Maybe this man was one of the other clowns and dressed similarly."

"That's what I suggested to the sheriff's man, but the dead man had Gary's pass in his vest pocket. We all signed our passes, remember?"

There was a long silence. 'So what you're saying," Tilby finally said, "is that Gary *gave* his pass and costume to his man."

"It seems so."

"But why?"

"I don't know. I'd hoped you could provide me with some insight."

They both stared at me. I noticed Corinne's face had gone quite blank. Tilby was as white-lipped as when I'd come upon him and Nicole in the dressing room shortly after Fitzgerald's disappearance.

I said to Tilby, "I assume you each have more than one change of costume."

It was Corinne who answered. "We brought three on this tour. But I had the other two sent out to the cleaner when we arrived here in San Francisco . . .Oh!"

"What is it?"

" I just remembered. Gary asked me about the other costumes yesterday morning. He called from that hotel where he was staying. And he was very upset when I told him they would be at the cleaner until this afternoon."

"So he planned it all along. Probably he hoped to give his extra costume to the man, and when he found he couldn't, he decided to make a switch." I remembered Fitzgerald's odd behavior immediately after we'd arrived at the pavilion—his sneaking off into the audience when he'd been told to stay backstage. Had he had a confederate out there? Someone to hand the things to? No. He couldn't have turned over either the costume or the pass to anyone, because the clothing was still backstage, and he'd needed his pass when we returned to the dressing room.

Tilby suddenly stood up. "The son of a bitch! After all we've done—"

"John!" Corinne touched his elbow with her hand.

"John," I said, "why was your cousin staying at the hotel in the Haight?"

He looked at me blankly for a moment. "What? Oh, I don't know. He claimed he wanted to see how it had changed since he'd lived there."

"I thought you grew up together on your father's ranch near Clayton and then went to Los Angeles."

"We did. Gary lived in the Haight before we left the Bay Area."

"I see. Now, you say he 'claimed' that was the reason. Was there something else?"

Tilby was silent, then looked at Corinne. She shrugged.

"I guess," he said finally, "he'd had about all he could take of us. As you may have noticed, we're not exactly a congenial group lately."

"Why is that?"

"Why is what?"

"That you're all at odds? It hasn't always been this way, has it?"

This time Tilby shrugged. Corinne was silent, looking down at her clasped hands.

I sighed, silently empathizing with Fitzgerald's desire to get away from these people. I myself was sick of their bickering, lies, backbiting, and evasions. And I knew I would get nowhere with them—at least not now. Better to wait until I could talk with Kabalka, see if he were willing to keep on employing me. Then, if he was, I could start fresh.

I stood up, saying, "The Contra Costa authorities will be contacting you. I'd advise you to be as frank as possible with them."

To Corinne, I added, "Wayne will want a personal report from me when he comes back; ask him to call me at home." I took out a card with both my All Souls and home number, lay it on the coffee table, and started for the door.

As I let myself out, I glanced back at them. Tilby stood with his arms folded across his chest, looking down at Corinne. They were still as statues, their eyes locked, their expressions bleak and helpless.

VII

Of course, by the time I got home to my brown-shingled cottage the desire to sleep had left me. It was always that way when I harbored nagging unanswered questions. Instead of going to bed and forcing myself to rest, I made coffee and took a cup of it out on the back porch to think.

It was a sunny, clear morning and already getting hot. The neighborhood was Saturday noisy: to one side, my neighbors, the Halls, were doing something to their backyard shed that involved a lot of hammering; on the other side, the Curleys' dog was barking excitedly. Probably, I thought, my cat was deviling the dog by prancing along the top of the fence, just out of his reach. It was Watney's favorite game lately.

Sure enough, in a few minutes there was a thump as Wat dropped down from the fence onto an upturned half barrel I'd been meaning to make into a planter. His black-and-white spotted fur was full of foxtails; undoubtedly he'd been prowling around in the weeds at the back of the Curleys' lot.

"Come here, you," I said to him. He stared at me, tail swishing back and forth. "Come here!" He hesitated, then galloped up. I managed to pull one of the foxtails from the ruff of fur over his collar before he trotted off again, his belly swaying pendulously, a great big horse of a cat . . .

I sat staring at the foxtail, rolling it between my thumb and forefinger, not really seeing it. Instead, I pictured the hills surrounding the pavilion as I'd seen them the night before. The hills that were dotted with oak and madrone and chapparal . . . that were sprinkled with people on horses . . . where a lone horseman had stood under the sheltering branches of a tree, his binoculars like a signal flare in the setting sun . . .

I got up and went inside to the phone. First I called the Contra Costa sheriff's deputy who had been in charge of the crime scene at the pavilion. No, he told me, the dead man hadn't been identified yet; the only personal item he had been carrying was a bus ticket—issued yesterday—from San Francisco to Concord which had been tucked into his shoe. While this indicated he was not a resident of the area, it told them nothing else. They were still hoping to get an identification on his fingerprints, however.

Next I called the pavilion and got the home phone number of Jim Hayes, the guard who had been on the performers' gate when Fitzgerald had vanished. When Hayes answered my call, he sounded as if I'd woken him, but he was willing to answer a few questions.

"When Fitzgerald left he was wearing his costume, right?" I asked.

"Yes."

"What about makeup?"

"No. I'd have noticed that; it would have seemed strange, him leaving with his face all painted."

"Now, last night you said you thought he'd come back in a few minutes after you returned from your break. Did he show you his pass?"

"Yes, everyone had to show one. But—"

"Did you look at the name on it?"

"Not closely. I just checked to see if it was valid for that date. Now I wish I *had* looked, because I'm not sure it was Fitzgerald. The costume seemed the same, but I just don't know."

"Why?"

"Well, there was something different about the man who came in. He walked funny. The guy you found murdered, he was crippled."

So that observation might or might not be valid. The idea that the man walked "funny" could have been planted in Hayes' mind by his knowing the dead man was a cripple. "Anything else?"

He hesitated. "I think . . .yes. You asked if Gary Fitzgerald was wearing makeup when he left. And he wasn't. But the guy who came in, he *was* made up. That's why I don't think it was Fitzgerald."

"Thank you, Mr. Hayes. That's all I need to know."

I hung up the phone, grabbed my bag and car keys, and drove back out to the pavilion in record time.

The heat-hazed parking lots were empty today, save for a couple of trucks that I assumed belonged to the maintenance crew. The gates were locked, the box office windows shuttered, and I could see no one. That didn't matter, however. What I was interested in lay outside the chain-link fence. I parked the MG near the trucks and went around the perimeter of the amphitheater to the area near the performers' gate, then looked up at the hill to the east. There was a fire break cut through the high wheat-colored grass, and I started up it.

Halfway to the top, I stopped, wiping sweat from my forehead and looking down at the pavilion. Visibility was good from here. Pivoting, I surveyed the surrounding area. To the west lay a monotonous grid-like pattern of tracts and shopping centers, broken here and there by hills and the upthrusting skyline of Walnut Creek. To the north I could see smoke billowing from the stacks of the paper plant at Antioch, and the bridge spanning the river toward the Sacramento Delta. Further east, the majestic bulk of Mount Diablo rose; between it and this foothill were more hills and hollows—ranch country.

The hill on which I stood was only lightly wooded, but there was an outcropping of rock surrounded by madrone and live oak about a hundred yards to the south, on a direct line from the tree where the lone horseman with the signal-like binoculars had stood. I left the relatively easy footing of the fire break and waded through the dry grass toward it. It was cool and deeply shadowed under the branches of the trees, and the air smelled of vegetation gone dry and brittle. I stood still for a moment, wiping the sweat away once more, then began to look around. What I was searching for was wedged behind a low rock that formed a sort of table: a couple of tissues smeared with makeup. Black and red and white greasepaint—the theatrical makeup of a clown.

The dead man had probably used this rock as a dressing table, applying what Fitzgerald had brought him in the canvas bag. I remembered Gary's insistence on taking the bag with him to the men's room; of course he needed it; the makeup was a necessary prop to their plan.

While Fitzgerald could leave the pavilion without his greasepaint, the other man couldn't enter un-madeup; there was too much of a risk that the guard might notice the face didn't match the costume or the name on the pass.

I looked down at the dry leaves beneath my feet. Oak, and madrone, and brittle needles of chapparal. And the foxtails would have been acquired while pushing through the high grass between here and the bottom of the hills. That told me the route the dead man had taken, but not what had happened to Fitzgerald. In order to find that out, I'd have to learn where one could rent a horse.

I stopped at a feed store in the little village of Hillside, nestled in a wooded hollow southeast of the pavilion. It was all you could expect of a country store, with wood floors and big sacks and bins of feed. The weatherbeaten old man in overalls who looked up from the saddle he was polishing completed the rustic picture.

He said, "Help you with something?"

I took a closer look at the saddle, then glanced around at the hand-tooled leather goods hanging from the hooks on the far wall. "That's beautiful work. Do you do it yourself?"

"Sure do."

"How much does a saddle like that go for these days?" My experience with horses had ended with the lessons I'd taken in junior high school.

"Custom job like this, five hundred, thereabouts."

"Five hundred! That's more than I could get for my car."

"Well . . . " He glanced through the door at the MG.

"I know. You don't have to say another word."

"It runs, don't it?"

"Usually." Rapport established, I got down to business. "What I need is some information. I'm looking for a stable that rents horses."

"You want to set up a party or something?"

"I might."

"Well, there's MacMillan's, on the south side of town. I wouldn't recommend them, though. They've got some mean horses. This would be for a bunch of city folks?"

"I wasn't aware it showed."

"Doesn't, all that much. But I'm good at figuring out about folks. You don't look like a suburban lady, and you don't look country either." He beamed at me, and I nodded and smiled to compliment his deductive ability. "No," he went on, "I wouldn't recommend MacMillan's if you'll have folks along who maybe don't ride so good. Some of those horses are mean enough to kick a person from here to San Jose. The place to go is Wheeler's; they got some fine mounts."

"Where is Wheeler's?"

"South too, a couple of miles beyond MacMillan's. You'll know it by the sign."

I thanked him and started out. "Hey!" he called after me. "When you have your party, bring your city friends by. I got a nice selection of handtooled belts and wallets."

I said I would, and waved at him as I drove off.

About a mile down the road on the south side of the little hamlet stood a tumble-down stable with a hand-lettered sign advertising horses for rent. The poorly recommended MacMillan's, no doubt. There wasn't an animal, mean or otherwise, in sight, but a large, jowly woman who resembled a bulldog greeted me, pitchfork in hand.

I told her the story that I'd hastily made up on the

drive: a friend of mine had rented a horse the night before to ride up on the hill and watch the show at the Diablo Valley Pavilion. He had been impressed with the horse and the stable it had come from, but couldn't remember the name of the place. Had she, by any chance, rented to him? As I spoke, the woman began to frown, looking more and more like a pugnacious canine every minute.

"It's not honest," she said.

"I'm sorry?"

"It's not honest, people riding up there and watching for free. Stealing's stealing, no matter what name you put on it. Your Bible tells you that."

"Oh." I couldn't think of any reply to that, although she was probably right.

She eyed me severely, as if she suspected me of pagan practices. "In answer to your question, no, I didn't rent to your friend. I wouldn't let a person near one of my horses if he was going to ride up there and watch."

"Well, I don't suppose my friend admitted what he planned to do—"

"Any decent person would be too ashamed to admit to a thing like that." She motioned aggressively with the pitchfork.

I took a step backwards. "But maybe you rented to him not knowing—"

"You going to do the same thing?"

"What?"

"Are you going to ride up there for tonight's concert?"

"Me? No, ma'am. I don't even ride all that well. I just wanted to find out if my friend had rented his horse from—"

"Well, he didn't get the horse from here. We aren't

open evenings, don't want our horses out in the dark with people like you who can't ride. Besides, even if people don't plan it, those concerts are an awful temptation. And I can't sanction that sort of thing. I'm a born-again Christian, and I won't help people go against the Lord's word."

"You know," I said hastily, "I agree with you. And I'm going to talk with my friend about his behavior. But I still want to know where he got that horse. Are there any other stables around here besides yours?"

The woman looked somewhat mollified. "There's only Wheeler's. They do a big business—trail trips on Mount Diablo, hayrides in the fall. And, of course, folks who want to sneak up to that pavilion. They'd rent to a person who was going to rob a bank on horseback if there was enough money in it."

Stifling a grin, I started for my car. "Thanks for the information."

"You're welcome to it. But you remember to talk to your friend, tell him to mend his ways."

I smiled and got out of there in a hurry.

Next to MacMillan's, Wheeler's Riding Stables looked prosperous and attractive. The red barn was freshly painted, and a couple of dozen healthy, sleek horses grazed within white rail fences. I rumbled down a dirt driveway and over a little bridge that spanned a gully, and parked in front of a door labeled OFFICE. Inside, a blond-haired man in faded Levi's and a T-shirt lounged in a canvas chair behind the counter, reading a copy of *Playboy*. He put it aside reluctantly when I came in.

I was tired of my manufactured story, and this man looked like someone I could be straightforward with. I showed him the photostat of my license and said, "I'm

cooperating with the county sheriff's department on the
death at the Diablo Valley Pavilion last night. You've
heard about it?"

"Yes, it made the morning news."

"I've got reason to believe that the dead man may
have rented a horse prior to the show last night."

The man raised a sun-bleached eyebrow and waited,
as economical with his words as the woman at MacMillan's had been spendthrift.

"Did you rent any horses last night?"

"Five. Four to a party, another later on."

"Who rented the single horse?"

"Tall, thin guy. Wore jeans and a plaid shirt. At
first I thought I knew him."

"Why?"

"He looked familiar, like someone who used to live
near here. But then I realized it couldn't be. His face was
disfigured, his arm crippled up, and he limped. Had
trouble getting on the horse, but once he was mounted, I
could tell he was a good rider."

I felt a flash of excitement, the kind you get when
things start coming together the way you've hoped they
would. "That's the man who was killed."

"Well, that explains it."

"Explains what?"

"Horse came back this morning, riderless."

"What time?"

"Oh, around five, five-thirty."

That didn't fit the way I wanted it to. "Do you keep
a record of who you rent the horses to?"

"Name and address. And we take a deposit that's returned when they bring the horses back."

"Can you look up the man's name?"

He grinned and reached under the counter for a

looseleaf notebook. "I can, but I don't think it will help you identify him. I noted it at the time—Tom Smith. Sounded like a phony."

"But you still rented to him?"

"Sure. I just asked for double the deposit. He didn't look too prosperous, so I figured he'd be back. Besides, none of our horses are so terrific that anyone would trouble to steal one."

I stood there for a few seconds, tapping my fingers on the counter. "You said you thought he was someone you used to know."

"At first, but the guy I knew wasn't crippled. Must have been just a chance resemblance."

"Who was he?"

"Fellow who lived on a ranch near here back in the late sixties. Gary Fitzgerald."

I stared at him.

"But like I said, Gary Fitzgerald wasn't crippled."

"Did this Gary have a cousin?" I asked.

"Yeah, John Tilby. Tilby's dad owned a dairy ranch. Gary lived with them."

"When did Gary leave here?"

"After the old man died. The ranch was sold to pay the debts and both Gary and John took off. For southern California." He grinned again. "Probably had some cock-eyed idea about getting into show business."

"By any chance, do you know who was starring on the bill at the pavilion last night?"

"Don't recall, no. It was some kind of kid show, wasn't it?"

"A clown festival."

"Oh." He shrugged. "Clowns don't interest me. Why?"

"No reason." Things definitely weren't fitting together the way I'd wanted them to. "You say the cousins took off together after John Tilby's father died."

"Yes."

"And went to Southern California."

"That's what I heard."

"Did Gary Fitzgerald ever live in the Haight-Ashbury?"

He hesitated. "Not unless they went there instead of L.A. But I can't see Gary in the Haight, especially back then. He was just a country boy, if you know what I mean. But what's all this about him and John? I thought—"

"How much to rent a horse?"

The man's curiosity was easily sidetracked by business. "Ten an hour. Twenty for the deposit."

"Do you have a gentle one?"

"You mean for you? Now?"

"Yes."

"Got all kinds, gentle or lively."

I took out my wallet and checked it. Luckily, I had a little under forty dollars. "I'll take the gentlest one."

The man pushed the looseleaf notebook at me, looking faintly surprised. "You sign the book, and then I'll go saddle up Whitefoot."

VIII

Once our transaction was completed, the stable man pointed out the bridle trail that led toward the pavilion, wished me a good ride, and left me atop one of the gentlest horses I'd ever encountered. Whitefoot—a roan who did indeed have one white fetlock—was so placid I was afraid he'd go to sleep. Recalling my few riding lessons, which had taken place sometime in my early teens, I made some encouraging clicking sounds and tapped his flanks with my heels. Whitefoot put his head down and began munching a clump of dry grass.

"Come on, big fellow," I said. Whitefoot continued to munch.

I shook the reins—gently, but with authority.

No response. I stared disgustedly down the incline of his neck, which made me feel I was sitting at the top of a long slide. Then I repeated the clicking and tapping process. The horse ignored me.

"Look, you lazy bastard," I said in a low, menacing tone, "get a move on!"

The horse raised his head and shook it, glancing back at me with one sullen eye. Then he started down the bridle trail in a swaying, lumbering walk. I sat up straighter in correct horsewoman's posture, feeling smug.

The trail wound through a grove of eucalyptus, then began climbing uphill through grassland. The terrain was rough, full of rocky outcroppings and eroded gullies, and I was thankful for both the well-traveled path and Whitefoot's slovenly gait. After a few minutes I began to feel secure enough in the saddle to take stock of my surroundings, and when we reached the top of a rise, I stopped the horse and looked around.

To one side lay grazing land dotted with brown-and-white cattle. In the distance, I spotted a barn and a corral with horses. To the other side, the vegetation was thicker, giving onto a canyon choked with manzanita, scrub oak, and bay laurel. This was the type of terrain I was looking for—the kind where a man can easily become disoriented and lost. Still, there must be dozens of such canyons in the surrounding hills; to explore all of them would take days.

I had decided to ride a little further before plunging

into rougher territory, when I noticed a movement under the leafy overhang at the edge of the canyon. Peering intently at the spot, I made out a tall figure in light-colored clothing. Before I could identify it as male or female, it slipped back into the shadows and disappeared from view.

Afraid that the person would see me, I reined the horse to one side, behind a large sandstone boulder a few yards away. Then I slipped from the saddle and peered around the rock toward the canyon. Nothing moved there. I glanced at Whitefoot and decided he would stay where he was without being tethered; true to form, he had lowered his head and was munching contentedly. After patting him once for reassurance, I crept through the tall grass to the underbrush. The air there was chill and pungent with the scent of bay laurel—more reminiscent of curry powder than of the bay leaf I kept in a jar in my kitchen. I crouched behind the billowy bright green mat of a chapparal bush while my eyes became accustomed to the gloom. Still nothing stirred; it was as if the figure had been a creature of my imagination.

Ahead of me, the canyon narrowed between high rock walls. Moss coated them, and stunted trees grew out of their cracks. I came out of my shelter and started that way, over ground that was sloping and uneven. From my right came a trickling sound; I peered through the underbrush and saw a tiny stream of water falling over the outcropping. A mere dribble now, it would be a full cascade in the wet season.

The ground became even rougher, and at times I had difficulty finding a foothold. At a point where the mossy walls almost converged, I stopped, leaning against one of them, and listened. A sound, as if someone were thrashing through thick vegetation, came from the other side of the narrow space. I squeezed between the rocks and saw a heavily forested area. A tree branch a few feet from me looked as if it had recently been broken.

I started through the vegetation, following the sounds ahead of me. Pine boughs brushed at my face, and chapparal needles scratched my bare arms. After a few minutes, the thrashing sounds stopped. I stood still, wondering if the person I was following had heard me.

Everything was silent. Not even a bird stirred in the trees above me. I had no idea where I was in relation to either the pavilion or the stables. I wasn't even sure if I could find my way back to where I'd left the horse. Foolishly I realized the magnitude of the task I'd undertaken; such a search would better be accomplished with a helicopter than on horseback.

And then I heard the voices.

They came from the right, past a heavy screen of scrub oak. They were male, and from their rhythm I could tell they were angry. But I couldn't identify them or make out what they were saying. I edged around a clump of manzanita and started through the trees, trying to make as little sound as possible.

On the other side of the trees was an outcropping that formed a flat rock shelf that appeared to drop off sharply after about twenty feet. I clambered up on it and flattened onto my stomach, then crept forward. The voices were louder now, coming from straight ahead and below. I identified one as belonging to the man I knew as Gary Fitzgerald.

" . . . didn't know he intended to blackmail anyone. I thought he just wanted to see John, make it up with him." The words were labored, twisted with pain.

"If that were the case, he could have come to the hotel." The second man was Wayne Kabalka. "He didn't have to go through all those elaborate machinations of sneaking into the pavilion."

"He told me he wanted to reconcile. After all, he was John's own cousin—"

"Come on, Elliott. You knew he had threatened us. You knew all about the pressure he'd put on us the past few weeks, ever since he found out the act would be coming to San Francisco."

I started at the strange name, even though I had known the missing man wasn't really Gary Fitzgerald. Elliott. Elliott who?

Elliott was silent.

I continued creeping forward, the mossy rock cold through my clothing. When I reached the edge of the shelf, I kept my head down until Kabalka spoke again. "You knew we were all afraid of Gary. That's why I hired the McCone woman; in case he tried anything, I wanted an armed guard there. I never counted on you playing the Judas."

Again Elliott was silent. I risked a look over the ledge.

There was a sheer drop of some fifteen or twenty feet to a gully full of jagged rocks. The man I'd known as Gary Fitzgerald lay at its bottom, propped into a sitting position, his right leg twisted at an unnatural angle. He was wearing a plaid shirt and jeans—the same clothing the man at the stables had described the dead man as having on. Kabalka stood in front of him, perhaps two yards from where I lay, his back to me. For a minute, I was afraid Elliott would see my head, but then I realized his eyes were glazed half blind with pain.

"What happened between John and Gary?" he asked.

Kabalka shifted his weight and put one arm behind his back, sliding his hand into his belt.

"Wayne, what happened?"

"Gary was found dead at the pavilion this morning.

Stabbed. None of this would have happened if you hadn't connived to switch clothing so he could sneak backstage and threaten John."

Elliott's hand twitched, as if he wanted to cover his eyes but was too weak to lift it. "Dead." He paused. "I was afraid something awful had happened when he didn't come back to where I was waiting with the horse."

"Of course you were afraid. You knew what would happen."

"No . . ."

"You planned this for weeks, didn't you? The thing about staying at the fleabag in the Haight was a ploy, so you could turn over one of your costumes to Gary. But it didn't work, because Corinne had sent all but one to the cleaner. When did you come up with the scheme of sneaking out and trading places?"

Elliott didn't answer.

"I suppose it doesn't matter when. But why, Elliott? For God's sake, *why?*"

When he finally answered, Elliott's voice was weary. "Maybe I was sick of what you'd done to him. What we'd *all* done. He was so pathetic when he called me in L.A. And when I saw him . . . I thought maybe that if John saw him too, he might persuade you to help Gary."

"And instead he killed him."

"No. I can't believe that."

"And why not?"

"John loved Gary."

"John loved Gary so much he took Nicole away from him. And then he got into a drunken quarrel with him and crashed the car they were riding in and crippled him for life."

"Yes, but John's genuinely guilty over the accident. And he hates you for sending Gary away and replacing him with me. What a fraud we've all perpetrated—"

Kabalka's body tensed and he began balancing aggressively on the balls of his feet. "That fraud has made us a lot of money. Would have made us more until you pulled this stunt. Sooner or later they'll identify Gary's body and then it will all come out. John will be tried for the murder—"

"I still don't believe he killed him. I want to ask him about it."

Slowly Kabalka slipped his hand from his belt—and I saw the knife. He held it behind his back in his clenched fingers and took a step toward Elliott.

I pushed up with my palms against the rock. The motion caught Elliott's eye and he looked around in alarm. Kabalka must have taken the look to be aimed at him because he brought the knife up.

I didn't hesitate. I jumped off the ledge. For what seemed like an eternity I was falling toward the jagged rocks below. Then I landed heavily—directly on top of Kabalka.

As he hit the ground, I heard the distinctive sound of cracking bone. He went limp, and I rolled off of him—unhurt, because his body had cushioned my fall. Kabalka lay unconscious, his head against a rock. When I looked at Elliott, I saw he had passed out from pain and shock.

IX

The room at John Muir Hospital in Walnut Creek was antiseptic white, with bright touches of red and blue in the curtains and a colorful spray of fall flowers on the bureau. Elliott Larson—I'd found out that was his full name—lay on the bed with his right leg in traction. John

Tilby stood by the door, his hands clasped formally behind his back, looking shy and afraid to come any further into the room. I sat on a chair by the bed, sharing a split of smuggled-in wine with Elliott.

I'd arrived at the same time as Tilby, who had brought the flowers. He'd seemed unsure of a welcome, and even though Elliott had acted glad to see him, he was still keeping his distance. But after a few awkward minutes, he had agreed to answer some questions and had told me about the drunken auto accident five years ago in which he had been thrown clear of his MG and the real Gary Fitzgerald had been crippled. And about how Wayne Kabalka had sent Gary away with what the manager had termed an "ample settlement"—and which would have been except for Gary's mounting medical expenses, which eventually ate up all his funds and forced him to live on welfare in a cheap San Francisco hotel. Determined not to lose the bright financial future the comedy team had promised him, Kabalka had looked around for a replacement for Gary and found Elliott performing in a seedy Haight-Ashbury club. He'd put him into the act, never telling the advertisers who were clamoring for Fitzgerald and Tilby's services that one of the men in the whiteface was not the clown they had contracted with. And he'd insisted Elliott totally assume Gary's identity.

"At first," Elliott said, "it wasn't so bad. When Wayne found me, I was on a downslide. I was heavy into drugs, and I'd been kicked out of my place in the Haight and was crashing with whatever friends would let me. At first it was great making all that money, but after a while I began to realize I'd never be anything more than the shadow of a broken man."

"And then," I said, "Gary reappeared."

"Yes. He needed some sort of operation and he contacted Wayne in L.A. Over the years Wayne had been sending him money—hush money, I guess you could call it—but it was barely enough to cover his minimum expenses. Gary had been seeing all the ads on TV, reading about how well we were doing, and he was angry and demanding a cut."

"And rightly so," Tilby added. "I'd always thought Gary was well provided for, because Wayne took part of my earnings and said he was sending it to him. Now I know most of it was going into Wayne's pocket."

"Did Wayne refuse to give Gary the money for the operation?" I asked.

Tilby nodded. "There was a time when Gary would merely have crept back into the woodwork when Wayne refused him. But by then his anger and hurt had festered, and he wasn't taking no for an answer. He threatened Wayne, and continued to make daily threats by phone. We were all on edge, afraid of what he might do. Corinne kept urging Wayne to give him the money, especially because we had contracted to come to San Francisco, where Gary was, for the clown festival. But Wayne was too stubborn to give in."

Thinking of Corinne, I said, "How's she taking it, anyway?"

"Badly," Tilby said. "But she's a tough lady. She'll pull through."

"And Nicole?"

"Nicole has vanished. Was packed and gone by the time I went back to the hotel after Wayne's arrest." He seemed unconcerned; five years with Nicole had probably been enough.

I said, "I talked to the sheriff's department. Wayne hasn't confessed." After I'd revived Elliott out there in the canyon, I'd given him my gun and made my way back to where I'd left the horse. Then I'd ridden—the most energetic ride of old Whitefoot's life—back to the stables and summoned the sheriff's men. When we'd arrived at the gully, Wayne had regained consciousness and was attempting to buy Elliott off. Elliott seemed to be enjoying bargaining and then refusing.

Remembering the conversation I'd overheard between the two men, I said to Elliott, "Did Wayne have it right about you intending to loan Gary one of your spare costumes?"

"Yes. When I found I didn't have an extra costume to give him, Gary came up with the plan of signaling me from a horse on the hill. He knew the area from when he lived there and had seen a piece in the paper about how people would ride up on the hill to watch the concerts. You guessed about the signal?"

"I saw it happen. I just didn't put it together until later, when I thought about the fragments of leaves and needles they found in Gary's clothing." No need to explain about the catalyst to my thought process—the horse of a cat named Watney.

"Well," Elliott said, "that was how it worked. The signal with the field glasses was to tell me Gary had been able to get a horse and show me where he'd be waiting. At the prearranged time, I made the excuse about going to the men's room, climbed out the window, and left the pavilion. Gary changed and got himself into white face in a clump of trees with the aid of a flashlight. I put on his clothes and took the horse and waited, but he never came back. Finally the crowd was streaming out of the pavilion, and then the lights went out; I tried to ride down there, but I'm not a very good horseman, and I got turned around in the dark. Then something scared the horse and it threw me into that ravine and bolted. As soon as I hit the rocks I knew my leg was broken."

"And you lay there all night."

"Yes, half frozen. And in the morning I heard Wayne thrashing through the underbrush. I don't know if he intended to kill me at first, or if he planned to try to convince me that John had killed Gary and we should cover it up."

"Probably the latter, at least initially." I turned to Tilby. "What happened at the pavilion with Gary?"

"He came into the dressing room. Right off I knew it was him, by the limp. He was angry, wanted money. I told him I was willing to give him whatever he needed, but that Wayne would have to arrange for it. Gary hid in the dressing room closet and when you came in there, I asked you to get Wayne. He took Gary away, out into the audience, and when he came back, he said he'd fixed everything." He paused, lips twisting bitterly. "And he certainly had."

We were silent for a moment. Then Elliott said to me, "Were you surprised to find out I wasn't really Gary Fitzgerald?"

"Yes and no. I had a funny feeling about you all along."

"Why?"

"Well, first there was the fact you and John just didn't look like you were related. And then when we were driving through Contra Costa County, you didn't display much interest in it—not the kind of curiosity a man would have when returning home after so many years. And there was one other thing."

"What?"

"I said something about sound from the two pavilions being audible all the way to Port Chicago. That's the place where the Naval Weapons Station is, up on the Strait. And you said, 'Not all the way to Chicago.' You didn't know what Port Chicago was, but I took it to mean you were making a joke. I remember thinking that for a clown, you didn't have much of a sense of humor."

"Thanks a lot." But he grinned, unoffended.

I stood up. "So now what? Even if Wayne never confesses, they've got a solid case against him. You're out a manager, so you'll have to handle your own future plans."

They shrugged almost simultaneously.

"You've got a terrific act," I said. "There'll be some adverse publicity, but you can probably weather it."

Tilby said, "A couple of advertisers have already called to withdraw their offers."

"Others will be calling with new ones."

He moved hesitantly toward the chair I'd vacated. "Maybe."

"You can count on it. A squeaky clean reputation isn't always an asset in show business; your notoriety will hurt you in some ways, but help you in others." I picked up my bag and squeezed Elliott's arm, went toward the door, touching Tilby briefly on the shoulder. "At least think about keeping the act going."

As I went out, I looked back at them. Tilby had sat down in the chair. His posture was rigid, tentative, as if he might flee at any moment. Elliott looked uncertain, but hopeful.

What was it, I thought, that John had said to me about clowns when we were playing gin in the dressing room at the pavilion? Something to the effect that they were all funny but, more important, that they all made people take a look at their own foibles. John Tilby and Elliott Larson—in a sense both broken men like Gary Fitzgerald had been—knew more about those foibles than most people. Maybe there was a way they could continue to turn that sad knowledge into laughter.

Notes
About the
Contributors

"The Toys of Death"   (1939)

G.D.H. and Margaret Cole were extremely prolific writers between the two world wars: individually and collaboratively, they published well over two hundred books of fiction, nonfiction, and verse. G.D.H. is noted primarily for his studies in social and economic history; his five-volume *A History of Socialist Thought* (1953–1960) is considered a landmark work. Dame Margaret is best known for her biographies *Beatrice and Sidney Webb* (1955) and *The Life of G.D.H. Cole* (1971). In the field of detective fiction, the Coles co-authored more than thirty "Golden Age" novels, beginning with *The Brooklyn Murders* (1923) and ending with *Toper's Web* (1942); many of these feature the detective talents of Superintendent Henry Wilson, of Scotland Yard. They also published six volumes of short stories, of which *Mrs. Warrender's Profession* (1938) is the most prominent. Unfortunately, the deductions of the delightful Mrs. Warrender are confined to short stories: she does not appear in any of the Coles' novels.

"The Calico Dog"   (1934)

Over the past half century Mignon Eberhart has published more than fifty novels, two plays, five collections, and numerous uncollected stories. She has been called the queen of the modern Gothic—justifiably and in the best sense of the term, as such fine nonseries novels as *The White Cockatoo* (1933), *Hunt with the Hounds* (1950), *R.S.V.P. Murder* (1965), and *Nine O'Clock Tide* (1978) attest. But she is also adept at the formal detective story. Her first few novels featured the exploits of nurse Sarah Keate and detective Lance O'Leary; among the best of these are *The Patient in Room 18* (1929) and *While the Patient Slept* (1930). Susan Dare, herself a writer of mysteries and an accomplished amateur sleuth, is another of Ms. Eberhart's memorable detective creations. *The Cases of Susan Dare* (1934), her only book, is considered by aficionados to be a minor classic.

"The Book That Squealed"   (1939)

The ability to create an atmosphere of palpably mounting terror and suspense was the primary reason Cornell Woolrich achieved his substantial reputation as a master of the crime story. No writer past or present rivals him in the art of expressing the kind of raw-nerved tension found in such novels as *The Bride Wore Black* (1940), *Black Alibi* (1942), *Phantom Lady* (1943, as by William Irish), and *The Night Has a Thousand Eyes* (1945, as by George Hopley) and in such story collections as *I Wouldn't Be in Your Shoes* (1943, as by William Irish), *The Dancing Detective* (1946, as by Irish), and *The Ten Faces of*

Cornell Woolrich (1965). The cinematic quality of his work is another reason for its success, and accounts for the remarkable total of twenty-eight feature films and twenty-five teleplays based on his novels and stories. "The Book That Squealed" is less horrific, and more a straightforward detective story, than most of his work; but the suspense that permeates these pages is nonetheless high—Woolrich at his edge-of-the-chair best.

"The Broken Men"   (1985)

Marcia Muller's San Francisco—based detective, Sharon McCone, was the first fully realized and believable female private investigator in crime fiction. She made her debut in *Edwin of the Iron Shoes* (1977), and has appeared in five other novels since then, among them *Ask the Cards a Question* (1982) and *There's Nothing to Be Afraid Of* (1985). McCone has also appeared in three short stories, of which "The Broken Men" is the longest and most accomplished. Ms. Muller has also published two novels—*The Tree of Death* (1983) and *The Legend of the Slain Soldiers* (1985)—featuring another pioneering detective character: Elena Oliverez, a Santa Barbara museum curator and the genre's first Chicana sleuth. Her other books include a nonfiction compendium of reviews of mystery, detective, and espionage fiction—*1001 Midnights* (1986)—and several anthologies, all in collaboration with Bill Pronzini.